Something about K
she'd drawn her shie
She was hurting an
should have found

Ross admitted what had been lurking in the back of his brain for weeks. He wanted to see Kelly Young without the shadows clouding her eyes, relaxed, carefree. He wanted to be the one who saw behind that icy mask of tightly leashed control.

Kelly Young had everything he'd been denied— two parents who had adored her, a job she clearly loved, friends who were nearby whenever she needed them. Her life was full, happy, the kind of tale children's storybooks were made of. Reaching out to Sandra Lange would cost her so little.

Yet she seemed terribly afraid of even meeting with Sandra now.

Why?

TINY BLESSINGS: Giving thanks for the neediest of God's children, and the families who take them in!

* * *

Books by Lois Richer

Love Inspired

LOIS RICHER

Sneaking a flashlight under the blankets, hiding in a thicket of Caragana bushes where no one could see, pushing books into socks to take to camp—those are just some of the things Lois Richer freely admits to in her pursuit of the written word. "I'm a bookaholic. I can't do without stories," she confesses. "It's always been that way."

Her love of language evolved into writing her own stories. Today her passion is to create tales of personal struggle that lead to triumph over life's rocky road. For Lois, a happy ending is essential.

"In my stories, as in my own life, God has a way of making all things beautiful. Writing a love story is my way of reinforcing my faith in His ultimate goodness toward us—His precious children."

PAST SECRETS, PRESENT LOVE

LOIS RICHER

Steeple
Hill®

Published by Steeple Hill Books™

Special thanks and acknowledgment are given to Lois Richer
for her contribution to the TINY BLESSINGS series.

This book is dedicated to moms all over the world who love above and
beyond. You are reflections of the Father's love for His children.

And this book is dedicated to my mom who never believed them
when they said it couldn't be done. You go, Mom!

STEEPLE HILL BOOKS

**Steeple
Hill**®

ISBN 0-373-87338-7

PAST SECRETS, PRESENT LOVE

Copyright © 2005 by Harlequin Books S.A.

www.SteepleHill.com

Printed in U.S.A.

You are the Lord, You alone; You have made
heaven, the heaven of heavens, with all their hosts,
the earth and all that is on it, the seas and all
that is in them; and You preserve all of them;
and the host of heaven worships You.
—*Nehemiah* 9:6

Ross—From the Scottish or Latin,
which means "from the headlands."
It is a German variant of Roswald or the
English variant of Roswell or Russell.

Kelly—From the Irish, which means "warrior or
bright-minded." It was originally a boys' name.

Sandra—A variation of the Greek Alexandra,
which means "defender of mankind."
A feminine form of Alexander.

Chapter One

You or Ben Cavanaugh may be the adult child of Sandra Lange.

The words echoed through Kelly Young's brain with the rhythm of a marching band on Independence Day. No matter how furiously she worked at cleaning out the old utility closet, she couldn't silence them.

"Aren't you leaving to get ready for Ben and Leah's wedding?"

She glanced up, saw Florence Villi scowling at her and nodded. Scour was a word that suited the cleaning lady at Tiny Blessings Adoption Agency to a T.

"I'm leaving soon," Kelly assured her. "Just a few things to tie up first."

"You're getting to be a workaholic." Florence's brown eyes hardened as she noticed what Kelly was doing. "I'm not responsible for any messes you make, and I've already cleaned this hall."

"I'll clean it up—don't worry, Florence."

"You looking for something special?"

"Just a little more space." Kelly lifted out yet another broom, held it up. "Do you ever use this stuff?"

"Not my job to clean out all the closets in this building," Florence grumbled. "I keep my stuff in the basement. I'm not responsible for this."

"I wasn't implying you were, I was just wondering—" Kelly felt the anger emanating from the other woman and decided retreat was wise. "Never mind. Are you working late tonight?"

"Same as any other night, isn't it?" Florence eyes narrowed. "Nobody ever had a complaint about that. I do my job and I do it right."

She did, Kelly agreed. Usually not with a happy face, but Florence kept the place clean and minded her own business. Except for the time she'd leaked information to the *Richmond Gazette* about some botched birth records. As she watched the over-painted lips on that grim mouth turn down, Kelly decided not to remind her of that faux pas. Florence already didn't like her, why make it worse?

"I suppose everyone else is gone," she murmured, trying to ease some of the articles back inside the closet.

"They left long ago. Could be that they all have people at home waiting for them."

Unlike you.

Having uttered her unspoken little dig, Florence pushed her mop down the hallway, nose in the air as she studiously avoided the mess Kelly had made.

"'Be ye kind, one to another. Tenderhearted, *forgiving*—'" Kelly recited her mother's favorite verse until some of her frustration drained away. Carol Young had loved life, refused to let someone else's unpleasantness drain her joy. She'd set a good example for her daughter.

Thank goodness her mom had never known about Sandra Lange and this search she was conducting for her long-lost child. Of course Kelly wasn't Sandra's child. It must be Ben.

Kelly checked her watch, gasped. How had it grown so late? Ben and Leah's wedding was important to her, there was no way she wanted to miss it. Fortunately her house was only minutes away. She could make it if she hurried.

"You are not watching me do this, Mom," she muttered as she shoved the jumble of brooms back into the closet willy-nilly. Of course they wouldn't go in as easily as they'd fallen out. Kelly wiggled and pushed, determined to get them inside, but something solid seemed in the way.

"What on earth is back here anyway?" she grumbled, standing on a gallon paint can to peer over the mess. "A filing cabinet? What's that doing here? It can't have anything in it."

Kelly scoffed at the very idea. There was no way Tiny Blessings Adoption Agency kept its outdated files in a utility closet, not with her as director. Although stranger things had happened under the previous director's orders. She stretched an arm over a pile of old rags and yanked on the handle to open it, but the drawer of the cabinet wouldn't open.

"Figures." Her watch bleeped the time. One hour and counting. "Rats!" She abandoned that effort and stuffed everything else inside. By using her body to hold the door closed, she managed to finally lock it.

"Later," she promised the steel gray door. No doubt there'd been some reason to put a lock on a utility closet. To keep people away from the mops, maybe? Mocking her own foolishness, Kelly got her coat.

It took five minutes to get home and fifteen minutes to shower, fix her hair and change. A record by any standard. The ringing phone delayed her a few minutes more, but when no one answered, Kelly quickly hung up. Then she was out the door and on the road.

At least for ten minutes.

That's when the ability to steer suddenly left her car. Without warning she found herself careening all over the road. Something was definitely wrong!

Kelly prayed for help as she tried to maneuver around a parked car with a combination of braking and intermittent steering ability. She touched the brakes just a little too hard and found herself sliding across an ice-slicked street toward a child with a sack of newspapers who was doing his best to skate his sneakers across the road in front of her.

Kelly held her breath, tapping gently on the brake pedal as she dragged at the stiff, unyielding wheel, afraid to honk lest she frighten him into turning into her path. As it was, he slid a little too close. She jerked the wheel hard right, begging it to obey.

At the last moment the car turned and skidded over the sidewalk. Kelly came to a shuddering halt smacked against a massive oak tree, right beside the busiest intersection in town. The little boy glared at her, then walked away, mouth pursed in an angry line.

Kelly switched off the key before resting her forehead against the steering wheel.

"That was close, Lord," she whispered, her entire body weak with thoughts of what could have happened. What on earth was wrong with the steering? She'd checked with the dealer a few weeks ago, made sure she was prepared for whatever nature tossed out. Obviously her steering wasn't okay. Maybe she'd bought a lemon.

Once she'd regained her equanimity, Kelly dragged her coat lapels over her best red silk dress and climbed out of the car to inspect the damage. Her silk-clad ankles stung at contact with the wet snow.

The front bumper was a mess, the tire on the passenger side was half-flat and the undercarriage was lodged against the cement curb, making it perfectly clear that she was going nowhere fast.

"Out joyriding, Miss Young?"

Kelly wheeled around, met the dark blue gaze of Ross Van Zandt. As usual, one hank of dark hair flopped over his left eye. More than a hint of dark stubble accented the rigid line of his jaw. He had the kind of jaw people sculpted—rock solid, determined.

He cleared his throat. Kelly realized she'd been staring at him. Her face flushed a hot embarrassing red.

"I'm sorry, what did you say?" It would have to be *him,* wouldn't it? The one man in town she did not want to see.

"I just wondered if you'd begun living on the wilder side of life." His voice held that hint of amusement that always made her bristle. One black eyebrow lifted as he took in her predicament. "Party dress, fast car—you know."

"Oh, of course," she muttered, gritting her teeth against the icy chill that her silk dress did nothing to block. "Party animal that I am, there's nothing I like more than parking my car against a tree when I've just put on my best heels and a silk dress."

"You're on your way to the wedding." It wasn't a question. He leaned over and unlatched the passenger side door, thrust it open. "Get in. I'll give you a ride. You don't have much time."

"But my car—" Kelly hugged into the warmth of her white cashmere coat while he pulled out a cell phone, dialed, then began speaking.

"Vinnie? Ross. Got a little problem."

In less than fifty words he'd conveyed the problem and formed a solution. That was Ross. Succinct didn't begin to describe his use of language.

The wind was bitter, filled with piercing bits of ice that stung when they hit the skin. Kelly shivered again, wondered if she'd be doing something illegal if she left. But then Ross was a private detective. He'd know all about this stuff, wouldn't he?

"I'll drop you off, then come back and watch while Vinnie loads your car and tows it. Now will you get in?"

"Oh. Okay. Thanks. Just let me get my bag." Kelly stepped daintily through the soggy mess underfoot, dragged out her black beaded bag and her car keys, then locked the door. By the time she made it into Ross's car her feet felt like icicles.

He watched, one inquisitive eyebrow raised, as she slipped her toes out of the delicate shoes, burying them in the carpet.

"Very pretty, Ms. Young, but not exactly weather-appropriate footwear," he mumbled, then quickly flicked the heater on high.

"They're very appropriate. It's a wedding, not a trapper's festival," she snapped, then wished she hadn't. "Sorry," she murmured when his eyebrows rose.

Kelly hated snarky people and had long ago decided not to become one of them. But something about Ross Van Zandt and his piercing scrutiny always made her tense. Maybe it was because he made a living probing into people's secrets. More likely it was because he was the one Sandra Lange had hired to find her child. That would be reason enough, especially since it was Ross who only days ago had informed her and Ben Cavanaugh that one of them might be the long lost child Sandra had been looking for. He had no idea how wrong he was.

Of course, Kelly felt sorry for Sandra. As director of Tiny Blessings Adoption Agency, Kelly spent every day dealing with people who were giving up their children for adoption. It was often a difficult and heartrending event. Sandra must have suffered terribly when she was forced to give up her own child.

But Kelly did not want to be her daughter.

Of course she knew she'd been adopted, had known it for years. In fact, she'd been the first child whose adoption Tiny Blessings had handled back when Barnaby Harcourt had been in charge. But being adopted had never been an issue with Kelly. Marcus and Carol Young were the best parents a girl could have. Living with them, being part of their family—that's all she'd ever known. They'd showered her with so much love she never wanted anything to spoil it, especially not now when they were both gone, especially not with Sandra Lange's problems.

"How'd you do it?"

Kelly twisted in her seat, stared at Ross. "Excuse me?"

"Your car, pasted against that tree. How'd it happen?"

"I'm not sure." She tried to recreate the sequence of events in her head. "The steering seemed wonky," she mused.

"Wonky?" Ross put on his left signal and waited for a car to pass before he turned toward the church. "What does that mean?"

"Soft, spongy. Unresponsive." What part didn't he understand?

"Has it happened before?" He frowned when she shook her head. "It's a new model, isn't it?"

Kelly nodded. "I just got it in the fall."

"Then it shouldn't be a maintenance problem. Maybe some manufacturing defect is to blame."

Remembering, she shuddered.

"I'm just glad I wasn't on a freeway when it happened. As it was I missed a little boy by inches." She chided herself for forgetting her manners. "I'm glad that you were driving past. Thank you."

"No problem."

She studied his thick jacket and jeans. "You're not going to Ben and Leah's wedding?"

"Nah. I'm not all that big on church stuff." He pulled up near the door, glanced around. "Looks like you beat the bridal party to the church."

"That's a blessing. Thank you very much for coming to my rescue and for handling the tow for me, Ross." She handed over her keys, then rested her hand on the door handle, wondering if she should say it. "You know they'd love you to come. Why don't you at least attend the reception?"

"I'm waiting for a call from the lab," he told her. "About the DNA tests."

Kelly froze. She knew exactly what he was talking about. Both she and Ben had given samples for testing last week. *Don't let me be her daughter!*

"I didn't realize you'd find out so soon," Kelly whispered, staring at her feet. They were bare. She used her toes to grope for her shoes.

"You mean you were hoping." His voice held a hint of condemnation.

"I have a full, rich life," she told him, bristling a little. "I loved my parents. They gave me a wonderful life. It's not that easy to suddenly accept that someone I've known for years could be my biological mother."

"Someone you feel would take away the glory from your mother, is that what you're saying?"

"I guess. Sort of." It was more complicated than that, but Kelly had deliberately avoided probing her feelings to discover what lay beneath her sense of fear about this situation.

"Sandra's not asking for anything, Kelly." He reached out, touched the hand she'd clenched on her lap. "She just wants to know the child she gave birth to all those years ago."

"So you've said." Kelly opened the door, felt the sting of the cold crisp air hit her in a wave. Impulsively she turned, faced him. "But I already had a wonderful mother whom I dearly loved," she blurted out. "Nobody can take her place."

Kelly didn't wait for the argument she knew would follow. She didn't want to hear it. Instead she swung her legs out of the car, and rose. Then she bent and met his frowning stare.

"Tell Vinnie I'll manage without the car until he gets it fixed. And thanks for the ride. I appreciate it very much." She swung the door closed and hurried toward the church door, stuffing away all the doubts that had surfaced in the last few minutes.

"Please let it be Ben," she murmured over and over as she hung up her coat, then was shown to her seat. "Please, please let Sandra's child be Ben and not me."

She sat in her pew, unable to relax until Reverend Fraser had taken his place at the front and Olivia, Ben's precocious seven-year-old daughter began her stroll down the aisle, preceding the bride. She heard a rustle at the back and twisted in time to see Caleb and Anne sneak into a back pew. So they'd made it back from their honeymoon for the wedding! Caleb still had a week off from his duties as youth minister for the Chestnut Grove Youth Center and she'd specifically told Anne to forget about the books at Tiny Blessings for two weeks. Kelly suspected they'd disappear as quietly as they'd arrived to finish celebrating their own nuptials.

Anne looked so happy, so content. A frisson of envy twigged at her. It must be nice to have somebody to share with, somebody to help when life got to be too much.

Kelly pushed away the longing and turned back to concentrate on the ceremony. By the time the wedding march sounded, she'd almost convinced herself that everything in her world was just the same as it had always been.

Almost.

He didn't belong here—not among these happy people, certainly not at a wedding reception where people celebrated marriage. The only thing Ross Van Zandt knew about marriage was that it didn't work. Not for his dysfunctional family anyway.

Ross thrust away the past and concentrated on finding her among the guests now milling freely through the hall. He'd deliberately waited until the toasts were made, the speeches given, hoping not to ruin this lovely day.

Kelly was seated at a table with three other young women. Sandra had told him that four women had been friends for many years—Meg, Rachel, Pilar and Anne, who wasn't at the table—and had a habit of meeting at Sandra's Starlight Diner for brunch on Sundays. It was clear from their giggles and boisterous laughter now that they were trying to talk Kelly into joining them. By contrast, Kelly's response sounded more restrained. He wondered if she was always so uptight, so restricted. If she ever let herself forget all the rules and relax.

"Ross?"

He wheeled around at the sound of his own name, found the groom standing to one side of the doorway, partially hidden by the massive potted palm that guarded the entrance.

"Hey, Ben. Congratulations."

"Thanks." Ben shook his hand while he studied his face. "You need to see Kelly," he guessed.

"Yeah, I do. I just got a call from the lab and—"

Ben held up one hand. "You don't have to explain. I understand. I'm not Sandra Lange's child."

"I was going to tell you after I told her." As an apology, it lacked a certain something, Ross sighed. "Could my timing be any lousier?"

"It doesn't matter, man. Really."

"Yes, it does. I haven't been able to find anything to lead me to your birth parents. That's got to bother you."

"Maybe it should," Ben admitted with a grin. "And probably it will when I've got time to sit down and think about it. But right now all I can think of is that God gave me the most beautiful woman in the world to be Olivia's mother and my wife. We just kissed Olivia goodbye. My brother is taking her to his house. Now Leah's waiting for me to get out to that car so we can start the first phase of our life together. That's pretty awesome, don't you think?"

Ross smiled broadly. He liked Ben's attitude. "Yes, it is."

"Later I'll have a lot of questions I'll want answers to, and maybe I'll hire you to find the truth, but not today. Today is for celebrating."

"And you're wasting time standing here because?" Ross raised one eyebrow.

"Because I forgot that I left my car keys with my dad. I was hoping to snag someone who wouldn't mind getting them for me. Leah's a wonderful woman and more patient than most, but she's sitting in the car waiting to go on our honeymoon. If I show my face in that room again we'll be delayed even longer. I barely got away unscathed the first time we left."

Joy, anticipation and a certain confidence filled Ben's voice. Ross's discomfort at telling him the news today of all days eased a fraction. The man was clearly looking forward to some time alone with his new wife. The least he could do was help him.

"I'll get the keys," he told the beaming groom. "Stay out of sight and I'll be right back."

"Great! Thanks a lot."

Ross stepped into the beautifully decorated reception room and breathed in the scent of flowers that mingled with burning candles, fully aware of exactly when the conversation stalled as curious eyes fell on him. Kelly's friends were less than subtle in their nudges and winks, but Kelly ignored them to stare at him, a tiny frown pleating the smooth skin of her forehead.

Ross kept his course steady, approached Ben's parents and quietly explained the problem. His father slipped him the keys while teasing, "Your P.I. technique of going unnoticed needs a little work," he chuckled.

Ross tossed back his own witty retort then strode toward the door. Kelly rose, said something to Meg, and met him halfway.

"So you did come," she murmured, her voice low, for him alone. "But you've missed the bride and groom."

"Not quite. I'm on my way to see him right now."

"Ben's still around? Oh." She trailed along beside him toward the door, stepped through and looked around. A soft chuckle burst from her. "Ben, why are you skulking behind that palm?"

"Shh!" He took the keys Ross held out and grinned. "Thanks a lot, pal." He paused, spared a look for Kelly, glanced at Ross, saw the shake of his head and nodded once, understanding immediately that she didn't yet know the truth. "See you guys later," was all he said before he turned and disappeared.

"Well." Kelly watched him for a few moments then turned to face Ross. "Are you coming in to share the rest of the party?"

"Maybe later, thanks." He took a deep breath. The time was now. "Kelly, have you got a minute? I need to talk to you. Privately."

"Certainly." She stood, tall, slim and poised, waiting innocently. "Go ahead. Is it about my car?"

He'd hoped for a quiet time when no one was around, when no one could interrupt. The soft sounds of music, laughter and the tinkle of glasses wafted out from the reception. Apparently this was as good as he was going to get.

"The lab phoned." There was no easy way to say it. "The DNA was conclusive. You are Sandra Lange's biological daughter."

She froze—there was no other way to describe it. Her entire body slowly immobilized until she resembled a statue in the town square. Her brown eyes remained open but Ross doubted if she saw anything through the glaze shielding them. Her clear, pure skin blanched, then became a marble mask that gave away no emotion.

"Kelly?"

"Yes?" She faced him politely.

"Did you hear me?"

"Yes, thank you."

So polite. He waited, leaning on one foot first, then the other, expecting a reaction—something. Kelly Young offered nothing but icy silence. Impatient, Ross scoured his brain for some answer to her strange response. He put himself in her place, tried to imagine how she must feel.

"Sandra doesn't want anything from you, Kelly. Except maybe a chance to get to know you better. She's a lonely woman who's going through a traumatic fight with cancer. Her prognosis is good, she's doing everything she can to make a full recovery. The diner is running smoothly so she has no worries there. The only end that's been left untied is finding the child she gave birth to thirty-five years ago. That child is you."

"Yes, you've said that."

"Do you want to see her?"

Kelly seemed to snap out of her fog, faced him with a frown.

"Now? It's nine-thirty at night, and I'm at a wedding reception. I'm sure Sandra is busy."

"I don't think she's too busy to see her daughter."

She gaped at his words, then quickly shook her head, the multitoned blond facets in her chin-length hair catching the light of the massive chandelier overhead.

"I don't—can't see her just yet. I need some time to think about this." Her hands knotted and unknotted as she stared at him. "I'm sure you can understand that."

"Of course." He motioned to the doorway, wondering if she ever just relaxed and let people see what was inside. "Do you want to go back to the party?"

"No." She was firm about that. Her eyes darkened to bittersweet-chocolate drops. "Not now. Most of the festivities are over anyway. I—I'd rather go home."

"I'll give you a ride, if you want." He felt sorry for her then. Beautiful, composed Kelly Young looked so confused, as if she couldn't quite make sense of her world.

She opened her mouth to decline, then obviously realized that her car was still at the garage.

"Thanks," she murmured. It took her only a moment to say goodbye to her friends and retrieve the little bag she'd brought. She handed her ticket stub to the attendant and smiled her thanks when Ross held her cashmere coat open. "I'm ready."

"My car's in the parking garage. Do you want to wait out front?"

"I'll go with you."

Despite the height of her heels, Kelly matched his stride with no problem. She offered little by way of conversation so Ross tossed around for something to say.

"Was it a good wedding?"

"Aren't all weddings good?" she asked, one perfectly arched brow lifted. "But, yes, this was a lovely wedding. Choosing to marry on the third day of the new year was a great idea. A fresh start, a fresh year."

Once started, Kelly kept talking. Great food, great decorations, great music. Everything was great or wonderful or fantastic. Ross knew she was simply marking time until he pulled up in front of her house, filling the spot a sleek silver car had just vacated.

"I'll walk you up," he offered, but she waved one hand in decline.

"I'll be fine. You probably have somewhere to be. Don't worry about me."

He ignored that, lending an arm for her to cling to as she balanced precariously on the icy path. She flashed him a smile once they reached the door.

"Thank you for saving me from a broken neck."

"You're welcome." He waited till she'd unlocked the door. "Are you sure you'll be all right?"

"Of course." She kept her face averted, refused to meet his eyes. "Thank you very much. Good night."

"Take care."

Kelly responded in kind, then closed the door.

Ross waited a few moments on the porch, leaning on a column as he watched the inside lights flare on. After a moment he slowly walked back to his car, his mind recreating the forlorn beauty of her face when he'd given her the news tonight.

What was Kelly Young so afraid of?

As he drove back to his apartment, Ross ruminated on Sandra Lange, pictured her sad green eyes peering at him, her newly grown silver-blond hair a shimmer of fuzz that feathered her scalp.

"If I could just know for sure," she whispered to him that first day when she'd hired him to find her child. "Then maybe I could let it all go."

Since then she'd become like a second mother to Ross, fussing with worry about the hours he spent on her case, the move he'd made from Richmond to Chestnut Grove to facilitate his work here, the time he'd spent following leads that ended in blanks. He'd never known concern like that, especially not now since his mother's Alzheimer's had made him a stranger to her. Maybe that's why he felt an odd responsibility to Sandra, a need to be sure she was all right. She'd become closer to him than his mother and so he did whatever he could to help her realize her goal.

It struck him that his part in this story was over, that he'd done what Sandra had asked, found the child she'd lost. He should be thinking about moving back to Richmond.

But all he could think about was Kelly—a slim, pale woman who held her emotions inside as if she were afraid someone wouldn't like her if they saw the truth.

He'd just rocked her world with his news. She would need time to think and digest what the knowledge could mean. Ross decided to visit Sandra while he gave Kelly an hour to regroup. Then he'd call, check up on her. Sandra would want him to do that.

But as he drove to Sandra's, Ross knew that concern wasn't all he was feeling. Something about Kelly's reaction—as if she'd drawn her shields up, enclosed herself behind them—bothered him. She was hurting and it was his fault. He should have found a better way to tell her.

Ross admitted what had been lurking in the back of his brain for weeks.

He wanted to see Kelly Young without the shadows clouding her eyes, relaxed, carefree. He wanted to be there to see her when she'd been freed from whatever held her back, he wanted to be the one who saw behind that icy mask of tightly leashed control.

Kelly Young had everything he'd been denied—two parents who had adored her, a job she clearly loved, friends who were nearby whenever she needed them. Her life was full, happy, the kind of tale children's storybooks were made of. Reaching out to Sandra Lange would cost her so little.

Yet she seemed terribly afraid of even meeting with Sandra now.

Why?

Chapter Two

Kelly leaned against the door and listened to the engine of Ross's car as he drove away. She was odd man out, alone. Again.

Her friends each had someone special in her life. She had no one. It was a pathetic admittance, but the truth could not be denied. Kelly had no desire to return to the reception. Ross's news had leeched away the spirit of fun she'd shared with the others. Now all she could think about was Sandra Lange. She was Sandra Lange's daughter. Sandra was her mother.

The knowledge filled her with unbearable angst that she couldn't explain. It was fear, she knew that much. But the basis of it couldn't bear exploring, not now. Kelly moved through the house slowly, scanning each room looking for something she could do to keep her hands busy, her mind occupied. But the big house was as neatly pristine as she'd always kept it. Just like the rest of her life.

Except for this business with Sandra. She skittered away from that. What to do?

Her mind flew to the storage closet she'd been cleaning

at the office. Now there was a project that would take her complete attention. So what if it was ten o'clock at night—on a weekend?

She thought about it for the space of two seconds then bounded up the stairs to change her clothes. Clad in a thick gray wool sweater and black pants, she tied on her hiking boots, pulled on her parka, beret, scarf and gloves, then reached for the doorknob. The winking light on her answering machine made her pause.

"Hi, Miss Young. This is Vinnie at the garage. I took a look at your car and—well, I don't know exactly how to say this. It looks like your steering has been tampered with. What I'm looking at had to be deliberate." A sigh. "Maybe you better call me tomorrow or Monday. We'll talk about it then. Bye."

Tampered with? Surely he was mistaken—overreacting, perhaps. Nobody cared about her car, or about tampering with it. Besides, she kept it in the garage when she was home.

Still, he'd been so definite. Kelly had no idea how steering on a car worked, but she knew Vinnie knew his car stuff. If anybody could fix it, he could. Until then she'd walk back and forth to the office. It wasn't that far and she needed the exercise after many Christmas indulgences. Kelly pulled open the door and stepped outside.

It was a lovely night—cold, clear, crisp. A promise of things to come?

Deliberately stuffing away thoughts of Sandra Lange, Kelly crunched down the street, admiring the lights and decorations that twinkled in the darkness. Usually she loved the holiday season. Celebrating Christ's birth, welcoming in another year—they were beloved traditions her parents had taught her to note as milestones. It didn't matter that the couple was gone now; she kept their traditions alive just the same, as a way of honoring them. Only this morning she'd written about the coming year in her journal.

I hope it's a year I can move away from the past, put my mistakes behind me and look forward to the future. I need to be free of the fear. Unable to delineate exactly what she was afraid of and unwilling to explore it further, Kelly had stopped there. She only knew that worry had lurked at the back of her mind for years, as long as she could remember she'd had this dream that someday someone would show up and tell her it was all a lie, that nobody cared about her, that she was all alone.

Kelly stopped, turned around and looked back at her house. White Christmas lights glimmered and twinkled under the eaves, above the wooden snowmen her father had created so long ago. Her house, though lovely, was also a reminder of the past. She'd chosen it with Simon, before he'd told her he'd made a mistake, that he didn't want to marry her. She loved the old colonial with its four big bedrooms, where she'd dreamed of tucking in her own children. Children she wasn't so sure she'd ever have now.

Was that why she'd hung onto it when he'd left, to keep alive the dream?

The dream was gone. It was time to admit that to herself and stop waiting for Simon to return. He'd made it clear that last morning before summer holidays began.

"I'm taking a new job, a better one, in New York. I don't want to hang around this pokey place forever, meeting at the diner for lunch, spending Sunday evenings with couples whose only interests are babies. I have big plans."

Plans that didn't include her. She knew that now, but then she couldn't accept that he would walk away without even discussing it.

"What about me, Simon? I thought you loved me."

"So did I. I'm sorry. I made a mistake."

A mistake. The words had devastated her.

"I need freedom. You're afraid of it. You won't take on the challenge of life, Kelly. You sit in your comfy world at that adoption agency and you spend your days handing out babies. Why? Because everyone expects you to?" His scathing tone had hurt. "You could do so much more, but you're afraid to venture beyond this place. I wanted to talk about moving, to discuss our future, but then I realized, you see your future here. I don't."

In a way, Simon had been right. The thought of leaving this place, of going to a spot where she knew no one, where she was the oddball, where nothing was familiar—that made her blood run cold. The only thing she didn't understand was why.

The familiar tightness in her chest signaled tension that she didn't want, so Kelly thrust away the past and sped up her steps. She concentrated on breathing so she couldn't think of anything else. Within minutes she was unlocking the front door of Tiny Blessings, punching in her security code. She locked it solidly behind her, then climbed the steps to her office. Once she'd removed her parka and winter accessories, she hung them neatly, then glanced around.

Her office was as she'd left it—clean and orderly. No papers marred the blank surface of her desk. Not that she felt like doing paperwork anyway.

What then?

The closet. It was the weekend. She could drag everything into the hall and leave it there till tomorrow. No one would notice or complain, especially not Florence, who wouldn't come back until four o'clock Monday afternoon.

Kelly picked up her keys and walked into the hall. As

soon as she turned the lock, the door burst open and broom handles pushed their way out, one knocking her on the temple.

"Ouch! Stop that or I'll throw the lot of you in the garbage," she warned, glowering at them as she propped the offender in one corner. With the brooms and the massive pail out of the way, Kelly could remove several dented, and probably useless, half-full paint cans. That left enough room for her to squeeze inside.

"Okay, now what have we got here?" She grasped the handle of the top drawer of the filing cabinet and yanked, but aside from a groan, the drawer never budged. Kelly tried the bottom one. Locked.

Why would someone lock a filing cabinet they'd left in a storage closet?

"Because they don't want anyone to look inside, dummy." She grimaced at her own answer. "So now what do I do? Pry it open?"

She couldn't think of any good reason why she shouldn't know what was inside, so Kelly asked herself where she'd find something to pry it open with.

"Florence's basement," she muttered and turned to the door.

To her utter shock, the steel door slammed closed in her face.

"Hey!" She grabbed the handle and twisted it but the door didn't open. "Open this door," she yelled. "I'm locked inside."

No answer.

"Florence? Can you let me out?"

But Florence never answered. She'd probably left long ago.

"Wait a minute." Kelly recalled using her key to unlock

the door. *The lock was on the outside.* She should be able to open the door from the inside. She slid her hands over the knob, tried to find a button, *something,* that would release the door. She found nothing. The knob would not turn.

Panic began to thrum inside her. There was no way this door should remain closed unless someone was deliberately preventing her from getting out.

"Let me out!" She lifted her hands, clenched them into fists and began banging. After several minutes, the only result she achieved was sore hands.

At least the light was still on. Kelly flopped down on the edge of the file cabinet and wondered how long she'd have to wait. Tomorrow was Sunday. The office would be closed all day. It was unlikely that Pilar, who placed Tiny Blessings' children, would come to the office—she was a newlywed. And Anne and Caleb hadn't stuck around after the wedding so she'd hardly come in to take a look at the agency's books on the weekend. One by one, Kelly ticked off her employees, heart sinking at the realization that she was alone—and going to be here for a while.

But not by herself.

Someone was out there, someone had deliberately closed that door. Rising panic filled her throat and she had to fight for calm. So many questions whirled around her brain—questions like who and why and how did they get into the building.

"It looks like your steering has been tampered with."

She'd dismissed Vinnie's words too easily. Now they returned with greater impact. Someone had deliberately tampered with her car? Maybe that same someone had shut her in this room.

Fear crawled up and lodged itself in her brain as a voice sounded outside the door.

"Move out of town, Kelly Young. Forget about the past." The voice wasn't clear, but ragged, not unlike a hoarse whisper—a sound made by someone who didn't want to be identified, or someone with a bad cold.

"Who are you?"

"There's nothing in Chestnut Grove for you anymore. Leave before it's too late."

Leave? But this was her home. She'd been raised here, found friends here, been a part of the church all her life. Where would she go?

"Why? Just tell me why." She waited for an answer. But the voice was gone. All that remained was an eerie silence filled with foreboding. She was alone—something she'd always dreaded.

Maybe not quite alone. Though the room wasn't cold, Kelly shivered. She could feel evil waiting just outside that door.

Ross pulled up in front of Kelly's house and scanned the yard. Three times he'd called her from Sandra's, three times he'd heard her voice on the machine.

"Maybe she's more upset than she let on. Please go talk to her," Sandra had urged him. "I'll feel better if I know she's all right."

Maybe Kelly wasn't answering the phone on purpose. He got out of the car, walked up the path and rang the doorbell, waited. When she didn't come to the door, he tried the knob.

"Kelly?" It was quarter past ten. Where would she go?

In a flash the answer was there. Tiny Blessings. She loved her work, was dedicated to finding the perfect home for every child. It had to be emotional, heartrending work and yet in the months he'd spent here he'd never seen her show the least amount of frustration.

Ross had learned a lot about her these past few months. Kelly Young rigidly adhered to every rule and regulation she'd set in place, but perhaps that was simply her way of dealing with the job. And of never making the same mistakes her predecessor, Barnaby Harcourt, had made. Mistakes that had only come to light a few months ago which she'd had to explain to the media. Though falsifying documents hardly classified as a mistake.

Ross knew Kelly was a stickler for routine. But if his revelation about her relationship to Sandra had caused more angst than he realized— He knocked again, twice. Bothered by the lack of response, Ross climbed back in his car and drove the few short blocks to the narrow stone-fronted building that housed Tiny Blessings Adoption Agency.

A big black car sat in front, in the no-parking zone, causing Ross to speculate that Kelly might be meeting someone. He knew from previous visits that Kelly's office faced Main Street and he could see the light in her office, but no matter how many times he dialed, she didn't answer the office phone. He parked behind the black car, where it was legal, and pulled on his gloves to protect his hands from the frigid air.

Ross checked the front door. Locked, of course. Kelly wouldn't dream of leaving the building open to anyone who happened to pass by. Defeated, he returned to his car and sat in the cold and dark, trying to think of some way to contact her. It seemed important that Kelly not be alone tonight. Because of Sandra, he told himself.

From the corner of his eye, Ross saw a movement at the side of the building. He squinted into the darkness, watched a figure slip out an emergency exit door, wait at the edge of the building till a vehicle drove past, then scurry across

the sidewalk and plunge into the poorly parked black car.
With a squeal of tires it pulled away from the curb, red tail-
lights disappearing into the night.

Not a client, Ross decided. Kelly would have let them
out the front door. The hair on the back of his neck prick-
led. Something wasn't right. People with legitimate business didn't sneak out side exits.

In two seconds he'd left his car and raced toward the
door, which was slightly ajar, thanks to a chunk of ice that
had caught in the frame. He dragged it open, stepped into
the dimly lit hall and made sure the door was closed se-
curely behind him.

The silence of the place irritated his already cranky
nerves. Why didn't she have some music playing, a radio
talk show—something to break the ominous quiet of the
old bank building?

Moving with stealth, he walked past the picture displays
that lined the walls—Tiny Blessings' children and their
adoptive families. Another time he would have stopped to
study them, but Ross glimpsed a sliver of light coming under Kelly's office door and quickly rapped his knuckles
against the solid oak, hoping he wouldn't startle her.

"Kelly?"

No response. Ross peeked inside. The room was empty,
but her coat hung neatly on the coatrack. So she was here.
Somewhere.

He stepped back into the hall, wishing he knew where
to find the switch that would illuminate the area instead of
trying to see in this dim gray-green glow. He jerked to a
halt just in time to avoid bumping into some objects litter-
ing the hall. What in the world?

Mops, brooms, a pail, paint cans—they were strewn all
over. Messy. Now that wasn't like Kelly. Not at all. He

didn't have time to think it through before his gaze snagged on a chair shoved under a doorknob, holding a gray metal door closed.

Why? his brain demanded. He worked the chair free, grasped the knob and tried to turn. The door wouldn't open.

"Kelly? Are you in there?"

"Y-yes. I can't get the door open."

He heaved a sigh of relief, then concentrated on the task at hand.

"There was a chair blocking it. I've moved that but I can't budge the knob. Is there a lock on the inside?"

"I—I don't know. Just a minute."

The doorknob rattled but didn't turn. He tried to twist it, to no avail. Ross stepped back, studied it, caught a glimmer of silver.

"Just a minute. I see something." A metal rod had been shoved under the door, tilting it just enough to jam it closed. He grabbed a mop handle and inserted it in the space. At last the metal rod rolled out. "Try the door now, Kelly."

The knob turned, she stepped out and stood there, tall, slim and more afraid than he'd ever seen her. Her brown eyes looked glazed, glossy with unshed tears, and her hand trembled as she lifted it to smooth her shoulder-length sun-kissed strands of hair.

"Someone locked me in," she whispered.

He could have handled the weak trembly note in her voice. He might even have managed to ignore the teardrop clinging to her long spiky lashes. But as he watched her face, saw how she grappled for that mantle of self-possession and couldn't find it, he couldn't ignore that.

Ross reached out, gathered her into his arms.

"It's okay, Kelly. You're safe. You're okay."

"Yes. Thank you." Her hands wrapped around him and she clung for timeless moments.

He held her until the fragile weight of her body stopped shaking, until the strong, capable Kelly returned, took control and stepped away.

"Okay now?" he asked quietly.

She nodded.

"I think so. It was just a little nerve-wracking when I started thinking I'd be locked in there for two days. I'd didn't think anyone would come into the office on the weekend."

So she'd come here to be alone.

"How did you get it open?" She listened carefully as he explained. "That couldn't have been an accident," she whispered when he'd stopped speaking. "Could it?"

"I doubt it." He frowned as suspicion niggled at the back of his mind. "Who would have done something like that?"

"I don't know. I thought I heard something, someone. But I guess it was just nerves."

She wasn't telling the truth. Ross had been reading people for a long time and he knew Kelly Young wasn't telling him something. That was okay. She could tell him later. But right now he needed some questions answered.

"Kelly, when I arrived I saw someone leaving via the side exit. They drove away in a black car. I didn't get the plate number."

"From the side? The emergency exit?" She bit her lip. "But it's always kept closed. How could they get in? The building was locked up when I arrived."

Maybe not as tightly as she thought, Ross surmised.

"I don't know who it was. They were dressed in black, a smallish person—maybe a kid who's angry at you, a teenager?"

"Angry? At me?" She blinked, her eyes dark and confused. "It's possible, I guess, but I don't think so."

"Then maybe—"

Kelly's eyes widened. She reached over and flicked on the hall light, then she bent over to pick up something from the floor.

"What's that?"

"A note."

The shaky tone was back, threading through her soft voice. Ross glanced down, saw the sheet of paper in her hands.

Leave town. Or pay the consequences.

Kelly felt Detective Zach Fletcher's intensive scrutiny even though she wasn't looking at him. Ross had insisted on calling him away from the wedding reception and Zach had come immediately. Now, half an hour later, Tiny Blessings was swarming with police.

"You're sure you can't tell me anything more?"

"I didn't see anything, Zach. I was working in the closet. I turned to leave but the door slammed closed. I couldn't get it open."

"But you heard a voice?"

She nodded.

"It said there was nothing in town for me anymore and that I should leave before it's too late. I told you all this."

"Yes, you did. And they left this." He stared at the note for a moment, flicked a finger against the plastic covering it, then glanced at her, his blue eyes softening. "Are you sure I can't call Pilar? She'd want to be here. For that matter, so would Meg and Rachel."

"Please, no. Nobody else needs to know about this right now. I've already spoiled your evening. I don't want to ruin anyone else's. You should be with Pilar, celebrating Ben and Leah's wedding."

He smiled. "We'll celebrate, don't worry. But I'm concerned about you. I don't want you to go home alone."

"I'll go with her," Ross volunteered.

Kelly jumped at the sound of his voice from behind her. She'd almost forgotten he was still there.

"You don't have to—"

"Thanks, Ross. I'd really appreciate that." Zach overrode her weak objections. "I'll get the lab working on things as soon as I can, but with holidays and everything, it might take a while to get any answers."

"Doesn't matter. I'll be in town for a while longer." Ross and Zach exchanged a funny look before Ross turned to her, raising one eyebrow. "Unless you object?"

Even the thought of being locked in that room again, with someone outside the door, whispering, it made Kelly shiver.

"I'd very much appreciate your help," she murmured. "After the thing with the car and now this, I'm a little nervous."

"What *thing?*" Zach was all ears while Ross explained the accident.

"I gave her a ride, then came back and watched while they towed the car. Vinnie should be able to tell you more when he gets back to work, but the way Kelly described her steering seemed odd for a simple malfunction."

"Actually, Vinnie left a message on my machine." She glanced from one ruggedly handsome face to the other. "I think he said the steering had been tampered with."

Kelly watched the two men exchange a glance and wished she'd kept silent. Now they'd think she was paranoid. "It's probably nothing, a mistake. In fact, I'm sure it's a mistake."

"I've never known Vinnie to make a mistake like that."

Zach scribbled something on a pad. "I'll talk to him. In the meantime, why don't you head home? We'll finish here and lock up for you. I should be able to set the security system by myself, shouldn't I?"

"Just press the set alarm button and leave within twenty seconds." Kelly chewed her bottom lip. "Um, Zach? The system wasn't on when I came in."

"Wasn't on?" More writing.

"I punched in my code, but I didn't need it," she explained. "It wasn't on. I'm sure someone just forget to set it in the hectic rush before the wedding today." She wasn't going to blame Florence.

"Anybody ever forgotten that little detail before?" Zach's blue eyes were dark as thunderclouds.

"No. Not that I know of."

"Uh-huh." He scribbled in his little book some more, then peered at her through his lashes. "Anything else you can think of?"

"I don't think so." He kept staring at her, his gaze narrowed. "Really, Zach. I think that's it."

"Okay." He flipped the pad closed. "Go home, Kelly. I'll get hold of you if I need you again."

"Thanks." She glanced at her watch, grimaced. Quarter to eleven. What a way to spend an evening.

"I'll take you whenever you're ready," Ross murmured.

"Thanks. I just have to get my things."

Moments later they were in his car, rumbling toward Kelly's home. When they arrived, she was surprised to see a police cruiser sitting outside, waiting.

"If you'll go inside and check things out, ma'am," the officer asked. "Zach asked me to make sure."

She stared at him, the implication hitting home.

"You think someone has been here, in my house?" She

felt a pressure on her arm, turned to study Ross's face. "Surely no one would break in here?"

"He's not saying they would," Ross reassured. "He just wants to make sure you're all right. Come on, Kelly. I'll go with you. We'll check things out together."

She responded to the tug on her arm, followed Ross to the door. He took her keys, opened it and stepped inside, glancing around first, then waved her in. "Everything look the same as you left it?"

Her white cashmere coat was lying across the arm of the sofa where she'd thrown it, black heels nearby.

"I think so."

"We'll go through each room down here, move upstairs, then check out the basement. Don't worry, I'll be right beside you." His fingers grasped hers, squeezed. "You deserve some peace of mind after what just happened. Checking everything will ensure that."

Kelly squeezed back, but kept her hand in his, drawing him along with her. She felt weak, silly, afraid—the emotions jumbled together as she took him from room to room, nodding each time he asked, "Okay?"

By the time they'd returned to the foyer she'd regained some of her equanimity. With an apologetic look, she slid her fingers from Ross's.

"Thanks," she whispered, feeling the heat rise into her cheeks.

"Anytime," he growled, grinning at her blush. Then he opened the door and addressed the officer. "We've been through the house. Everything looks fine."

"Good. We'll be patrolling past here every little while. You need anything, you dial 911." He stared straight at Kelly, waiting for her nod.

"Thanks." Ross closed the door, twisted the dead bolt,

then turned to face her. "Would it be too much to ask for a cup of hot chocolate?"

"Of course not. I should have offered. Come on into the kitchen and I'll put on some water to warm."

Kelly found her feet moving slowly, as if by rote, and wondered why she couldn't snap out of this cocoon that weighed her down. She wanted to tell Ross she was fine, that she could manage on her own. She didn't want him to see her here in this big empty house, looking like a pathetic figure with no one in all of Chestnut Grove to turn to.

But wasn't that exactly what she was?

"Have a seat. Would you like something to eat with your cocoa?" she asked, hoping he'd say yes.

Kelly had baked a mountain of things before Christmas, thinking she'd have plenty on hand when she invited people over. But holidays were family times and, because she hesitated to break into that laughing closeness that existed between reunited families who got together only once or twice a year, Kelly had ended up asking only a few guests. That left her with a freezer full of fattening food. Oh well, the food bank might take it.

"You wouldn't have any chocolate cake, would you?" Ross asked. "I love chocolate cake, but no matter how well I read the cake mix instructions, I just can't make a decent cake."

The very thought of him mixing and blending made her smile, but she hid it by opening the fridge.

"You certainly are the man of the moment. I happen to have two of them sitting here, but only one is waiting to go to the church outing tomorrow." She held the door open so he could see. "Is that what you'd like?"

At the sight of her mile-high chocolate layer surprise, his eyes grew huge. He licked his lips.

"Perfect. But are you sure you want to cut into one? If you were supposed to bring two—"

"Just one. But I always make two because the filling is a double recipe. Somehow it doesn't taste right if you cut it in half so I always make two cakes. There's plenty for you. I'll give Pilar's dad Salvador a quarter, take some to work, maybe even sneak a piece or two to Rachel's father Charles if I think her mother won't catch me."

"Why shouldn't she catch you?"

"Beatrice is vegan, vegetarian in the extreme. This cake is worse than red meat to her." She giggled at his squinched-up face. "If nothing else, I can always throw what's left away."

"In the garbage?" Ross looked scandalized.

"What else? If I had a dog, I'd feed it to him, but then he'd probably get sick. It's pretty rich," she warned as she set the cake on the counter in front of him.

Ross seemed content to sit there, staring at the cake, so Kelly busied herself making two big mugs of hot chocolate, adding water to the gourmet mix she'd purchased. Then she laced both drinks with some leftover whipped cream. She sprinkled some peppermint mint chips on top, then added a striped candy cane poking through the cream.

Kelly carried her favorite etched mugs to the counter, set one in front of him and one at her own place. She got a plate, a knife, a cake lifter, two forks and a couple of festive napkins. In minutes she had two place settings on each of the quilted placemats she'd made for the holidays. With a flick of a button, the radio began playing soft music that filled the room and helped drain away some of the emptiness she felt inside.

"Aren't you going to taste it?" she asked when Ross made no effort to pick up his fork.

"Uh-huh." But he remained transfixed, his eyes riveted on the dark chocolate layers that sat on regal layers of pure white cream.

The sound of her grandfather clock chimed twelve and sent the sound echoing from the living room throughout the house.

"I'm a bit late but I don't think I ever wished you a happy New Year, Ross," she murmured, holding up her mug.

His eyes met hers. He reached out, grasped his mug and lifted it, touching the rim against hers.

"Happy New Year, Kelly."

The phone chose that precise moment to ring. Kelly set down her untouched mug and lifted the receiver.

"You've been warned," a voice cackled. Then the line went dead.

Chapter Three

Her silence wasn't normal.

Ross glanced up from his drink, took one look at Kelly's face and lifted away the receiver. He clamped it against his ear, but heard nothing.

"Who was it?"

"I don't know." She took the phone from him and hung it up. "They're gone." Her hand was shaking. "Before you ask, whoever it was said only one thing. Apparently I've been warned."

Ross hated to see her so disturbed on what should have been a night for celebrating her friends' marriage. Barricading her inside that closet had been no accident and a threatening phone call proved someone had malicious intent. But he wasn't going to say it and add to her concerns, not now. He reached over, squeezed her fingers with his.

"I'll call Zach."

But Kelly stopped him. "Please, let it alone for now. Telling him in the morning will be soon enough. I don't want to ruin the entire night for him."

He didn't like it but her tone was so beseeching that he

finally nodded and let it go. "I guess they wouldn't be able to set up tracers tonight anyway." He hit * 69 and listened as a bodiless voice told him the call could not be traced.

"Probably used a cell phone. Or a pay phone." She pretended lack of concern, though her cheeks were paper white. "Let's take our food into the den. I'll light a fire and we can reminisce about happier times."

Though he followed her out off the kitchen and into the oak paneled den, cake and cup in tow, Ross knew he didn't have a whole lot of memories he wanted to reminisce on. It was all right for Kelly, she'd had a happy childhood. His, not so much.

"Here we are." She lit the fire then sank into a big armchair and waved him to a nearby seat. "Now tell me about yourself. You came here from Richmond?"

"Yes." He knew from experience that not responding only elicited more questions in Chestnut Grove. "Originally from New York," he muttered. "Brooklyn."

"Wow! I've never lived in such a big city. It must be interesting." She paused, waited for him to embellish, and when he didn't she turned her attention to the fire. "Someone told me you used to be a cop. What was that like?"

"Ugly." Her blink of surprise told him his one word had said too much to stop now. He took a sip of his drink while his brain organized his thoughts. "I was assigned to some pretty nasty areas. Too many drugs, too many weapons, too much poverty."

"And you burned out?" She nodded, her brown eyes soft with compassion. "I can understand that. Sometimes I feel that way when an adoption doesn't go through. The adoptive mom loves that child so much but all she can do is watch the child be taken away. It's heartbreaking for both of them."

Kelly fell silent, the cup still clasped between her hands though her mind was obviously on just such a case. Ross fidgeted, wished he could think of something to change the subject.

"Was there something specific that made you leave?" she asked several moments later. "I've heard that it usually takes a life-altering event for a police officer to move away from that line of work."

"Private investigation isn't that far off," he murmured and sighed at her expectant gaze. "But yes, I did have a reason to get out. I almost killed a kid."

He waited for the shock and horror those words always induced. Kelly Young displayed none of that. She simply sat in her chair, legs curled under her, watching him as if she knew there was more to the story.

Why was he telling her this when he'd kept it to himself for so long? Ross didn't know but he blamed it on the fire and the intimacy it brought.

"He was strung out—crack, heroin, I don't know which. Didn't really matter. All of fifteen years old and he looked thirty." He dragged a hand through his hair as his stomach knotted into a hard lump of anger. "He'd robbed a convenience store, assaulted the owner and taken his gun. When I got there the kid was strutting his stuff in the street, waving that gun like it was Excalibur and he was Arthur."

Ross closed his eyes, relived the moment.

"I tried to talk him down, tried reason, control, everything I could think of. He was too high. A little girl came around the corner. He grabbed her, pointed the gun at her head." He stared at Kelly, prayed she'd understand. "I had to take my best shot. I couldn't let another innocent die. I couldn't stand there and let it happen."

"Of course you couldn't. I understand that." She leaned

forward, her hair slanting over her smooth pale cheek as she set her untouched drink on the table. Then she reached out to touch his knee. "You did your job, Ross."

"Yeah, I did." He pinched his lips together. Some job. Shooting a fifteen-year-old addict. "It was the third drug call that night, all of them violent. By the time I got back to the station I knew I couldn't do it anymore. So I handed in my notice, worked my time and left."

It was a little more complicated than that, but she didn't need to know.

"And came to Richmond." A soft sweet smile tilted up her lips. "That was when?"

"Two years ago."

"And you've never gone back?"

"A couple of times." He did not want to get into this now.

"I suppose you miss your friends from the precinct. Or is it the fast pace of the work?"

"Neither." He swallowed, sucked in a breath. "I went to see my mother. And my sister, Trista."

"That's nice. Your mother must love having you back to spoil." The look in her eyes told him she'd shared a lot of happy times with her adoptive mother.

"Hardly. I doubt she even knew if I was there. She has Alzheimer's. Most of the time she doesn't even know who I am." Ross couldn't stop the rush of words. He'd have to get out more often. Maybe that would help him get control of his tongue.

Something, possibly pity, washed over Kelly's face. He hated seeing it, didn't want her to offer him that. Ross blurted out the first thing that came into his head.

"When are you going to see Sandra?"

Kelly's alabaster skin lost some of the faint glow it had begun to regain and stretched a little tighter. "I don't know."

"Soon?"

"I told you, I don't know when. Too much has happened, I haven't had a chance to really think about it." She stared at her hands, fingers threaded together. "I suppose after the holidays."

"This is after the holidays. Tomorrow?" he persisted, knowing she hated being pressed but he was worried on Sandra's behalf. She'd waited so long for that special moment when she'd finally meet her long-lost child. Surely Kelly could understand that.

Kelly shook her head. "I can't tomorrow. I told you, we're having a church social. We usually spend the afternoon at the ski hill. After that we go to the Morrow mansion. Lindsay Morrow—do you know her?"

"Know of her." He nodded. "The mayor's wife."

"Yes. Around here she's known for her big society events. Remember the Christmas tree lighting and reception? Well, every year she hosts a second event at her home a few days after the festive season is finished—to celebrate the New Year, she claims. It's always a big deal, casual, but something we all talk about for weeks to come."

"Talk about, why?" He couldn't fathom what that odd little note in her voice alluded to.

"I guess you'd have to know Mrs. Morrow to understand." Kelly nibbled on her fingernail, her smooth forehead furrowed. "They go to our church sometimes, but… well, she's not a joiner. She's more high society than most of us, moves in a different circle."

"There are circles in little old Chestnut Grove?" he teased, then watched her cheeks flush a warm clear rose.

"Sort of. People like the Morrows belong to the country club set. You know, the wealthy, perfect people. I mean, have you ever looked at Lindsay Morrow? She could have been a model with that rail-thin body of hers. Makes the rest of us envious."

"Really?" He thought Kelly was far more attractive. Judging by tonight, he'd found her comfortable to be around, friendly, the kind of person you could easily talk to. She was also gorgeous; the whole package was perfect. By contrast, Mrs. Morrow, whenever he'd met her, seemed cold, standoffish. "I guess she looks okay, but—"

"Okay?" Kelly laughed. "Lindsay Morrow is pure glam. The way her glossy black hair swoops across that aristocratic jaw, never a hair out of place. Those deep, dark midnight eyes, the straight confident set of her shoulders—she's regal. Her clothes only reinforce her image—nothing but designer labels."

"Huh." He mulled it over. "Ambitious, powerful, privileged. It's intimidating. She's the opposite of Sandra, I guess. I think I'd feel like an overgrown oaf around Mrs. Morrow, but Sandra always makes me feel welcome. She gets this look, kind of a shy smile that makes you glad you came to see her."

"Really?" The temperature of Kelly's voice dropped several degrees.

"Really." Ross frowned. "Why do you hate her?"

"Me? I don't hate Sandra Lange. Not at all." Bright red spots of color appeared in her cheeks. To hide it, she fiddled with her mug of hot chocolate, then rose to her feet with some excuse about cookies and rushed out of the room. When Kelly finally came back she carried a dish of gingersnaps and a glass of milk.

She held out the plate.

"These used to be my dad's favorite," she murmured, then froze, her eyes flying to his. "My adoptive father," she corrected. She took a deep breath, met his gaze head on.

"I just realized—if you know who my birth mother is, you must know who my biological father is as well?"

He hated lying to her, hated the secretiveness Sandra had insisted upon. But the secret was not his to share.

"You'll have to ask Sandra," he murmured. "It's something she should tell you."

"Of course." She stared at the big round cookie, took a bite. After a moment she pointed to the bowl. "Help yourself."

He moved to take one, then realized that the luscious piece of chocolate cake still sat on the plate on the table in front of him.

"I'd rather eat this," he told her with a grin. "What's with that glass of milk?"

"I've changed my mind. I don't feel like hot chocolate tonight. Too much of a good thing at Christmas, I guess. Anyway, Dad always said gingersnaps and milk were made to go together."

They sat together in front of the fire, he with his chocolate overload, she with her cookies and milk. She had the art of dipping down to a science, holding the cookie in the milk just long enough to saturate it, but not long enough for it to fall apart. Then she'd slip the sopping bit into her mouth. She caught him staring and grinned.

"Help yourself," she offered. "I can get you a glass of milk if you want."

"No thanks. The cake was great, more than enough." Ross leaned back, watched her drink the last of the milk. She dabbed at her lips with a napkin covered with nutcrackers as she stared into the fire. That's when he knew he had to press the issue, for Sandra's sake.

"Why not tomorrow, Kelly? Just for a few minutes. Sandra would love to see you."

"I told you, tomorrow's busy."

"The next day then."

"I have to be at work. It's a busy time, cleaning up details from the end of the year, some staff on extended holidays. Things like that."

"So busy you can't make time for Sandra—a half hour out of your busy schedule to see a woman who's waited all those years?"

"Waited?" The anger on her face blazed at him, her voice altered, brimmed with outrage. "She *gave* me away."

"But—"

Kelly held up a hand. "I'm not saying that was wrong, I don't know her circumstances. But surely if she'd wanted me—"

He couldn't let her go on. "Sandra didn't give you away willingly, Kelly."

"What?" Her frown was part puzzlement, part fury. "She signed the papers, she had to. It's the law. Without her consent—"

"Yes, but she was under the effects of anesthetic when she did that. Once she woke up, she'd changed her mind." He had to keep going, had to make her understand. "She wanted to raise you herself but she was manipulated into giving you up and then you were gone. She's spent years regretting that she wasn't stronger, that she didn't argue to hang on to you. She's always wondered about you, tried to find out who you were, where you went."

"Wondered…about me?" The whisper slipped out from her white lips. Her eyes grew huge. "She didn't even know me. She never looked before, did she?"

"No," he admitted. "Because she thought it would be selfish to disrupt your new life. But she never forgot her child. And she dearly wanted that child back, in her arms."

"Wait a minute!" Kelly jerked back. "You said she was

manipulated. Are you saying my parents tried to persuade her? Because I will never believe that."

"No, not your parents. From what I've been able to learn, they had no idea of your connection to Sandra, or that your adoptive mother ever wanted to know about you. That was deliberately kept from them."

"By whom?"

"Barnaby Harcourt, for one."

She stared at him. "Mine was the first adoption he arranged," she whispered. "I knew he did some terrible things, changed official records, but—" She shook her head. Tears squeezed from the corners of her eyes, rolled down her cheeks. "My parents gave me my birth records years ago. They said my parents were deceased. He must have altered them, just like all the rest. That's why there were two sets."

"I'm sorry, Kelly."

"I thought I was Kelly Young. That was my history," she whispered, staring at him. "I liked my life, loved my parents, found a job in the town where I grew up. Taking on the directorship of Tiny Blessings, that was my way of giving back to the community where I belonged. And now you're telling me that everything I ever believed was a lie."

She wasn't talking to him. Ross understood enough about Kelly Young to realize that her questions were directed toward heaven and the God she trusted. He'd seen this in others in Chestnut Grove.

"It isn't all a lie. Your parents loved you, cared for you. That won't ever change. You have that to hang on to forever." She seemed frozen so Ross tried again, choosing a different tack this time. "Knowing about Sandra, that could be for the good. You could find out your real history." That sounded lame. "Just see her—it only has to be a few moments. Talk to her. Maybe you'll find the answers you need. Please?"

He'd tried everything short of begging, but Ross was even willing to go that far if it would get Sandra the meeting she craved. She'd been like an expectant child when he'd left her, hardly able to control her excitement as she planned and dreamed of that special moment in time when she'd finally get to meet her child as a mother.

What if it never happened?

A change seemed to come over Kelly. She drew herself erect, blinked away her tears.

"I suppose I can't put it off forever." Her dark gaze narrowed, fixed on him intently. "I'll go on one condition."

Uh-oh.

"What condition?"

"I'll go see Sandra if you'll come to the church social tomorrow." She met his gaze, her own implacable. "Well? You're so big on me experiencing new things, how about walking your talk? Is it a deal?"

Kelly looked like she expected him to refuse and normally he would have. Ross had steered clear of the church for years. There was enough guilt in the world, he didn't need someone else telling him he was a mess. But in that moment he made a split-second decision he hoped he wouldn't regret.

He'd go to that church social for Sandra, because her faith was different than any he'd ever seen. She didn't rail at God, or spend days and hours weeping for what she'd lost, as his own mother had. Sandra took what she was dealt and pressed on, made what she had into something better. She needed to meet her daughter, needed the closure it would bring to her aching heart.

"Fine." He lifted his head, glared at her. "It's a deal."

"You'll come?" Kelly's surprised look was laughable.

"That's what I just said." He gulped down the trepidation that filled him, pretended it wouldn't bother him in the least to be around a bunch of goody-two-shoes. "What time should I pick you up?"

Her eyes turned bittersweet, secrets fluttering through them.

"We usually go skiing after church. By any chance would you consider coming to the morning service—"

"Don't push it, Kelly." Next she'd be trying to suck him into thinking God cared whether Ross Van Zandt had paid for his sins.

"Okay, I won't push it." She shrugged. "But you don't have to pick me up. I can catch a ride with someone and meet you there."

Leaving him to walk into the hornet's nest of church people alone? No way.

"I'll be here," he reiterated. "What time?"

They'd just decided on a time when the front doorbell rang.

"Pretty late for callers," he muttered, more to himself than her. He had a sudden replay of her hunched in that closet and made sure he was two steps behind when Kelly opened the door.

A uniformed officer stood on the step, face peeking out from beneath her cap. "Glynis Barnes. Zach sent me over to stay with you tonight."

"Oh. How thoughtful of him," Kelly murmured. "Please, come in."

"Wait a minute." Ross stepped forward, blocking her path. "Do you have identification?"

Officer Barnes nodded, pulled out her badge and waited until he'd studied it. Satisfied, Ross handed it back, caught a bit of movement from the corner of his eye and turned.

Kelly's eyes grew huge, then she seemed to waver. He grasped her arms, held her upright.

"Hey! What's the matter?"

"I don't know. All of a sudden I don't feel very well."

"I'm the one who should be woozy after all that chocolate. You didn't even have any."

"Yoo." But she barely smiled at his joke, her face blanching as her fingers clutched his arm. "Oh, my."

"You need to sit down." He guided her back into the den, helped her into a chair. "Better?"

She shook her head "yes" once, but that changed to a violent "no" as she lurched to her feet and headed out of the room as if on fire.

"She's sick. I'll look after her," the cop told him calmly, then followed Kelly.

Left on his own, Ross paced the den for several minutes, wondering why she'd suddenly become so sick. Probably the gingersnaps, he decided with a grimace. That particular cookie had never been one of his favorites, though in his childhood years he'd never had a choice between the kinds of cookies he'd enjoyed. He'd considered it a good day if there was bread in the house. Treats of any kind were a luxury.

He wasn't sure how long he waited until Kelly returned. She was whiter than cotton wool and her eyes were glossy.

"I'm sorry," she whispered, her voice wobbly. "I don't know what happened. I don't feel very well. I think I'll go to bed."

"Probably the best thing," he agreed. "Now that you've got—" he glanced at the cop standing nearby, raised one eyebrow, her name forgotten in the excitement.

"Glynis," she supplied.

"Now that you've got Glynis here, I guess I'd better go,

too. Take it easy, okay? If you don't feel better tomorrow, we can cancel."

"You wish!" A bit of her fighting spirit had returned to those expressive eyes and Ross was glad to see it.

"No, I don't wish. I think I might even be looking forward to it." Which was more truth than she needed to hear. But the simple fact was, something about Kelly Young made him want to stick around.

She nodded, but her skin was turning that sickly shade of green again and Ross figured this was a great time to get out. He headed for the door, grabbed his coat, slid on his shoes and waved a hand.

"Take care."

"Yes. Thank you for everything."

A moment later Glynis closed the door behind him. He walked into the chilly night air, climbed into his car and revved the engine, hoping it would warm soon and send out some heat. He decided to visit Sandra. She'd want to know what happened and he needed to see her, to let her know he'd told Kelly the truth.

He wouldn't explain that Kelly had been less than ecstatic about meeting her birth mother. Later, of course. But not now, not tonight. Tonight he just wanted Sandra to know that her daughter, Kelly, knew she had a mother nearby.

The streets were deserted and Ross made good time. He'd phoned Sandra on his cell to make sure she was up to receiving guests and learned she'd been sitting by the phone, waiting and wondering. Several minutes later he pulled up in front of her pretty little house and walked up to the door. She opened it before he could knock, her face brimming with questions.

"How did it go?" Sandra asked after she'd hugged him.

He'd begun to enjoy those bursts of affection she showered on him.

"Kelly was surprised but I think she took it okay." He'd already decided not to tell Sandra about the rest of the events that night. She would only worry. "She's going to need a bit of time to absorb it all."

"Of course." Sandra perched on the edge of the piano bench and knotted her fingers together. "Did she seem upset?"

Ross chose his words carefully.

"Not upset. But it's hard for her to understand. I think she's fighting her feelings, as if getting to know her birth mother means somehow betraying her adoptive mother. When I told her you'd been pressured to give her away, she was pretty amazed."

"Shocked, you mean. I don't blame her. I've wondered for years how I could have let him talk me into it." Sandra jumped to her feet. "I think I'll make some tea. And I've got a piece of pie for you. I brought it back from the diner."

"No, thanks, Sandra. Nothing for me. Please." He rose and grasped her hands when they would have reached to fill the kettle. "You need to rest. Come and sit down," he cajoled. "Stop fussing over me and take some time to let things sink in."

Sandra had pushed her way through the cancer treatments with a will and determination Ross admired. She'd come through like a trooper, was on the mend now. But he'd glimpsed those times when she sagged from her battle against the deadly disease. He'd seen firsthand how her need to seem all right in front of her staff and customers at the diner had left her sapped of energy when she came home where no one could see. He was prepared to argue with her now if it would make her conserve whatever strength she could muster for what might lay ahead. Emotionally she was needy. What happened with Kelly could drain her and make her physical recovery more difficult.

Ross led her to the nearest easy chair, waited until she was seated, then pulled up a footstool and sat down in front of her. He took her hands in his.

"You had a baby girl, a daughter," he murmured, knowing she hadn't yet begun to absorb that detail, though he'd told her about the DNA results hours ago.

"I know. A girl named Kelly." Tears rushed to her eyes and she dashed them away. "And such a pretty girl. Did you notice her hair? Those streaks—gold and silver and bronze, all mixed up together. I used to try so hard to get my hair those exact shades when I was her age. Of course hairdressers didn't do highlights nearly as well back then and my parents condemned me for coloring my hair, but still…" She stretched a hand to the area just above her ear, rubbed her fingers against the downy tendrils that had begun regrowing after her chemo treatments.

"Kelly is as beautiful as her mother," he murmured, his heart pinching at the soft sheen of love that radiated from Sandra's pretty face. "She has to love you, Sandra. She won't be able to help it. Just give her time."

"You're so sweet to me, Ross." She enveloped him in another tight hug, then leaned back and pinched his cheek. "Why hasn't some smart woman snapped you up?"

He didn't want to hurt her, so he laughed, drew away. "Because I'm smarter and besides, I don't want to be snapped."

"Don't you believe in marriage, Ross?"

"Not the ones I've seen," he muttered, keeping his face averted as he thought of his alcoholic parents and their notorious brawls.

"Then you haven't seen the right ones. Marriage can and should be a true meeting of two minds, not to force one to be like the other, but to complement each other. The wife a blessing to her husband and vice versa."

He grinned. "How'd you become such an expert?"

"Watching my own parents." Sandra smiled at the memory. "They had this bond that made them complete. I always wanted what they had. Sometimes I felt a little bit left out because their world seemed complete when they had each other. Maybe that's why I tried so hard to find love, maybe that's what scared away—" She stopped, peered up at him. "Never mind."

"You were going to say that's what drove him away, weren't you?" He shook his head. "It isn't. He was a cheater before you met him, Sandra. Men like that feed on women who trust them. He was a creep. The fact that he made you believe you had to give away your baby only proves it."

"He told me she was with a family in California." She struggled to keep her voice even. "He claimed she had everything a child could need."

"Well, we know the Youngs did live in California for a while. You couldn't have known they'd move back here when she was just a few years old." He chewed his bottom lip. "For the rest of it—I think Kelly did have everything she needed. She speaks of the Youngs with great love. You must have known them so you'd know how they were with her."

"They loved her the way a precious child should be loved." Sandra sighed. "I couldn't have chosen anyone better myself."

He remained silent a moment, thinking. But he had to prepare her. "That love they showered on her might be what will make it hard for Kelly to accept you as her mother, Sandra."

"What do you mean?" Her green eyes grew wide. "How can having loving parents make her hate me?"

"She doesn't hate you. But she won't want to betray them, either. The Youngs are the only family she's ever known. She was told her birth parents were dead. Loving you, calling you Mom—that might seem like betrayal toward the woman she's looked up to for so many years."

"I don't want to take away anything Marcus or Carol were to that child! I thank God every day that they were there when I couldn't be, that they loved her, raised her to trust God. It's because of them that Kelly is who she is today—a beautiful, strong, caring woman who loves God and gives back to the community." Sandra gulped. "Of course I wish it could have been me, but God directed otherwise."

God again. He bit his lip to stop the question—why hadn't God straightened out this mess thirty-odd years ago and saved her the heartache?

"I know you don't understand my beliefs, Ross. You're angry on my behalf, and that's sweet. But I've been without my child for many years and I've had to learn understanding. God knows what He's doing. He has a plan that is far bigger than what I see. Maybe I'll live long enough to find out what it is, but even if I don't, I still trust Him. He knows the plans He has for me, plans to prosper and not to harm."

Another of her Biblical quotes. How did you argue against faith like that? Ross studied the serenity filling her face and wished he could figure out her attitude. Sandra was the loser in this. She'd missed the special times he was pretty sure most mothers treasured in their secret hearts—first steps, first words, first day at school, first boyfriend, first kiss. All the things his own mother had never given a hoot about.

Like snowflakes dropping from the sky, the questions filled him. Why hadn't he been born to Sandra? Why hadn't her God looked after him, given him a loving home?

He knew why.

Because of Trista. His little sister would never have made it if he hadn't been there to protect her. For her sake he was glad he had been. But that didn't make the living hell of his past any less brutal. His father was dead, his mother seldom recognized him, let alone cared about him. The only one he had left was Trista.

"When is Kelly coming to see me?" Sandra's quiet voice brimmed with barely suppressed delight. "When can we talk?"

"Kelly promised that if I went to this church social she'll be attending tomorrow, she'd come to see you after that. I don't have a specific time yet, but I'll get one." He grinned, waggled a finger at her. "A skiing day! The things I do for you, Sandra Lange."

"Like dating Kelly is a hardship." She chuckled. "Puh-leeze."

"It's not a date, it's…reciprocity." His face felt hotter than the fire at Kelly's. "I go with her, she comes here. That's the deal."

"Martyrdom, here comes Ross Van Zandt." Sandra giggled, then quickly sobered. "I'm not so sure it's a good thing if you had to bribe her to see me."

"It wasn't a bribe." He huffed out a sigh. "Will you give it up, Sandra? She's coming to see you, that's what you wanted. Isn't that enough?"

"Shame on me." She reached up, touched his cheek with her fingertips in a gentle caress he would never tire of. "Yes, my dear man, it is more than enough. Thank you."

"Welcome," he mumbled, embarrassed by the soft glow

of love in her eyes. How could she love him? She didn't even know him, wouldn't want to if she did.

"It's been a long day. You're tired and with all you've done, who could blame you." She brushed her palm across his hair, pushed back a lock of hair and patted his cheek. "Go home and get some rest, Ross. Tomorrow's going to be a busy day."

"Yeah, skiing." He made a face. "I'll probably end up in the hospital with two broken legs and a concussion. People like me don't do skiing."

"People like you? It's not the technique, it's the attitude," she told him. "Stop expecting the worst. Besides, after that everyone goes to the Morrow mansion."

"Oh, goody," he mocked her. "The Ice Queen in her palace."

Sandra stared him down until he wished he hadn't made the comment.

"I'm old enough to be your mother, Ross, so let me give you some motherly advice. If you look hard enough, you'll always find something bad about people. But if you look hard enough, you'll always find something good, too."

"Okay, Mother. I'll try to see something good in her."

She rose, grasped his hand and tugged. Ross stood, would have pulled away, but her hands refused to let go.

"You've done so much for me and I don't know how I'll ever repay you. Finding Kelly—it's like a dream come true. I couldn't have asked for a more wonderful daughter. You gave her to me. You are a man to be proud of, Ross."

"Good night, Sandra." He bent, kissed her cheek, squeezed her hand, then let himself out.

Immediately, the warmth Sandra always shed was overpowered by the frosty winter night. He shivered, climbed into his car and without warming the engine, headed for home. Home—that was a joke.

He unlocked the door and stepped inside the miserable apartment. A fax machine, his surveillance equipment—hardly the comforts he'd found in Kelly's beautiful house. No silky drapes, plush sofas or comfy cushions here. Certainly nothing that would hint at time and attention spent on decorating the space. This was a strictly utilitarian area meant to remind him every time he stepped in it that he was here for one reason only—to reunite Sandra with her long-lost child.

As soon as that was done his purpose here would be over. Funny how he didn't want to think about leaving.

Ross walked to the window, picked up the plain wooden frame that held a photo of Trista taken at her campus in Atlanta. It still amazed him that she'd married some preppy fellow from an Ivy League school and chosen law for herself. Kelly was like Trista—reserved, pulled into herself, as if she were afraid to let anyone know she wasn't as strong as they thought.

He knew why Trista was like that, but what made Kelly Young so reticent?

And why did someone want her out of town so badly they would tamper with her steering, barricade her in a closet and threaten her over the phone?

All questions he'd like to ask Sandra's God.

Chapter Four

Kelly was almost out the door when the phone rang. She debated only a second before picking up the receiver.

"Hello?"

"So you're up and around this morning?" Ross's low voice held a hint of amusement. "I guess the gingersnaps couldn't keep you down, huh?"

"Not for long." She wasn't going to mention that her stomach was still doing odd little twists and turns or the horrible dreams she'd had. "Actually I'm just going out the door." She knew he wouldn't come. But she asked anyway. "Want to join me for church?"

"No, thanks. I just wondered what time I should pick you up." The chuckle in his voice was gone. Now it was all business.

"I'll meet you here at noon. We'll have a bite to eat, then head out to meet the others. Is that all right?"

"You don't have to cook for me, Kelly. In fact, I should be taking you out."

"Why?" She frowned into the phone. "Look, if I don't leave now, I'll be late. Dinner's already in the oven. Just be here. Bye." She waited until she heard his response, then quickly hung up the phone before he could think of another excuse. Just as quickly it rang again.

"You're coming," she said firmly. "You promised and you'd better be there."

No response.

"Hello?" Only silence. "This isn't funny, Ross."

His low grumble didn't answer, but there was someone there. She could tell by the slight breathy sound.

"Stop phoning me," she said sharply, then slammed down the phone.

Before it could ring again, Kelly was out the door, walking down the street toward Chestnut Grove Community Church. It was a longish walk, but fortunately the day was mild. Kelly began to enjoy herself as the sun shone glittering white against the snow that had drifted down sometime during the night.

She spared a thought for the newlyweds, wondered if Ben knew he wasn't Sandra's long lost child. Ross would have told him, she was sure. Poor Ben—he actually wanted to know about his birth parents. That had never been an issue with Kelly.

She remembered a day as clear as this morning. After the holidays, at home, waiting for school to begin. She'd been eleven when her mother had sat her down for a talk. Kelly had assumed the discussion would revolve around the birds and the bees, but to her surprise her mother had explained about her adoption.

"Are you upset?" her mother had asked.

"No. Not upset." How could she be upset that her parents had wanted her, loved her even though she'd been born to someone else? She'd told her mother that, but not about the secret rush of worry that tucked itself into her heart as she wondered if anyone could ever take her away from her parents.

Neither had she told them about the dreams she'd had, horrible nightmares where a woman tried to grab her, told her that it was all a mistake, that the Youngs weren't supposed to get her but another child—one who was prettier, smarter, one more worthy of being loved by them.

As she walked along the shoveled walks, Kelly could almost feel the oppression of those horrible dreams. After years of being nightmare-free, she'd had it again last night. Only this time it was worse. This time Sandra Lange had been the woman pulling her out of her mother's arms.

It was just a dream. It's not reality. Sandra isn't like that.

But though she repeated the words to herself over and over, she didn't feel comforted. It wasn't a good way to start the morning. Sunday school was the usual hectic hour it had always been. She loved team-teaching the senior girls but they were a challenge, and with Leah away, Kelly was forced to keep her mind on the topic at hand.

Kelly dismissed her class a few minutes early so she could take her place in the sanctuary. She tried to find a sense of peace to hush the whirlwind in her brain that rose up whenever she thought about Sandra and facing her, trying to feel that bond that had come so naturally with her own mother. What would Sandra expect?

The Morrows moved past her down the aisle, Lindsay Morrow dragging at her husband's arm when he would have sat on one of the back pews. Clearly she wanted more attention, Kelly mused and then checked herself for her lousy attitude. She was a little jealous of Lindsay's electric blue silk suit and the way it fit. The woman was made to wear beautiful clothes. Gerald, on the other hand, though his suit was no doubt custom-made, looked uncomfortable in it. He took his place at the end of the front pew beside his wife, then buried himself in the bulletin.

Eli and Rachel Cavanaugh sat down in front of her. "Wasn't the wedding lovely?" Rachel asked her, looking deliriously happy herself. "Leah was a beautiful bride."

"Yes, she was."

"I noticed you left early. Is anything wrong?"

"No. Just a personal detail I had to take care of." Kelly had no desire to admit to people she'd known for years that she'd just found out she was the illegitimate daughter of a woman she'd known most of her life. What would they think of her?

"I noticed you came to the wedding with Ross."

"Yes. I had a problem with my car and he gave me a ride. I was so late I was afraid I'd miss everything but I made it. I saw Caleb and Anne slip in for the ceremony."

"Yes. Anne said she couldn't possibly miss it. They left again right after. They looked pretty happy, too."

"Must be a love bug going around." Kelly heaved a silent sigh of relief as Pastor Fraser stepped to the podium and began his usual welcome speech. Meg Talbot Kierney slipped in on the other end of her pew, smiled, then turned to help her son Luke. Jared and Chance followed them minutes later.

Meg Kierney, Rachel Noble Cavanaugh, Pilar Estes Fletcher and Anne Smith—though now she was Anne Williams—usually lunched together at Sandra's Starlight Diner after Sunday morning service. Kelly had gone along sometimes, but she'd never really felt as close to the four women as they obviously did to each other. And never more so than now when each was happily married and she was dealing with a past she'd never expected, never wanted and didn't know how to face. Everything about Sandra's secret seemed tawdry, ugly.

"Now for just a few of the announcements. We want to make you aware of a new fund-raising event. The Noble Foundation will be hosting a Valentine's event and I know they'd be glad of your support. Details will be forthcoming, but if you're able to help in any way, there is a sign-up sheet in the foyer. A meeting will be called later."

Finally the litany of soon-to-happen events was finished and the congregation rose to greet each other. Kelly stood, welcomed Meg, Rachel and Eli and anyone else who offered their hand, but inside she squirmed. In a couple of days word would get out all over town and they'd all know she wasn't Kelly Young anymore. She'd be someone else, someone with a new mother, someone people talked about. She wanted to run home, lock herself inside and pray for the whole thing to be a dream. Which just went to show how un-perfect her perfect life really was.

Somehow she got through the morning, rose when the others did, mindlessly sang the songs she'd grown up with. At one point in the sermon she'd glanced over one shoulder and spotted Sandra Lange seated in the back, watching her. Kelly quickly glanced away, then felt a rush of guilt. That was her mother! And she was trying to ignore her.

Kelly didn't understand her own reluctance to face Sandra. She had nothing against the woman, felt she was a good member of the community. She'd heard that Sandra had stepped in after her own mother had been killed in a fire at the diner. At one time she'd lived in Richmond, or something—the details were sketchy. Kelly had heard that she'd moved back to Chestnut Grove, worked with her father and eventually inherited the diner from him. Sandra was a kind woman, she worked hard, there was nothing to be afraid of.

And yet Kelly couldn't rid herself of the fear that the

security she'd found in her past was forever destroyed. Whatever lay in the future frightened her because she was no longer in control.

At the end of the service Kelly sidestepped several people and made her escape through a side door. It would be better at the party, she told herself. Ross would be there and she could use him to block any unwanted discussions. It was unlikely Sandra would go skiing, even more unlikely that she'd show up at the Morrows'. The past two years when Kelly had attended she'd never once seen Sandra Lange attend.

"You'd better get in before you kill yourself."

She blinked, surprised to find Ross driving along beside her. "Why would I get killed?"

"Walking so fast on ice." He frowned. "Church must have been bad if you had to run away."

"Ha-ha." Aware that two of the town busybodies were only a half bock behind, Kelly climbed into the car. "What are you doing cruising around? Spying on someone?"

"My being a private investigator bugs you, doesn't it?" He shrugged. "Can't help it, Kelly. That's what I do."

"I'd hate it."

"Why?"

She scrounged for an answer and decided to be honest. "Poking into other people's private business." She shook her head. "Some people prefer their privacy."

"People like you." He drove toward her home at a snail's pace. "You know, ever since I came to town I've noticed something about you."

"Spying on me?" she snapped.

"No. Just taking note of human nature."

He smiled but Kelly wasn't fooled. "And I suppose now you're going to tell me about my human nature."

"Maybe. You're so reserved. I don't understand that. You grew up with the Youngs, never wanted for anything, your life was as stable as could be. Your parents loved you, you loved them." He frowned, shook his head. "To me it looks like you had the perfect childhood."

"Pretty close," she agreed. "Is there something wrong with that?"

"Of course not. But that's why I don't understand your attitude."

"My attitude?" She waited until he'd shifted into Park on her driveway, then opened her door. "There's nothing wrong with my attitude. I'm perfectly normal, so don't go putting my life under a microscope, Ross Van Zandt. I'm not one of your P.I. clients."

She climbed out, stomped her way up the path to the front door, angered by *his* attitude.

"Kelly, wait!"

She heard him pounding up the walk behind her and chose to ignore it, knowing very well that the neighbors wouldn't. Why couldn't she find her keys? Exasperated, she finally moved the brick at the bottom of the column and picked up her spare keys. A second later she had the front door open. Ross stepped in behind her.

"Now you're mad at me and I didn't mean to hurt you. Honestly. I guess I just spend too much time studying people."

That did nothing to appease her. Kelly kept her lips pressed together, headed for the kitchen. "I assume this means you are staying for lunch," she muttered as she lifted the chicken potpie from the oven.

"Would you rather I left?" he asked quietly. Something in his voice made her turn, look at him. His dark eyes crinkled at the corners as if he knew a secret that she didn't. "I could always eat the foot I've stuck in my mouth."

How did you stay angry with someone like that? Kelly sighed and shook her head.

"Of course you should stay. Look, I guess I'm a little touchy. This whole thing with Sandra is hard to deal with." She lifted the salad from the fridge and tossed it with some dressing. "I'm not exactly a teenager. I thought I had my life figured out. I knew who I was, where I came from, where I was going. Then this came along. It's like everything has shifted, as if it's off-kilter and I can't quite get a grip on things. I don't like that feeling."

"You're talking as if you've had something taken away. That's not the case, Kelly."

"Isn't it?" She set the dishes on the table, motioned for him to sit. "It feels like everything I thought was true, everything that defined who Kelly Young is, has shifted." She sighed. "Maybe you're right and I have cold feet or something. I don't know anymore. That's the hard thing about this. My parents, the people I trusted the most, are gone so I can't ask them for advice. All I have to go on is your word."

"Mine and Sandra's." He reached across the table, grasped her hand where it lay on the tablecloth. "If you want to know more, all you have to do is ask. She'd be happy to tell you anything she could. After all, she's been looking for you for a long time."

"Not me."

"You. Maybe she didn't know your name, but you are her child. She has the documentation. Barnaby Harcourt falsified some documents, tried to change the truth, but he couldn't. You are Sandra's child."

She pulled her hand away. Ross leaned back, his face troubled.

"I don't understand what's so terrible about it, Kelly. You have a chance to really know the woman who gave birth to you. Why aren't you grabbing it?"

"I had a mother," she told him, trying not to lose her temper. "I loved her dearly. Just because she died doesn't mean I want somebody else to fill in her place."

"But Sandra doesn't want to do that. She wouldn't even try. She knows how much your parents loved you and she understands how much you loved them."

"Then what does she want?"

"I think it's possible to love more than one person in your life, Kelly."

"That's what you want me to do? Love someone I've only known as a neighbor, a business owner?" She shook her head. "I can't."

"Not right now, perhaps. But you don't have to close the door completely. Maybe if you give it time, maybe if you gave her a chance you'd be surprised by what you and Sandra could share."

"Now that my adoptive mother is gone, you mean?" She was angry, unreasonably so, Kelly decided as she caught sight of herself in the mirror. She didn't understand exactly why, she only knew she wasn't yet ready to accept anyone other than the mother she's always known.

"That's not what I meant."

"That's what it sounded like." To cover the rush of emotions flooding her, she got up, plugged in the kettle for tea. Now, cream and sugar. No, she'd used up the cream in his hot chocolate. Milk then. He watched her the whole time, his gaze relentless.

"Leave that and sit down. Tell me what you're feeling. Please." He waited for her to return to the table then leaned forward. "I won't judge you, I won't try to talk you into anything. Just tell me what's going on in that lovely head of yours."

He was a nice man. She'd never really let herself think that before, hadn't wanted to admit that Ross Van Zandt was different. At the moment he sounded like he cared. He was certainly more determined than other men she'd known, especially Simon, who wouldn't have cared what she thought.

"Kelly? Talk to me."

"All right." She looked at him, held his stare. "How many people in town know the reason you're here?"

"A few, I suppose."

"Quite a few by now, I should think." She pleated and unpleated the nutcracker napkin by her plate. "How many know that I'm Sandra's daughter?"

"You, Ben and Sandra," he answered quickly. "I haven't told anyone else. Ben is away on his honeymoon and I don't think Sandra's broadcasting the news."

"Maybe not yet. But how do you think people will react when they find out?" She couldn't look at him, couldn't stand to see the pity in his eyes.

"Does it matter?"

That surprised her.

"Of course it matters." She did look at him then. "You said you were a student of human nature. Think about it. The gossip will go full force. Everyone will be speculating on every move I make when they find out."

"So?"

He truly didn't understand. Kelly took a deep breath and explained. "I think they'll react just the way you've reacted. I think they'll all wonder why Sandra and I aren't best buddies, why ungrateful Kelly doesn't embrace her true mother with the appropriate devotion an illegitimate child should."

"I'm not—"

"Not what? Sure? I am. To most people, I won't be me anymore. I won't be Kelly Young, daughter of Marcus and Carol Young." Tears welled in her eyes and she could do nothing to stop them rolling down her cheeks. "That's what it says on their headstones you know. Marcus and Carol, always loved by their daughter, Kelly. Their *daughter.* Not some stray who stayed with them because she had nowhere else to go. They were my parents. Carol was my *mother.* She was not a substitute for anyone else, to be pushed out of my heart when the one who gave birth to me came along."

"Oh, Kelly, I don't think anyone would expect you to feel that way, least of all Sandra."

He was appalled by her words, she could tell. But Kelly was beyond caring what Ross thought. She couldn't keep it inside anymore. She had to say it.

"My mother loved me through my temper tantrums, my bossy phase, my know-it-all era. She was there for me whenever I needed her to be. Every year she accepted my silly homemade Mother's Day gifts as if they were gold and kept them in a place of pride, just because I made them. She taught me how to pray, how to read my Bible, she taught me what a mother did. Carol Young was, and always will be, my mother." She glared at him. "Sandra isn't," she whispered, and then returned to the counter as the kettle boiled.

Ross remained silent while she made the tea, carried it to the table and poured them each a cup, adding milk to her own. She dished up a plate for him, one for herself, though she suspected neither of them would be able to eat much. That was all right. The queasiness in her stomach hadn't completely abated anyway.

"It's interesting that you feel like this," he said when she thought the silence could stretch no longer.

"Interesting?" Kelly sipped her tea, watched him. "Why?"

"Well, I was comparing my experience with yours. I've always known who my mother was. She was lousy at it, but I didn't know that, until I got a lot older. I thought all mothers were like that. I listen to you now and I wonder why Sandra couldn't have been my mother. She has so much love to give."

"Maybe she'll adopt you." Kelly managed a smile at her poor joke.

"She already has," he murmured. "But the hole in her heart is because of you. She'll understand that you have reservations, Kelly. I'm sure she has a few of her own. But can't you just push all that worry and speculation back until you meet with her, find out firsthand what she's thinking?"

"I suppose I'll have to." That seemed to settle the issue and after a few awkward moments, they managed to consume some of the chicken potpie she'd made.

"Do you like cooking?" Ross speared the last bit of cucumber from his plate, his eyes on her. "Chocolate cakes, this meal today, those gingersnaps—you must get some pleasure out of creating this great food."

"I didn't used to. But when I came back here after college I decided I needed to learn to cook for—" She stopped and gulped. Why had she said that?

"A man?" he guessed.

What was the point of pretending? He'd hear about it from any of the locals if he asked.

"Yes. My fiancé, Simon. We were engaged. Actually we planned to buy this house together."

"Really." He glanced around in interest. "I didn't realize. Could he cook?"

"Simon?" She blinked. "I don't think so. At least, he never offered. He liked to come over to my place for dinner, but I always prepared it. Why did you ask that?"

"No reason." He shrugged. "Just seems like most men nowadays at least have the basic knowledge of how to take care of themselves."

"Simon was devoted to his business."

"And you, of course."

"Of course." But he hadn't been, not really. Kelly skittered around that truth. "He was good at what he did. Eventually he found himself stifled by Chestnut Grove. He wanted to move on. I didn't. I like my job as director at Tiny Blessings. He wanted to sample the bright lights of New York. We called the wedding off, I bought the house, renovated and voila."

"You renovated this place yourself?"

"No, silly. But I did most of the designs, then I hired someone to do the work." She sipped her tea, added some more milk. "It's turned out pretty well, I think. Simon didn't want to make any changes right away. He needed all his cash to pour into his business and remodeling wasn't a priority with him."

"He sounds like an…unusual fiancé. Any guys I've seen who intend on getting married are usually prepared to make their wife and home a priority."

"He did. But he was self-employed and he had to look to the future. That's why his business was so important to him. I offered to help him with it but he didn't like my suggestions. Eventually I figured out that it just wasn't a meeting of the minds. I guess that's why we broke up." They'd broken up because Simon refused to consider her opinion on anything.

"So all of this—" Ross waved a hand around the room "—is your own personal style?"

"Most of it, yes, though I took a few suggestions from the contractors. Is that good or bad?"

"Good. Very good. Your home has a very warm and welcoming feel."

"Thank you." She met his glance, felt her heart give a bump and looked down at her plate. "That's what I was striving for. I guess decorating is a legacy from my mother. I'm not nearly as good at it as she was, but I try. She had this knack of knowing exactly how to make the most of a room. I have to use good old trial and error."

Her mother had been good at everything, particularly at raising a daughter. Kelly had always wanted to emulate her, to measure up, to be the child Carol Young could be proud of.

"In fact, my parents bought the sofa and chair in the living room as my Christmas gift a couple of years ago. Mom thought the fabric was practical and would wear well. I guess it will. I don't use that room much. I kind of prefer the den." Her father's big clock boomed the hour from the living room. "I didn't realize it was so late. We'd better get a move on. Would you like anything more?"

He laughed and rubbed his washboard-flat stomach. "No way. I'll probably roll down the hill as it is."

"I'm afraid the ski hill people don't allow rolling," she murmured, turning her back so he wouldn't see her grin.

"Then I'm in trouble because that's about as much as I know about skiing." He carried the dishes to the counter, where she began scraping them clean. "Should I wash?"

"I wouldn't dream of subjecting you to that torture." She giggled at the relief flooding his face. "We'll shove them in the dishwasher."

They worked well together, with Ross seeming to anticipate her next move. It took only minutes to restore the kitchen to its usual state.

"Okay, I'll just go and change, then we can leave." She started out of the kitchen but his next words made her pause.

"Do you mind if I look around? I'd like to see what else you've done with your house."

Was he looking for something? Kelly chided herself for the thought. Was that what it was going to be like now, suspicious of everyone and everything? She motioned forward.

"Help yourself. I'll be down in a minute."

She found him in the garden room ten minutes later.

"So now you know all my secrets," she murmured, unsure as to her own feelings, knowing he'd found her special place.

"You added this?"

Kelly nodded. "My mother—" She hesitated, hearing the defensiveness in her own voice. She cleared her throat, then continued. "My mother always said I should have been a farmer because I spent so much time poking in the dirt. I just like puttering around with plants so I had this room added on."

"It looks like you've got the right touch." His fingers brushed over the rich ruby leaves of the massive poinsettia she'd left on the bench.

"I don't know about that. This particular plant was supposed to bloom in time for Christmas but here it is the first week in January and it's just begun. I guess my timing's off."

"Does it matter when it flowers?" Ross stared down at her, his dark eyes glowing. "Isn't it just as beautiful now as it would have been then?"

It was like being locked onto a laser beam when he stared at her like that. Kelly couldn't look away.

"You have a point there," she whispered. The silence

stretched long and taut between them. There was something going on—she knew it, felt an emotional connection to him that she'd never felt before. It wasn't just that he was so good-looking. It was that he seemed to understand the things she hadn't said. Which was a silly thing to think when she considered his words about Sandra. Kelly shook her head to dislodge the feelings she didn't want to have. "We need to go."

"Yes. Though it's hard to leave. With the sun shining, this room is like a little bit of the tropics." He took one last look at her abundance of plants, then stepped back, allowing her to precede him through the door.

"I need to get my skis." She moved to the opposite side of the house, toward the door that let to the garage. "They're probably covered in dust," she babbled, needing to fill the silence. "I haven't been skiing in a long—"

Kelly stared at the open door. It had been closed, locked. She remembered checking last night and she certainly hadn't used it this morning.

"Is something wrong?"

"I thought I'd locked this."

Something moved in the cavernous space beyond. Kelly looked again, saw nothing. Maybe she'd only thought she'd seen something. Maybe the nightmares from last night had made her prone to hallucinate. Or perhaps it was the accident. Either way, Kelly wasn't about to explain that she'd just seen something. Ross probably already thought she was a basket case. Why add to that impression when she wasn't even sure?

"No. Everything's fine. Just have to get my gear." She flipped on the overhead light and when she saw nothing heaved a sigh of relief. Her car was still at Vinnie's, of course, so there was no reason for her to have used the garage, but the tiny lights at the bottom of each automatic door still winked green, signaling that the door opener was still active. She'd forgotten to turn it off. And the side door was unlocked.

She locked that, then walked over to the kill switch that blocked power to the overhead doors and flicked it off. Now no one could possibly get in unless the switch was turned on. To do that they'd have to get inside. She lifted her skis down from the rack and carried them toward the house, where Ross immediately lifted them from her arms.

Kelly grabbed her ski boots and poles from a nearby shelf, then closed and locked the connecting door from the garage to the house. When she turned she saw Ross watching her.

"Are you sure you're all right?"

"Yes. Just wanted to turn off the garage doors. No point in having them on since my car's in the shop. Shall we go?"

"Sure." He followed her to the front door. "This is all your gear?"

"It's bright so I should take my goggles, and I need my jacket of course, but yes. Other than those items, I'm ready." He took her boots and poles while Kelly pulled her ski suit out of the closet. She tugged on the jacket but folded the ski pants over one arm. "I'll put these on when we get there. My gloves are in my pocket and my goggles—yes, here they are." She took them from the shelf and smiled at him. "Don't worry, we'll rent you some skis at the hill." She locked the front door, tested it and felt a rush of relief when it stayed firmly closed.

"Thanks a lot. You realize I'm probably courting suicide by going along with this," Ross muttered as he attached her skis and poles to his roof rack.

"Hardly suicide. Anyway, I think you're putting me

on." Kelly pointed. "Why do you have a roof rack if you don't ski?"

"Came with the car when I bought it in Richmond. Seems a lot of people around this area ski. I guess my day has come." He held the door, waited for her to get in.

But Kelly's attention was on something else, someone else. A figure dressed in black scurried out of the hedge at the side of her property and after a quick glance at them hurried down the street in the opposite direction.

"Look. Who is that?"

"Who is what? Where?" Ross turned to look at her, followed her pointing finger down the street. "What do you mean?"

Kelly knew he saw nothing. The figure was gone.

Or maybe it had never been there.

Chapter Five

Although he was grateful for Kelly's obvious preoccupation, Ross couldn't help noticing the furtive glances she kept tossing over her shoulder as she slid alongside him down the bunny hill. What was she looking for?

He'd been at this long enough to know he was no good, so Ross deliberately flopped on his rear, wincing at the pain that came from having already hit that area about a gazillion times. Why had he ever thought snow was soft?

"Had enough?" Kelly bent over, reaching out to help him up.

"Yes. More than enough. I need a break. Hot chocolate would be nice." He brushed away her hand. "Don't help me. I'll end up pulling you over just like last time."

"And the time before that!" She giggled, her laugh a musical treat in the clear sharp air. "But I don't mind."

She didn't seem to. In fact she looked as if she were enjoying herself. He couldn't help but stare at her. Her ski outfit was a soft baby pink that showed off her gorgeous hair to advantage. Her brown eyes twinkled with fun, worry-free now, but he'd seen shadows flicker through off and on all afternoon.

"It strikes me as odd that you ski," he mumbled, struggling to his feet with the grace of an elephant.

"Me? Why? It's really not that hard. My mother started me when I was five."

"That might explain it." He concentrated on getting to the ski lodge without mishap and without taking another header down the hill. Talk about embarrassment.

"Explain what?" Kelly grabbed his pole and tugged on it, directing him out of the line of traffic. "I don't know what you're talking about."

Finally they were there. Ross grabbed on to the railing like a lifeline and heaved a sigh of thanksgiving that he'd survived without mangling his body.

"You're usually so reserved," he puffed, struggling to get his feet free of the long narrow skis, which he personally felt should be called lethal weapons. "I wouldn't have guessed you to be a person who takes chances. From what I've seen, you consider most things before you act. Yet here you are, not in the least afraid to hurl yourself down the side of a mountain going the speed of light."

"Ross," she remonstrated, her smile huge as she watched him move awkwardly in the clompy boots, "technically, I don't think you could call this a mountain. And skiing is not generally considered a suicide sport."

"Until now," he muttered.

"It just takes a certain balance, persistence and skill. Anyone can learn to do it. But you're right. I'm not the type to take unnecessary risks. I like life too much." She pointed to an empty space in the crowded lounge. "Anyway, I'd hardly call what I've been doing on that hill hurling myself down a mountain."

He collapsed onto a nearby bench without answering.

"I'll get us a couple of drinks, okay?"

"My entire body thanks you." He shifted his leg, groaned. "I'd do the gallant thing and offer to get you a drink but I don't think I can walk that far without falling down. I never thought of myself as particularly clumsy but this sure brings it out in me."

"You just need practice. Oh, look, there's Lindsay Morrow. I didn't think she'd be here with the party at her place afterward. But then of course she has servants to look after those things." Kelly hurried toward the food counter, her walk in the stiff boots almost normal.

"Practice, she says. As if I'm ever doing this again!"

"Talking to yourself is the first sign of a very serious disorder." Detective Zach Fletcher flopped down beside him, his grin stretching from ear to ear. "I'm a little surprised to see you sitting again, Van Zandt."

"What do you mean?" Ross finally got one boot undone and dragged his foot out, groaning at the sensation of having one ankle free. He glared at the detective. "I just got in here."

"Yes, but from what I've seen, you've been sitting down most of the afternoon."

"Oh, that's too funny." Ross pressed his cramping toes against the floor boards. "Everybody thinks he's a comedian."

"Okay, since you're in serious pain and trying so hard not to show it, I'll let up and tell you what I've found. I requested a trace on Kelly's phone but that won't happen until tomorrow. From what you said this morning it sounds like a crank, but these days cranks come in all shapes and sizes and some of them are dangerous. We'll see what develops."

"She said she saw someone this morning."

"Doing what?"

Ross explained as best he could. "I didn't see this phantom figure so I'm not much help there, but I can tell you Kelly saw something, or thought she did. Her face was so white I thought she'd pass out. She's not letting on, but I think she's pretty unnerved. Then she was sick last night, too. I don't suppose that helped."

"According to Glynis she had some pretty bad nightmares. My guess is Kelly's having a hard time dealing with your DNA results."

"You know?" Ross was constantly amazed by how little escaped the folks at Chestnut Grove Community Church.

"I can guess. I saw you talking with Ben at the reception. He left with his new wife and you left with Kelly. Doesn't take a genius to figure out the situation."

"Well, don't let it get around. I'm not too sure Kelly's ready for the world to know she's Sandra's daughter." He saw her coming and changed the subject. "Why aren't you working today?"

"Even us lowly cops get days off." Zach smacked him on the shoulder, then rose. "You're courting danger traveling with this guy, Kelly. If he falls on you, you'll be toast. Better get him some private lessons."

"I tried." Kelly handed Ross a steaming cup of rich dark chocolate and winked at Zach. "He *said* he didn't need them," she explained, eyes dancing.

"My advice—next time don't listen to a word he says."

"There isn't going to be a next time. I might be stupid but I'm not a total fool. My skiing days are over," Ross said, finally having pried off his second boot.

"Hey, you guys." Meg Kierney hailed them from a nearby table. "Want to join us or is that a private meeting?"

Ross surveyed the faces. "Us" included Rachel Noble

Cavanaugh, Pilar—Zach's wife—and Jonah Fraser, eldest son of Reverend John Fraser. He also noted the quick glance Kelly gave him before she spoke.

"We'd love to join you, wouldn't we, Ross?"

"Sure." He handed his drink to Zach. "Make yourself useful, will you?" He eased to his feet, wincing at the joint and muscular protests from his body. He hobbled over to the table feeling like a fool, but determined to try to fit in. "Why does anyone do this?" he asked, lowering his body gingerly.

"First-timer, huh?" Jonah patted his shoulder. "I share your pain, buddy. With this bum leg of mine, I'm beginning to think my skiing days are over." He held up a hand. "Don't ask. Old injury."

"You did very well out there, Jonah." Rachel patted his shoulder. "Next time we'll go a little slower. No point in trying too much at one time."

"Exactly my thoughts." Ross turned to Kelly. "Maybe I'll come back and try again next year. But I doubt it."

Pilar leaned close to Kelly. "Zach told me about the closet incident at Tiny Blessings and the phone calls. Are you all right?"

"I'm fine." Her smile looked forced. "I'm surprised to see you and Rachel here. You four usually choose the first Sunday of the month for brunch at the diner."

"To which you know you are always welcome. Maybe if you'd come today we would have gone." Meg winked at her. "Lately we don't get there as often as we used to. Each of us has other commitments. This week, with Anne still on honeymoon and Leah just beginning hers, there are only the two of us regulars. Since this outing was planned, we decided to come here instead. Maybe next week you'll join us?"

"Maybe."

Ross wondered why Kelly didn't accept the invitation and join the women. From all he'd heard, their Sunday brunches were hilarious occasions. That reticence again. He was getting more curious about that as time went on. Even now she seemed to listen more than participate. Of course, it could be she didn't want to go to the diner because she'd have to face Sandra.

"So what are we to expect at this shindig at Morrow Manor?" Pilar glanced around. "Should we go home and change? You think it's going to be very fancy?"

"You know the mayor's wife." Rachel made a face. "Of course it's going to be fancy. Lindsay Morrow lives to show off."

"She is one of the best hostesses we've ever had for a function like this." Kelly's words sounded automatic to Ross. She sipped at her tea, the mint aroma filling his nostrils as he leaned over beside her to rub his sore knee.

"I never did understand why you seem to admire her so much." Rachel sounded disgruntled. "She's such a show-off. Do you know she's even trying to take over my Valentine's Day thing for the foundation? She's bound and determined to make it some kind of charity costume party."

"That could be fun." Meg leaned forward. "What was your idea?"

"Less formal for starters. Lots of folks in Chestnut Grove might be intimidated by having to find something fancy to wear for just one occasion. Besides—" Rachel's voice dropped "—Lindsay always has to be in command at her things. I was hoping to get more community involvement going. That's hard to do when the mayor's wife is ordering everyone around."

Ross watched the interplay between the women, noted how Kelly held back, offered little comment.

"Someone who really knows how to get people involved is Sandra Lange. When I helped her with a teen class, she had them think up ways they could raise money to buy a new television for the seniors' lounge. We had more fun in that class—Sandra was a hoot." Meg sighed, shook her head. "But even if she was feeling up to it, I wouldn't dare ask her. Sandra and Lindsay could never work together. Their styles are too different."

At that point, Zach drew Ross into a conversation. Only later did he turn to say something to Kelly and notice she'd left the table.

"She said she wanted to take another run down the hill before we had to leave," Meg explained, seeing his confusion. "Her mother was a skiing champion, you know. She won all kinds of awards for her skiing prowess, even got a place on the Olympic team, but she broke a leg before the Games and couldn't participate."

"Wow."

Meg nodded. "She taught Kelly everything she knows about the sport, entered her in a ton of events. Kelly always did well, but she never had Carol's ability. So you see, you don't have to worry about Kelly on skis. She's an expert on these runs."

Ross nodded. There was a little more discussion, then the others gathered their things, prepared to leave for the Morrows'. When they were gone, he retrieved his own street shoes, turned in his skis, then sat to digest the information he'd just learned.

A glimmer of insight dawned. He'd wondered why she had no fear, but of course Kelly wouldn't fear skiing because she'd mastered it. It was like her work at Tiny Blessings—in that area she knew exactly what she was doing.

The wintry day grew cooler as the sun dropped over the hill. Still she didn't return. Ross didn't even realize he was worried until he glimpsed her pink suit swooping down the hill. She wasn't hurt. A rush of relief flooded him as he hurried outside.

"Ross, I'm so sorry. I completely lost track of time." Face glowing, eyes shining, she removed her skis, which he picked up. She led the way back inside and quickly pulled off her boots. "You should have gone ahead with the others. I would have caught up."

"I wouldn't dream of reneging on my deal." He picked up her poles and boots, as well. "Besides, I just remembered something. We forgot to bring along that cake."

Her eyes dimmed, her smile faded. "Yes, I guess we did."

She said nothing on the return journey to her home, refused his offer to go inside with her. "I don't want us to be too late," she murmured.

She emerged from the house a few minutes later in a different outfit, cake in tow.

"No fair," he teased when she climbed inside. Kelly lifted one eyebrow. He touched one corner of her lips. "Milk?"

"I was thirsty." A faint flush of red suffused her cheeks. "I should have offered you something. I'm sorry."

"I was just teasing you. I'm fine. You ready?" He waited for her to clip her seat belt, but she didn't respond. "Kelly? What's wrong?"

"There was another phone message," she whispered.

Anger filled him. Why would someone harass this beautiful woman?

"What did it say?"

"Same thing. Get out of town. Nothing for me here." She looked straight at him. "I don't understand why this is happening. What did I do?"

"Nothing. It's just some nutcase harassing you to get his jollies."

"It doesn't sound like a nutcase. It sounds like someone is quite serious." Finally she fastened her seat belt.

"Well, don't worry. The mystery will soon be cleared up. Zach told me they're putting a trace on your line." He started the engine and began the drive to the Morrow mansion. "Have you turned down someone recently, for an adoption, I mean?"

"No. I have three cases pending, but I'm sure it's not one of those would-be parents. By the time they come to me, they're usually so desperate to have a child, they'll do anything. Threats and nasty phone calls would be a definite black mark that would stop most adoptions." She met his look. "You have no idea how much some people long to be parents. That's the only part of my job I really don't like, turning someone away. It's heartrending to watch their hope die."

"I can imagine."

"Sometimes I'm their last hope." She sighed, shook her head. "But as my mother always said, you take the good with the bad. Some things in life just have to be done. I have to do my best to place the children where I think they'll flourish. I can't please everyone."

"Were your parents strict, Kelly?" He didn't know where the question had come from, particularly when she looked so shocked.

"Strict? As in mean?" She shook her head. "Not at all. They were very loving, kind people. Why do you ask?"

"I don't know. Just wondered. You don't have any brothers or sisters?"

"No. When I was little I asked my mother about that and she said that after they chose me, they moved to California. She said she had all she could handle just loving me." Her eyes glossed over. "Wasn't that sweet of her?"

"Mmm." He pulled into the driveway.

"Just drive up to the door. They always have someone who parks the cars. Mrs. Morrow is ultra-organized."

Which sounded good, until Ross noticed that his older car found a home out of sight with the other clunkers while the newer, fancier vehicles were displayed in plain sight on the long circular driveway. He made a mental note to reevaluate his impression of the Morrows.

"So you came, Kelly. I was beginning to wonder. It's grown so late." Mrs. Morrow barely paused for a breath, her speech was so smooth and practiced. "And you've brought your friend. I'm afraid I don't remember your name. Please, let Catharine take your coats."

"Thank you. This is Ross Van Zandt."

"Oh, yes. Of course. Shame on me for not remembering. How nice to meet a such handsome man."

"You, too." Ross helped Kelly out of her jacket, slightly annoyed by Mrs. Morrow's gushing tone.

"I'm so sorry we're late, Mrs. Morrow. I hope we haven't inconvenienced you. We were delayed at the ski hill. I brought this." Kelly handed over her cake.

"Isn't that sweet?" Lindsay Morrow handed off the plate to a passing waiter with barely a glance at the dessert. "It's so clever of you to think of those who aren't watching their figures and can gorge themselves on empty calories."

That disparaging comment got to him. Ross stepped forward.

"Kelly invited me to come with her. I'm quite sure we have met before, Mrs. Morrow." He held out his hand, forcing her to shake it or render a display of bad manners. The frail white fingers barely grazed his skin before she pulled away. "You may remember I'm a private investigator."

"Oh. Well, perhaps we have met. I go to a lot of functions and of course with Gerald as mayor—" She shrugged, her smile fixed firmly in place. But Ross knew something had rattled her. "Do enjoy yourselves, children. Excuse me."

"Children?" Ross looked at Kelly.

"It's just the way she talks. She's probably a little pre-occupied with so many people here," Kelly whispered. "We can talk to her later when things have calmed down, if you want. Don't you just love this house?"

Love it? Ross glanced around and shuddered. Pretentious, yes. Elegant, maybe. Overdone—totally. But then what did he know about interior decorating? He had no doubt that it cost the Morrows a mint.

"I guess it's all right. Look, there's Zach and Pilar. Should we head over their way?" He grasped her elbow and steered her toward the couple. Zach's arm was looped around his wife's waist and she was leaning against his shoulder. They looked utterly comfortable.

"You still walking, Van Zandt?" A mocking smile curved the detective's face.

"I'm walking. Barely." Ross waited a moment until the two women began chatting, then poked Zach with his elbow. "Maybe we should get these two gorgeous ladies something to drink?"

"I was wondering if that was going to happen soon." Pilar offered him a sweet smile. "Mayor Morrow has mixed up a new punch that he claims is better than ambrosia. I think I'd like some of that."

"Sure. Kelly?"

"Oh, punch would be fine. Thank you."

"Punch it is." He inclined his head toward the table where a punch bowl and little glass cups were laid out. "You heard them, Zach."

The other man waited until they'd moved away from the ladies.

"Okay, what's going on?" he asked, accepting the glasses Ross filled and handed him.

"Kelly had another phone message when we stopped by her place to pick up her cake. Just thought you should know."

"This guy's persistent."

"I hope you find out something soon." Ross took a sip of the punch, decided it wasn't bad and filled his glass. "Kelly's bothered, though she won't admit it."

"Understandable." Zach walked with him toward the women. "Ladies, the two of us have decided you both need a little excitement in your lives so we're moving into the den. I hear Mrs. Morrow has some games going on there. If we can't find excitement there, we'll keep looking."

"Keep looking?" Ross glanced at Kelly. "What does that mean?"

"You missed the announcement." Pilar motioned to several different areas of the house. "Mrs. Morrow has different activities set up in different rooms. Board games in the den, karaoke in the music room, a whole bunch of things. We're to sample a variety. The dining room is loaded with food we brought and a lot of other goodies besides. Anytime you want a snack you just help yourself. Clear as mud?"

Ross grinned. "Oh, very clear. We're going to the karaoke room. See you later."

"We are? Why karaoke?" Kelly didn't give in to the pressure on her arm but stayed put, her scrutiny intent. "Are you some kind of closet performer? Because I should warn you—I don't sing in public. Not at all. And I don't intend to let the rest of the world in on that secret tonight."

"I have other reasons for attending." He caught her hand and tugged her alongside him. "Come on. It will be fun."

"Fun?" They paused at the door of the music room, where Kelly sent him an arch look as someone who was obviously tone-deaf broke into a rather loud and distinctly off-key version of "Amazing Grace."

He nudged her inside anyway and found them both seats at the back. Once they were seated, he glanced around the room with interest. There were a few new faces, but most were people he'd been introduced to in the weeks since he'd moved to Chestnut Grove.

Issac Tubman took the stage next. The lovable cook from Sandra's Starlight Diner crooned a delightful western melody that had the crowd enthralled, especially when he knelt in front of Florence Villi at the end of the song. Even Florence had to chuckle. Dinah Fraser looked like a starlet as she belted out her song in perfect voice and clarity. Then Pilar's father, Salvador Estes, treated them to a wonderful Spanish medley.

"They're all very good, aren't they?" Kelly whispered as she clapped. "I can't believe we have this much talent in our town. Maybe Rachel should plan a talent show for her Valentine's fund-raiser."

"It's an idea." Ross knew she said something else, but his attention was fixed on a tall slender man with black hair and hazel eyes who was leaning against the door frame. His clothes looked expensive and fit him perfectly. "Who's that at the door?" he asked, leaning toward Kelly.

"Hmm?" She was studying the next performer, made a face as Pilar's dark-haired brother Ramon lip-synched a silly Italian aria about the fickleness of women. "At the door?"

"Yes."

Kelly glanced around him, a satin swath of her hair brushing his cheek as she got a better look.

"Andrew Noble." She leaned back, her warm breath flickering over his ear as she whispered, "He's Rachel's cousin. From New England, I think. He shows up every so often, usually if there's a party going on. I have no idea what he does but I can see him as something mysterious. Maybe that's because he so often wears all black."

Ross knew the Nobles were wealthy. This Andrew looked a little like he imagined a rich playboy would, but there was something distinctly unplayful about the man's eyes. He decided to keep an eye on him.

Samantha Harcourt took the stage next. In Ross's opinion she was thinner than a skeleton, but apparently models were supposed to look like that. After the first two notes, he grabbed Kelly's hand and tugged.

"Okay, I've had enough. Let's move on."

"Thank you." She waited till they were in the hallway, then let loose her giggles. "A little too loud for your taste?"

"A little too everything." He glanced around, but saw no sign of the man who'd been standing there a moment ago. "Want to get something to eat?"

"Sure." She walked with him to the dining room. "Since there's no one else around at the moment, can I ask you something?"

"Shoot." He glanced at the array of food and wondered why he hadn't thought to bring something. It looked like everyone else had contributed.

"Why did you want to go in there, Ross? Don't tell me it was because you couldn't wait to hear them, because I won't believe you."

He assessed her frown, decided truth was the best option.

"I wondered if you might connect any of the voices to the one that phones you." He held up a hand at her protest. "I know it was a long shot, but I figured it would be easier for you to identify if I didn't tell you, if it came naturally, so to speak."

"But those are my friends!" She stared at him, brown eyes wide. "Some of them have known me for most of my life. Why would they suddenly tell me to leave?"

He shrugged. "Maybe they wouldn't. It was just an idea."

"Don't get any more. I'm sick of wondering about that caller. I just want to relax and enjoy tonight."

But she wasn't relaxed. For one thing, her complexion had paled. For another, she dithered over the crudités, vacillating between a bit of cauliflower and a small stalk of celery.

"I didn't mean to upset you, but I can't help wondering, Kelly," he told her softly. "I am what I am. I like to solve mysteries. I want to know who is calling you."

"So do I. But I'm not going to subject my friends to an inquisition or suspect them of terrorizing me." She finally grabbed a ham sandwich and set it on her plate.

"Are you terrorized?" he asked softly.

She met his stare without flinching. "I don't know. I certainly don't like it that someone seems to be targeting me. But I don't know what I can do about it, either. I just have to—" Her voice faded to nothing, her eyes glazed and she grabbed the table as her plate tumbled to the floor. The sound of shattering china brought someone running.

"Kelly?" Ross set his own plate down, supporting her until he could help her to a nearby chair. "What's the matter?"

"What's going on in here?" Lindsay Morrow stood in the doorway. When she saw the broken plate, a frown marred her lovely face.

"Kelly almost fainted," Ross blurted out before she could lay into them for damaging her precious china, if that's what she intended. Though come to think of it, she didn't look like she was angry. She looked…strange.

"Does she need to lie down?" Mrs. Morrow pressed a button on the wall and a moment later a young woman in a black uniform with a white apron came running. "Please clean that up, Catharine."

"Yes, ma'am."

"I don't want to cause a fuss. I'll be fine if I just sit here for a moment." Kelly glanced at Lindsay, her eyes pleading. "Don't let me spoil your wonderful party. Not after you've gone to so much work."

"That's very kind of you to think of me, dear." Their hostess almost preened as she said the words. "But you're my guest. I don't want you to worry about my feelings. If you feel unwell you must lie down. Catharine, please show Miss Young to the blue bedroom, would you?"

"Yes, ma'am." The maid stepped forward as if to help Kelly.

"No, really, I don't want to intrude into your home."

"It's no problem at all." Lindsay Morrow looked unconcerned.

Ross took a second look at Kelly's face, which had gone whiter than white. He stayed where he was, blocking the maid who would have assisted her. "Maybe you should rest for a minute, Kelly. If you went upstairs, no one would know."

"I'm not some feeble invalid," she whispered, but her sudden wince decried her words. "All right, maybe just for a few minutes," she relented. "But I don't want to make a scene. Just walk with me naturally." She turned to Lindsay. "Maybe if we pretended that you're showing me around?"

"Showing you…?" Lindsay's dark brows lowered just for an instant before she recovered. "Yes, of course, my dear. A true lady never wants to display her private troubles. I applaud your discretion. Never mind, Catharine." The maid disappeared.

"Thank you." Relief flooded Kelly's weak voice.

Ross was surprised by how heavily she leaned on his arm. Her face was the same shade as the gossamer fluff on a dandelion gone to seed and it turned more pasty with every step she took up the circular marble staircase. He was relieved when they finally made it to the blue bedroom.

"I don't want to mess anything up," Kelly murmured from her perch on the side of the bed, arms crossed over her middle. "You have such a beautiful home. I love the way you've integrated the shades of blue in this room."

"Thank you, Kelly. Now don't worry about the room. Just lay back and relax. Perhaps you'd like a glass of ice water? I'll have Catharine bring one up. And maybe something to eat. You've gone a very strange shade of green."

Ross took a second look at Kelly and realized Mrs. Morrow was right.

"Perhaps I should call a doctor? Do you have pain?" Lindsay waited by the door.

"No, thank you." Kelly glanced at Ross. "I'm sure I'll be fine."

"All right. Rest then. If you need anything, you can send your boyfriend for help." She closed the door soundlessly behind her.

Boyfriend? She made it sound as if they were having some kind of childish affair. Ross would have liked to tell Lindsay Morrow off, but Kelly's groan distracted him. "What is it? Upset stomach again?"

"Sort of. It's mostly passed now. Just kind of spasmy. I

feel a bit woozy. Maybe if I eat something, though I'll feel terrible if I leave a mark on this gorgeous spread. Do you think it's silk?"

"Who cares?" He pulled a chair near, sank into it. "It's just a bedspread."

"But it isn't. Don't you see? It's custom-made for this room. She has exquisite taste. My mother would have loved this room."

Again with her mother. Ross was beginning to tire of hearing about the saintly woman who'd raised Sandra's child. Which wasn't nice at all, he supposed. But his feelings here were for the birth mother. How was Sandra supposed to compete in Kelly's mind with a woman who'd been so perfect?

Catharine arrived with a tray carrying a glass of water, a drink of punch for Ross, a plate filled with bits from many different dishes he'd seen displayed downstairs and some dessert samples. Kelly's chocolate cake was not among them.

"Can you eat anything?" he asked after the maid had left.

"Maybe." She sipped the ice water, took a cracker from the plate and bit off the pointed corner. "Actually I feel a little better now. Guess I was just hungry." But she didn't eat much, just a few bites of cracker, some cheese and the water.

"Would you like to leave? I don't mind going, particularly if you're not feeling well. You've had a busy day. It's no wonder if you're tired."

"It's Sunday," she murmured, her glance puzzled. "I haven't done much."

"You were ill last night, you got up and walked to church, made me lunch, went skiing, and then you rushed over here. Add on the holidays and the wedding and I think you're probably feeling the combined effects."

"Maybe." She swung her legs over the edge of the bed, stood gingerly as if testing her ability to remain upright. "Everything's staying where it's supposed to, so I guess I'm okay. Let's not leave just yet. I'd really like to see more of this house. You should meet people, too, and all you've done is spend the evening babysitting me."

"Hardly babysitting," he protested, holding open the door. "You're too strong for that."

"You think I'm strong?" She paused at the top of the staircase to stare at him. "Why do you say that?"

"Because you are." She looked skeptical so Ross ploughed on, slightly embarrassed that he was showing how much he admired her. "Zach told me about your work with the church. I heard all about the hours you spent on the Christmas toy drive for kids in foster care who are waiting for permanent homes."

"It was more fun than work."

"He also mentioned that you initiated a program which liaises with the church youth center. Even though those kids volunteer their time at Tiny Blessings, I know they have to be supervised and I know how wearing kids can be." He studied her beauty under the light of the huge chandelier. She looked gorgeous in her burgundy cashmere sweater and black slacks. Only her eyes were sad.

"These past few months I've been in Chestnut Grove, I've seen you involved in so many things. You've had a lot going on, Kelly. Not everyone can give so much back to their community and keep their lives balanced. It takes a very strong, giving person to manage so many things and do them well."

She stared at him, eyes wide with surprise. "I—thank you for saying that," she finally whispered. "I try but—"

"No more buts." He grinned at her. "Just accept the compliment, will you?"

"Yes, I will. Thank you."

After a soul-searching look she started down the stairs. Ross walked beside her, watching for any sign of unsteadiness. But Kelly had her "capable" mask back in place. If she was queasy, she didn't show it. He couldn't help wondering why she felt she had to be so strong.

They reached the bottom. Ross looked around. "Where is everyone?"

"Feeling better?" Mayor Morrow walked toward them. "Lindsay said you'd had a bad spell, that you were resting. Everything all right now?"

"Yes, thank you. I feel fine now." Kelly smiled at him, her face changing to show the awkward admiration of someone intimidated by his commanding presence.

"Then you'd better come along to the great room," the mayor decreed with what Ross privately termed his "photo-op" smile. "Lindsay's got something special planned."

Ross was left to walk on the opposite side of Kelly, content to listen as she chatted with the mayor.

"She's done a wonderful job, as usual. The Christmas tree lighting was spectacular."

"I'm glad you enjoyed it. We like to open our home to the citizens of Chestnut Grove as often as we can. After all, they put their faith in me two years ago and I want to show I appreciate it."

Not to mention the fact that he was up for reelection later that year and would need their support again, Ross thought to himself.

Gerald Morrow stood back and waited for them to precede him into the huge room. "Go ahead, find yourselves a place to sit. It looks like my wife's about to get the ball rolling. One thing about Lindsay, she plans everything to the nines."

Something about the way Gerald said that made Ross take a second look at him. The mayor wasn't movie-star handsome, though with his white hair and blue eyes, he was a very good-looking senior citizen. His custom suits compensated for his expanding waistline but still lent him the air of power and authority. He had the kind of face that brought one word to mind—tough.

"There are some seats over there, Ross." Kelly led the way to a couple of stools near the French doors that opened onto a pool.

As he stared at the area outside he noticed how some-one had made sure it was perfectly lit. Though the pool had been drained for the season, it now held a magnificent ice sculpture that looked like a crystal snowman. Some type of revolving light changed it from red to green to gold, then flickered a show of colors across the entire area, turning it into something like a fairy land. Evergreen shrubs pro-vided the backdrop for whimsical characters perched here and there around the pool. Sandra would have loved to see this display. Ross had enjoyed watching the festive season turn her into a little kid with great big eyes.

A movement to the left caught his attention and he turned to get a better look.

"Ross, what are you doing?" Kelly whispered, tugging on his arm.

Sensing he was drawing attention to himself, Ross ad-justed his position, slightly turned so he could keep his gaze trained on the corner of the patio. The light display moved higher against the firs and spruce trees, leaving the deck in shadow. Moments later he watched someone slip across the area. The movements were furtive and the fig-ure glanced over one shoulder. For a moment he seemed to glance at Ross. Then he hurried away.

An odd prickle of awareness skittered down his spine as Ross kept his attention focused on the patio. But the intruder was gone.

Who was he and why was he out there?

Chapter Six

"Ross, that's the third time we've missed our chance. At this rate we're not going to take home any of those great prizes Mrs. Morrow has up for grabs. What's going on?" Kelly followed his gaze through the window, then twisted to face him. "What are you looking at?"

"Nothing. Just the display." He smiled at her. "Sorry. Guess I'm just a little preoccupied. Anyway you don't really need another coffeemaker, do you?"

"No, but Tiny Blessings could sure use it. Ours takes forever to brew just one cup of coffee." She saw what was coming and shook her head. "Don't say it because I've already cleaned it ten times. It's just too old and I don't want to buy a new one until we can afford one of the better models—like that pour through one that Peggy Cavanaugh just won," she hinted.

"I promise I'll try harder," he whispered, but the saucy look in his eyes told her she was being humored.

"You wouldn't have to try hard if you'd just keep your eyes trained on what's inside this room," she reminded.

"I'm looking." He faked a leer at her and she poked him in the side. "And I like what I see."

"Be serious. I could use this next prize."

"What is it?"

"A day at the spa. For two."

"Not interested." He crossed his arms across his chest, his expression adamant, "I do not need a mud bath and I'd rather not have my follicles cleansed or exfoliated."

"Spoilsport." She couldn't quite smother her laughter at the mental picture he'd created. "It could be fun."

"No."

As it turned out they did win a prize—the last one. Kelly gaped as one of Lindsay's helpers placed a five-foot metal sculpture, outlining a man with a golf club, in front of them with a flourish. She endured the teasing of the others as they moved out of the room to listen as the pastor expressed thanks on behalf of everyone to the Morrows for a wonderful evening.

"I'm so glad that each of you could come." Lindsay Morrow's voice carried clearly from the other room. "And I hope you've enjoyed yourselves. Gerald and I are delighted to host this event each year. As mayor, he enjoys having the public in his home and I consider it my duty to be a leader in the community. I take that role very seriously. Which is why I want to invite each of you to the charity costume party I'm hosting on Valentine's Day to help support the Noble foundation. Please get your tickets early."

"Did you hear that?" Rachel stomped up to them, her face red. "The woman is not even in charge and she's issuing invitations. I'm going to set her straight this instant!"

"Now, honey." Eli Cavanaugh hung onto his wife's arm, preventing her from charging toward Lindsay. "Let's not be too hasty. You're the one in charge, everyone knows that the Noble Foundation is your baby. Let this go for now. Everyone's enjoyed their evening, don't spoil it. You can speak to her tomorrow when no one's around."

"I intend to," Rachel snapped, then patted his cheek. "Sorry. I'm taking it out on you, aren't I? Come on, let's go home." She waggled her fingers at Ross and Kelly. "See you and your, er, treasure." She and Eli left chuckling about the unusual item.

"Bye." Kelly looked down at the item, sighed, then felt Ross's arm nudge her ribs. "What?"

"What are we supposed to do with it?" Ross whispered after he'd made sure they were really alone.

"You're asking me? You won it." She walked around the piece, trying to come up with some purpose for its creation. "I suppose you could put it in a pot and let ivy creep all over it."

"Wonderful! And since you're the gardener, you should have it. I'll even carry it into your house for you." He grinned as if he'd been given a "get out of jail free" card.

"Maybe I could talk Peggy into trading," she mused.

"Would *you* trade this for a coffeemaker?" Ross asked, eyes dancing with fun.

"No." She fixed him with her most severe look. "It's all your fault. I should have taken Kimberly Forrester up on her suggestion to switch partners. She and Samantha won those gorgeous designer bags."

"I didn't even try to find an answer to that question when Mrs. Morrow asked it," he admitted, then shrugged at her glare. "Well, what would I do with a designer bag?" Quickly he raised a hand to stop the comment she was ready to offer. "Don't go there, Kelly. Come on, time to go home." He hefted the unusual piece into his arms, pretended to collapse, then carried it toward the front door where Catharine waited with an array of coats.

"Act grateful," Kelly whispered in his ear as they waited in line.

"That's a stretch when I'm lugging this monstrosity," he whispered back.

She smothered a giggle, delighted by his comical look. Ross was fun. It was nice to have someone to share special moments with. Simon would have been busy working the room, trying to make contacts. Ross didn't seem to care about that and suddenly it didn't seem so awful that he'd spent most of the game peering out the windows.

She glanced at the happy faces around her, content to watch the others repeat their appreciation to the Morrows for the wonderful party. At last it was their turn.

"Don't you love the Antoine DeTaurer?" Mrs. Morrow asked, one hand sliding down the side of the metal Ross had plunked on her marble floor. "He's up and coming, a local artist, you know. I'm sure it won't be long before his work is shown internationally."

The sculpture—she was talking about the sculpture and its creator. Kelly made a mental note to bone up on the local talent.

"It's a very nice piece, Mrs. Morrow. Ross and I will have to work out an agreement to share it." She didn't dare look at him for fear she'd start laughing. "Thank you for a fantastic evening. We had a great time."

"I'm so sorry you weren't feeling better. These after-New Year's colds always seem to hit those who've let themselves get a bit run-down. You'll want to take better care of yourself, dear."

It was so nice of her to be concerned, Kelly mused, flushing under Lindsay's intent scrutiny.

"Oh, I'm fine, don't worry about me. Ross was simply entranced by the display around the pool. I guess that's why we didn't do very well at your game."

"I did notice he spent a lot of time looking at it." Lindsay frowned. "Was there something wrong with the ice sculpture?"

"Oh, no. The snowman is great. Really something to see." He paused and looked at Kelly, who surreptitiously poked him in the ribs. "If I stared too long I guess it's because I happened to notice someone out there."

"On the deck?" Lindsay frowned, glanced at her husband. "Did you let someone outside?"

"Now, dear," he placated, looping his beefy arm around her slender waist. "We all know not to tamper with your displays. I'm sure it was just a shadow or something that Ross saw."

"Perhaps." Lindsay eased away from him, her smile a little stiff. "Anyway, I'm delighted you came, Kelly. Happy New Year."

"To you, too," Kelly replied but the Morrows had already turned away and were involved in a whispered discussion with each other.

"Come on. Let's vamoose while the getting's good." Ross held her coat, pulled on his own, then picked up the sculpture once again. "I hope I can get this monster into my car."

"Shh! They'll hear you."

"Those two aren't going to hear anyone but each other. Looks to me like the mayor is getting bawled out. She's a piece of work, isn't she?"

Kelly waited while one of the servants helped Ross load their prize into his car, that had been brought to the door. Once they were inside the vehicle and moving away from the mansion, she turned to face him.

"What did you mean?"

"About Mrs. Morrow?" He shrugged. "I don't care for her much. She's snarky and she makes those cutting remarks, like saying you're catching something because you're run-down."

"She was just being a good hostess, concerned for her guests."

"Ha!" He looked at her, shrugged. "Trust you to think the best of everyone. But I happen to know that the mayor was wrong. What I saw in that yard was no shadow. Someone was out there."

Kelly was getting a strange feeling about this. She took a second look at Ross, tried to judge whether or not he was serious.

"Perhaps one of the people from the party went outside to get a breath of air," she offered, thinking as she said it how strange that sounded. After all, the majority of the group had been outside in the cold most of the afternoon.

"How did they get out there?" he shot back, his eyes dark with curiosity. "When you were working on that puzzle I tried the door. It was locked and there was an iron bench blocking it on the outside so you couldn't have squeezed through the doors even if you could have jimmied the lock."

"There's probably a side door, Ross." She didn't understand his fixation with this. "Anyway, even if someone was out there, what does it matter?"

"There was someone and it matters because I'd like to know exactly who it was. I hate loose ends," he told her, his forehead pleated in a frown. "That's a loose end."

"Have you always been this obsessive?"

He cast her a funny look, then nodded. "I guess so. My sister Trista once told me I asked too many questions."

"What's she like?"

"Sweet, innocent. Gentle." He shrugged. "I used to think I had to protect her."

"From what?"

"Life."

Kelly blinked at the vehemence of that word. She'd gathered from other things he'd said that their childhood had not been happy. Had it also been abusive?

"You remind me of her a lot," he added, glancing sideways while they waited at a stop light.

"I do?" Was that good or bad? Since she didn't know his sister, Kelly couldn't judge. "How?"

"I told you I used to think I had to protect her. I didn't realize then how strong she really is. You and she are a lot alike in that you both have this spunk, the same kind of inner grit that propels you through life."

"No one ever told me I had spunk before." She grinned. "I think I like it. Tell me more about this wonderful woman I resemble."

"She's in law school in Atlanta. I don't know how long she'll be there though."

"Why? Doesn't she like it?"

"She likes it a lot. And she's good at it." He pinched his lips together. "She's having a tough go of it now, though. Her husband walked out on her."

"I'm sorry."

"Don't be. He isn't much of a loss. All talk, no substance."

Kelly flinched at the harsh words, thrust her chin forward.

"I think it's always a loss when a marriage fails. There's something terribly sad about watching two people who've committed themselves to each other turn on the very ones they once professed to love." She fiddled with her gloves. "It's bad enough when teenaged girls come in to Tiny Blessings after making the decision to give up their babies. It's heartrending to hear their stories of how they'd committed themselves, thought somebody loved them for better or worse and now they're alone and scared, aching because they know they can't care for the child they carry."

Ross didn't say anything to that but she knew he was thinking about it. Kelly pressed on.

"It must be infinitely harder when you've gone through the steps to marital commitment and then find out you made a mistake, that the person you trusted with your heart isn't trustworthy at all." She looked down at her hands, anxious not to show anything of her own feelings. "It must hurt so terribly."

"Yes." He drove on through the winding streets. "I suppose you've gone through some of that yourself with your Simon."

"With Simon?" She blinked, peered at him through the gloom. "What do you mean?"

"Well, you must have been committed to get engaged to him." He frowned at her. "You said yourself that it was he who left. All I'm saying is that it must have hurt."

"Yes. It did." But not for that reason. Not because her heart was broken. Kelly veered away from asking herself why and turned the focus back on him. "Trista is going to need her brother while she goes through this," she murmured, thinking how nice it would be to have family to share life's burdens with, to talk to when things got rough and you couldn't tell anyone else.

"She knows where I am, but I doubt she'll come running." "Why not?"

"Trista thinks she dumped on me enough when we were

kids. She carries this guilt thing." He pulled into her driveway, turned to look at her. "What's with all the questions?"

"I'm sorry if you thought I was intruding. It's just that it seems like you know so much about me and I know very little about you." Kelly grasped the door handle as a little ping of hurt shot through her. "Thank you very much for coming with me."

"Not so fast, lady." His hand on her arm made it impossible to get out of the car. "You're not leaving without The Thing, are you?" He jerked a thumb over his shoulder. His dark eyes sparkled with fun.

"You can keep it." She slid out of the car, then bent over. "But I would like my ski stuff."

"Oh, no. No way." Seconds later Ross was digging in the back seat trying to free the metal golfer. "Okay, he's out. Finally. Lead the way. I'll carry him to your sunroom. It's the least I can do."

Kelly grabbed her boots and ski pants and started up the walk, checking behind every few steps to make sure Ross was still making progress.

"I should probably warn you that I don't carry enough insurance to pay for back surgery," she warned as he plunked the object onto the step.

"Won't need it," he called as he returned to the car for her skis and poles.

Kelly let herself inside, breathed the familiar fragrance of cinnamon candles she loved. Behind her, Ross handed over the ski equipment, then toted in the sculpture.

"I'll have you know I'm perfectly capable—" he paused to puff out a breath "—of carrying a few pounds of metal into someone's house."

"I can see that. Let me take one end." She grabbed the base and lifted, and together they moved the piece into her sunroom. "I'm going to need a very special pot to bury this in," she muttered to herself.

"Why don't you just plant it somewhere in your garden outside? Preferably behind a bush. You could call it garden sculpture."

"Maybe." She followed him out of the room, paused to straighten a pot of ivy that had tipped over. When had that happened?

"Anything wrong?"

Ross's warm breath brushed her ear and it was as if a spring inside her wound a little tighter.

"Kelly? Are you all right?"

"Yes, fine. Thanks for asking." She stepped away from him, forced a smile to her lips as she led the way back to the front door. "Just thinking. Would you like a drink, something to eat?"

Ross shook his head, his expression giving away his puzzlement.

"No, thanks. I had plenty at the Morrows'." His gaze never left her face.

"Well, then." She didn't want to ask him to leave but the day's events had left her drained and her stomach was acting up again. Kelly only wanted to crawl into bed and go to sleep.

"When is a good time to go to Sandra's?"

The question sent a shaft of fear through her. It had been waiting at the back of her mind, she realized. Perched there like a black cloud ready to dump misery on her head.

"I'm not sure—"

"It's just a visit, Kelly. Nothing to get flustered over."

"Tomorrow evening," she whispered. "After work."

"Done." He feathered his fingers against her arm and gently squeezed. "She doesn't want to change anything, Kelly. She just wants to talk. Don't sweat it, okay? Good night."

With his leaving, Kelly felt a surge of panic billow inside her. For so long she'd managed to maintain her life on an even keel, tried to run her life like a ship by keeping the equilibrium constant. But now the ship was listing and she was losing control. She felt rudderless, prone to whatever someone else dished out.

At that moment her stomach lurched wildly. She raced for the bathroom. When the retching spasm was finally over, she crawled into her bed and lay huddled under a mound of blankets.

It seemed as if everything in her life had done a one-eighty and nothing made sense. This illness—she was never sick. Was it nerves?

In slow motion, the events of the past few days rolled through her mind. Being shut in that closet, the accident, seeing someone in the garage, the phone message—those weren't things she'd imagined.

And Sandra Lange wasn't, either. Maybe she could write the rest off as nerves, but Sandra—that was going to be difficult.

Waves of tiredness rolled over her and Kelly closed her eyes. Hand it over to God, her mother had always said. He'll help you.

Good advice. Except things had changed. Her mother wasn't really her mother anymore. Maybe God—

She rolled over, buried her face in the pillow, too weary and worn out to puzzle it through anymore. Finally sleep came, but with it, horrible dreams. The ringing phone broke through one of those.

Fighting her way through the grogginess, Kelly picked it up.

"Hello?"

No answer, only several soft breaths. The caller was letting her know someone was there.

"Leave."

Then the line went dead.

Chapter Seven

For the third time Ross listened to the chime of the door-bell echo through Kelly's house. For the third time he waited for the door to open, to no avail.

Something was wrong.

He tried the front door. Locked. Not that he'd expected differently. He was good at reading people and last night Kelly had been on edge. He pulled out his cell phone, dialed Sandra.

"We're going to be late," he told her without preamble. "Something's wrong."

"I don't know yet. I'm at her house. Kelly isn't answering the door or her phone. The lights are on so I'm sure she's here, but—" He didn't want to say any more.

"She left work early," Sandra told him. "I overheard Pilar at the diner this afternoon while I was making pies."

"You sure you're up to that?"

"I'm fine, Ross. The chemo was a bit hard to take, but I'm definitely on the mend and I need to make sure my business is on solid ground. The Starlight Diner succeeded because of my parents' hard work. I don't want it to fail because I wasn't paying attention."

"Surviving cancer can hardly be called neglect. Besides, your parents wouldn't want you to overdo it." He didn't like to think of her having to manage on her own. That's why he was certain if Kelly would only talk to her, understand that Sandra didn't want anything but to get to know her better, the two could begin to develop a closer relationship.

"I'm fine, Ross. Really. But I am concerned about Kelly. Pilar said she seldom gets sick. She couldn't even remember the last time Kelly had taken a sick day and yet today she left early."

"According to Lindsay Morrow, Kelly is run-down." The woman's words still grated on his nerves. Sandra muttered something and he realized she wouldn't know what had happened at the mansion. "Yesterday. We went to the Morrows' house after skiing, Kelly felt a little rough. Lindsay made some comment about her being run-down and susceptible to illness."

"That woman! Does she ever think before she speaks?"

Ross almost smiled as Sandra the mother hen bristled on her daughter's behalf. Then he sobered. "I think she thinks long and hard. On the one hand, she seems friendly enough but on the other, she's always ready with her put-downs."

"That's just Lindsay's way. She's all about her public persona. Any answer at the door yet?"

"No. I'm going to try round the back, see if she's left something unlocked where I can squeeze in. I'll let you know."

"Thanks, Ross."

He clicked the phone off, stuffed it into his pocket then made his way around the house. To his surprise, the side door of the garage opened on the first turn of the handle.

He stepped inside, looked around. Light from a window showed him a neat empty space and the way to the door into the main house. Now if only it was unlocked, too.

Ross wouldn't have said that it was God, but something was on his side. The door to the house opened without a problem and he stepped inside.

"Kelly? It's Ross. Are you here?"

There was no sound. In fact the entire house was strangely silent. He checked the kitchen, den, living room, her sunroom, then moved upstairs. A faint moaning sound emanated from the end room. The door was open, just a crack. He rapped on it.

"Kelly? Are you all right?"

"I think so."

Propriety was one thing, but sickness was quite another. Ross didn't hesitate.

"I'm coming in." He pushed the door open, walked into her room, his eyes straining to find her in the gloom.

"I'm over here. I'll put a light on." A second later a lamp illuminated the room.

She was still in her work clothes, though the conservative black suit had certainly seen better days. Her hair was scraped back from her face and hung limply to her shoulders. Her face was paler than the cream duvet covering her bed.

"Why were you sitting in the dark?"

She touched her temple. "I had a headache," she whispered. "The darkness seemed to help. I can go downstairs now, though. I feel better."

He watched her rise from the bed, noticed she'd slipped off her shoes. That was a good thing, the heels were way too high for someone in her condition. She walked slowly toward him until the light from the hall bathed her face. She seemed dazed. Maybe she'd taken something for the headache.

"Hang on to the rail," he ordered when he noticed her wobble a bit on the middle of the staircase.

"Yes." She paused on the bottom step.

Ross squeezed past her, thinking she might need help, but when he touched her hand, he found her skin burning hot.

"You're not all right," he chided, laying the back of his hand against her forehead. "You've got a fever, Kelly."

"Yes. But it will go down soon. I took something for that. Then we can go see Sandra." She moved from the last step to the floor, eyes huge, her voice resigned. "I just need to sit down for a few minutes before we go. Maybe the kitchen. It's warmer."

"Are you cold?"

"At the moment. But that could change anytime. It's a really weird flu." She offered him a sad smile then sank onto a barstool. "Would you mind putting the kettle on? I could really use a cup of tea."

"Sure." He switched on the element, then reached for the phone. "I'll call Sandra, tell her not to expect us tonight."

"I'll be fine. You said she wanted to see me, so let's go."

"Kelly, you're sick. You need to rest." She looked about to protest so he found another argument. "You might give it to her. With her weakened immunity, the flu or a cold could make her really sick."

"Then of course we won't go," she rasped, her voice merging into a dry cough. "I guess Lindsay Morrow was right. I am run-down."

The whistling kettle cut off what Ross wanted to say and by the time he had her chubby brown teapot filled with hot water and two tea bags from the decorative tin on the counter, Kelly was nowhere to be seen.

Ross carried the pot and two big mugs into her den. While he waited for her to reappear, he lit a fire and poked and prodded it until it began to blaze. The flames cast a golden glow on the room while adding a warmth and comfort he'd also found at Sandra's.

Kelly appeared in the doorway moments later and Ross saw the panic in her eyes before she lowered her eyelids.

"Thank you very much for making the tea and lighting the fire," she said huskily, sinking into the big armchair nearest the fire. "This is exactly right."

She'd changed into some kind of velour suit in chocolate brown that made her eyes look bigger than they were and emphasized the golden bronze tones in her hair.

Ross poured a cup for her, one for himself, then sat down across from her. But she barely glanced at him before she rose, mug in hand.

"I like my tea with lots of milk," she murmured. "Can I get some for you, too?"

He shook his head, watched her pad from the room, her slippered feet silent on the plush carpet. A moment later she was back.

"This tea is very good," she complimented. "Strong but not bitter. It sure hits the spot."

"Have you eaten?"

Kelly made a face. "My stomach is pretty upset. I don't think I could swallow anything but this tea right now."

The lamplight lit her face in such a way that Ross had a full view of her pale face. The hollows beneath her cheekbones were pronounced. "Maybe you should see a doctor. Whatever you've got, it's draining you. You can't let it drag on, Kelly."

"I know. It's a funny flu. Sometimes I feel perfectly normal and then wham, I'm clammy and shaky and sick. I even have nightmares. Everything tastes funny, too. Except this tea."

She drank it greedily, as if parched. When she put her cup onto the table Ross added more tea to it.

"This time I'll get the milk," he promised.

"There's not much left. Help yourself to some of that cake, too, if you want. I forgot to take it to work. I seem to have forgotten several things."

Ross emptied the tablespoon or so of milk into her mug, then tossed the carton into the garbage, his mind on the almost empty fridge. Even if she'd been able to eat, it looked like she had no food. He pulled out his cell phone.

"Sandra? The diner's still open, isn't it? Good. Can you get someone to make up a couple of plates of whatever the special is and send them over to Kelly's? No, she's okay. Well, a little sick. She says it's the flu." He listened, nodded. "Yes, maybe you're right. Okay then, some homemade chicken soup and whatever else you think would do the trick. She wanted to see you, but I told her she was probably contagious. Truthfully, I don't think she could have managed going out again. She's pretty weak."

A sound from the other room compelled Ross to end the call. He hurried back to the den, found Kelly sitting where he'd left her. She looked to be asleep, but her lips were moving. Ross stepped closer, leaned down to put her tea on the table.

"Don't hate me, Mom," she whispered. "I loved you. You're my mom, I always love you. Don't make me go. Please? I tried so hard not to make any mistakes, but things went wrong anyway. Don't go away, Mom. Mom!"

"Kelly. It's just a dream. Wake up now." Ross gently shook her shoulder, trying to ease her from her terror. Nightmare was right. He was relieved when her eyes finally opened and she looked at him.

"I don't want to see her, Ross," she whispered as tears rolled down her face. "What if she finds out I'm not the person she thinks? What if she tells me to go away?"

It was like weathering a sucker punch to the gut and Ross couldn't stand there and watch this beautiful woman suffer any longer. He bent, lifted her into his arms and sat her down on the love seat beside him.

"Sandra isn't going to tell you to go away, Kelly. Not ever." He brushed the damp tendrils away from her forehead, pressed a gentle kiss to her brow. "Why would she? Don't forget, she's known Kelly Young for years. She knows what your favorite foods are at the diner, she knows you love the color orange. She watched you change from a little girl to a teenager to a woman."

"But I'm not like her. I can't talk to total strangers like she does in the diner, on the spur of the moment. I could never run a business like the diner. Not in a thousand years. There are too many things going on."

"If you'd grown up with it the way Sandra did, you probably could handle the place with one hand tied behind your back." He couldn't believe she doubted her own ability. "Anyway, what about your work at Tiny Blessings? That's a very tough job that I don't think Sandra could manage. Yet you do it every single day."

"And every single day I'm afraid I've made the biggest mistake of my life."

Her whisper was shockingly revealing. Cool-as-a-cucumber Kelly Young felt vulnerable?

"Why?" Maybe if he kept her talking…

"You don't make the kind of decisions I have to make without a lot of second-guessing. Since I found out…since you told me that Sandra is…that we're connected—" She paused, shook her head. "You said I was taken away, Ross.

That she was talked into giving me away. What if I've done the same thing to some poor young girl who didn't really know her own mind? What if I've taken her child from her when in her heart of hearts she wanted desperately to keep it? What if thirty-four years down the road, some woman comes back to tell me her mother made her give up her baby, that she made a mistake and that I made it worse? What then?"

"Then you'll deal with it. If and when it happens." Ross leaned back so he could look directly into her face. "Nobody gets it all right, Kelly. Everybody makes mistakes. You can't control life, you can't manage what *might* happen. You can only live the best you know how."

"That's hard for me."

He grinned. "It's hard for everybody, honey. But we push on anyway." The sound of the doorbell echoed through the house. "I hope you won't mind, I took the liberty of having some food delivered. I think you should eat something."

He left before she could protest, pulled open the front door and stared.

"Nothing better than delivery service by the boss." Sandra smiled at him, patted his cheek. "I'm not worried about contagion, Ross. But I can't wait any longer. So am I coming in or what?"

He stepped back automatically, then held out one hand for the sacks she carried, the other for her coat. "She's in the den. Why don't you go on in while I set the table in the kitchen."

Ross pointed out the direction, then left to take the food to the kitchen. Maybe it wasn't an ideal circumstance for a meeting, but given what he'd just heard from Kelly, he was glad it had happened this way. Kelly's doubts were growing exponentially. If she waited much longer, she might change her mind about talking to Sandra at all.

Surely it would be better for her to face Sandra now—tonight—rather than keep wondering what might happen, right? He hoped so.

Kelly heard the voices and wondered what was taking so long. She rose, waited for the dizziness to fade, then slid her feet back into her slippers.

"Ross? Who is—" The words died on her lips as she stared at Sandra Lange.

"Hello, Kelly. I heard you were ill. I brought some chicken soup and fresh rolls for you. I hope you don't mind."

"That's very kind of you. Thank you." She could only stare at the woman who had given her life.

"Would you rather I left? Don't be afraid to tell me. I won't mind."

But she would. Kelly could read the hope in her eyes and that immediately sent a tremor of worry through her. Sandra wanted something, that's why she was here.

"Why don't we go to the kitchen?" Sandra suggested. "Ross was going to set the table."

"The table? Oh, yes, you said you'd brought food." Kelly followed her out of the room. "He didn't have to call you. I could have made something later."

"I understand you haven't been feeling well. Perhaps you should see a doctor?"

"It's just the flu." Kelly shrugged. "One of those bugs you have to work through your system, I guess." She stopped in the doorway, frowned. "I wouldn't want to give it to you," she murmured.

"You sound just like him." Sandra glanced at Ross and grinned. "I'm not that delicate. I'll be fine."

"Let's all sit down. The soup is hot and if you ladies are on a diet or something and can't eat, I won't mind. I'm starved."

"Missed dinner again?" Sandra guessed.

"Forgot. I had some things on my mind." He held Sandra's chair, then pulled back the one beside it so that Kelly was forced to sit beside her.

She sat down, tried to figure out what could possibly keep him busy now that his job of finding her was complete. Then it dawned on her.

"You're leaving," she murmured, staring at him.

"Not just yet. There are a few things I have to finish first. I took on another small job, won't take me more than a few days to complete." As he spoke he ladled the soup into bowls. Sandra declined, saying she'd already eaten. "I do have to pack up the apartment, though," Ross added, and made a face.

"Let me guess—it's a mess." Sandra laughed at his comical look, covered his hand with hers. "Poor Ross."

"A mess is an understatement. Another move should be child's play, I've done it so often. You'd think I'd have developed a system with all the moves I've made."

All the moves he'd made. He made it sound as though he'd rambled around half the country but Kelly had the impression that he'd really only made one move that impacted him personally—the one when he'd left New York.

"Can I suggest something?" Sandra said, seeming oddly hesitant.

"All suggestions gratefully appreciated. Great soup, by the way."

Kelly tasted hers, surprised to find that her stomach had settled enough to let her taste the delicate flavor of parsley in the chicken broth. But her attention was on those seated on either side of her. She was intrigued by the relationship between Ross and Sandra. *He should have been her child, not me,* Kelly thought as she watched them. It was obvious he doted on her and that Sandra reciprocated his feelings.

"I just thought you might want to phone that new maid service that started in town. I've heard good things about them."

"Thanks." He winked at Kelly. "She fusses over me as if I were her k—six."

An awkward silence fell. Kelly didn't know what to say to break it. She was probably supposed to make some witty remark about Sandra being her mother but she couldn't fathom how to say that without it sounding weird.

"I'm sorry if it's awkward to have me here, dear. I'll just go and leave you two to enjoy your food." Sandra half rose.

"No, please." Kelly never knew where the words came from. "I'd like to talk to you, if you're not too tired or don't need to be somewhere."

"I don't." Sandra leaned back against the chair, her face wary. "Did you have some specific things you wanted to talk about?"

"Kind of. When you had your ba—me, uh—" Kelly gulped, started again "—when you gave birth, you lived here? In Chestnut Grove?"

"No." A sad look washed through her eyes. "I was living in Richmond then."

Kelly wished she could just let it go and not hurt the poor woman any longer, but then the questions would always be there. She pressed on.

"Can you tell me about that time?"

"I came back after the ba—you were gone. I wanted to find you, to raise you myself, but I was broke and alone and no one would tell me anything about you." Sandra's eyes brimmed with tears, but she dashed them away and continued. "I had a midwife, you see. Everything was arranged. But after I gave birth, something went wrong. I ended up at Richmond Community Hospital in surgery. I had to have a hysterectomy and when I came out of the surgery, I was so groggy."

"I'm sorry, It must have been horrible." Kelly didn't know what else to say.

"It was, but mostly because all I could remember when I woke up the next morning was that I'd signed a form giving you up for adoption. The midwife had taken you and no one knew where. I tried and tried to get in touch with…someone, but he wouldn't answer my calls."

"My father," Kelly guessed, thinking how strange that sounded. Marcus had always been her father. Or so she'd thought. "I'd like to know who this man was."

"I'm sorry, dear. But I can't tell you that."

"You can't tell me who my birth father is?" A spurt of anger filled her heart. "Can't or don't know?" she demanded, then wished she hadn't taken such a cheap shot.

Sandra seemed unfazed. "I know who he is, Kelly. But I can't tell you. I made a promise and I have to keep it."

"This isn't happening." Kelly pushed away the food as her stomach protested. She hated chaos and yet her whole life was turning into one big twisted knot. "I thought the purpose of our meeting was for me to get some answers. But this is a dead end."

"Maybe you could tell her more about that time. Maybe that would help explain why you promised." Ross's soft dark gaze was steady on Sandra. Kelly felt a rush of longing for him to look at her like that, as if she were precious, valuable.

"All right." Sandra squeezed her eyes closed, then began speaking. "I phoned him and phoned him, begged him to tell me what had happened to you. The one time he actually spoke, he threatened me, told me to leave it alone or I'd regret it." Her green eyes begged Kelly to understand. "I didn't know what else to do so when I was released, I came home. I told my parents the whole story and they forgave me, put me to work in the diner. I kept writing letters to everyone I could think of, but no one would help. After a while I had to stop. It wouldn't have been right to try and come between a child and the family it had bonded to."

"You gave up?" Pain sliced through her heart. Her biological mother hadn't even wanted her enough to keep looking.

"I never gave up, Kelly. And I never, ever stopped loving you. I always hoped, always prayed I'd find you." Sandra's fingers closed around hers. "When I came back here, begged my parents to forgive me and let me come home, I was full of dreams of finding you. I even went to the police, begging them to start an investigation."

She paused, drew in a deep breath. Pain and regret clouded her eyes but she continued, though her voice was less steady than it had been.

"It wasn't long after that when someone set fire to the Starlight Diner. My mother died in that fire, Kelly." The tears did fall then. "He'd warned me when I was in Richmond, but I had no idea he'd go to that extreme. It took my mother's death for me to realize that this man would do anything to stop scandal from touching him. I was afraid he'd hurt my dad and me, if I continued to push about the adoption."

"So you stopped." Her own voice sounded flat, unsympathetic. Kelly felt as if they were talking about some other child who'd been taken, some other mother who'd suffered. She didn't want to feel the pain underlying Sandra's soft voice.

"I didn't have much choice. There were no leads, no one who could help me, not enough money to hire someone. I had to help my dad run the diner, I couldn't keep on looking. So I clung to the one hope I had."

"Hope?"

"He'd told me that you'd been adopted by a very loving couple who were living in California. You had parents who dearly loved you. I had to be content with that. So I forced myself to concentrate on doing what I had to. The diner was rebuilt and when my father passed on, I inherited it."

"You never married?"

Sandra shook her head, her face drooping with sadness. "I didn't think it was fair to any man knowing I couldn't have another child. My parents said that was God's punishment for my sin. They said that over and over until eventually I believed them."

"They sound awfully heartless."

"Not really." Sandra tried to smile. "They just had their beliefs and I trampled them with my willfulness. It wasn't until I learned for myself that God doesn't kick us and malign us when we make a mistake that I began to build my own spiritual relationship. God loves us. That was the one good thing that came out of working at the diner. I met a lot of people who helped me figure out that I needed Jesus in my life if I was going to keep from blowing it again."

"And you didn't see my father again?" Kelly thought the question was perfectly straightforward so she was surprised when Sandra didn't answer right away.

"I kept track of him, followed his career. But I stayed away from him."

"So he's still in Richmond. But if you were content with your life, if things were going okay, then why—"

"Why did I hire Ross to find you?"

Sandra's bittersweet smile touched a nerve that Kelly didn't want anyone to see.

"Cancer does funny things to you, Kelly. You begin to realize what really matters in life." Her voice softened. "You were on my mind a lot during the past thirty-four years. I'd wake up in the morning and wonder if you were okay, if you ever married, if I had grandchildren. I'd always wished I'd found you, spoken to you, let you know that I didn't let you go willingly."

"But you didn't."

"I was afraid of ruining your life."

"And now?"

"Things changed. Suddenly I was facing the possibility of death and I'd never learned what I most wanted to know—were you all right, were you loved, did you need me? I never told you I loved you."

"That's where I came in, to unravel the past."

Kelly had almost forgotten Ross was still there. She stared at him for several moments, then nodded.

"Sorry, my brain's a little foggy tonight. You're talking about Barnaby Harcourt's dirty little secrets, aren't you?" She shook her head. "It was horrible to learn that my birth certificate had been altered. I always knew I was adopted but to change something so basic—" She faltered to a halt.

"Finding out about his machinations was the first stone unturned. After that, things just began to unravel."

"That's what sin does, falls apart when the light of truth is shined upon it." Sandra's stare remained on Kelly. "Do you have anything else you'd like to ask, honey?" she asked softly. "I promise I'll answer as truthfully as I can."

"Except that you won't tell me the name of this man."

Sandra shook her head. "I can't."

"Then maybe you can tell me how you met him."

Sandra was silent for several moments. When she finally spoke her voice was so quiet Kelly had to lean forward to hear.

"I was twenty. I couldn't afford to go away to college right after high school, so I was working for my parents and saving money. I met him in the diner when he came for lunch. He was handsome, a professional, sure of himself and a charmer. I was shy, self-conscious and plump." She glanced at Kelly, nodded, her lips forming a half smile. "I'm sure it's a story you've heard a thousand times in your office at Tiny Blessings."

"That doesn't matter. This is your story. Please, go on."

"Well, that very first day he started to flirt with me. Nobody ever showered attention on me so I could hardly believe he'd even noticed me. He left me this really large tip and a note on the back of his bill. 'You have beautiful eyes.'" She snorted. "What a fool I was!"

"Don't beat yourself up. The guy was a creep looking for a place to show his true colors. You just got in the way."

"My parents were strict and they would have put a stop to it if they'd known, but I made sure they never did." Sandra's winsome smile made her look years younger. "At first we'd meet for coffee at a place out of town. We'd talk and talk. I heard all about his horrible marriage, his depressed wife and how he so wanted to be free of her but couldn't because she needed him."

"A married man?" Kelly could feel the color leaving her face. It was worse, far worse than she'd ever imagined. Somehow this scenario had never played out in her mind—she was the unwanted child of a married man!

"We started meeting more frequently. I was flattered that someone so good-looking, so smart, would notice little old me. He was ambitious and he had plans for the future.

I was living a fantasy." She shrugged. "Maybe I had dreams that he would take me with him up the corporate ladder, I don't know. I did believe him when he said he loved me, that he would divorce his wife as soon as she was mentally well enough."

"Don't say any more if it hurts too much," Kelly murmured. She could hear the pain in Sandra's voice and had no wish to cause more. "You can tell me some other time if you want."

"No, I'd like to finish. Then I can finally put it away." Sandra accepted the cup of coffee Ross offered to her. "Thanks."

"You're welcome." He had another for Kelly but she shook her head. Her stomach had started its tap-dance routine again and coffee wouldn't help.

"Anyway, the inevitable happened. I got pregnant." Sandra set her cup down, shook her head. "I didn't mean that quite the way I said it," she told Kelly. "I just meant—"

"It's okay. She understands. Go on." Ross smiled encouragingly.

"I actually thought he'd be happy about it. I was so naive."

"Most normal men would be," Ross muttered.

"He was furious at first. Then he told me he'd pay for an abortion. I couldn't do that. It went against everything my parents had taught me for years. I wasn't living a right life, but I knew what was wrong and I couldn't violate that. Thank God I didn't." She pressed her hands over her face to muffle her sobs. "Thank God."

"The louse changed tactics when she wouldn't go along with his great idea, probably because he was afraid of being exposed." Ross's mouth pinched into a grim line. "That would ruin his career ambitions for sure. So he told Sandra that he'd stand by her and the child, that he'd leave his wife, take care of her and the baby, but that she had to keep quiet about her pregnancy and not name him or everything would go up in smoke and he wouldn't be able to support her."

Kelly had heard the same story many times before from girls who'd been tricked just as badly. The fact that this time it was her mother who'd been duped was something she wasn't yet prepared to deal with.

"So he convinced you to move to Richmond, probably paid for your apartment and gave you a little allowance to scrounge by on while you waited to give birth. You were out of the way and he figured no one would suspect you carried his child." She smiled at the surprise written all over Ross's face. "You might say I've heard it before in various shapes and forms."

"It must sound tawdry and horrid to you," Sandra murmured, eyes downcast. "I guess it was. At the time I didn't see that, of course. I loved him. I thought he loved me. He'd promised me marriage and I wanted to believe him."

"There's nothing wrong with that. Sometimes hope in people is all we have to hang on to." Her stomach was roiling again. The weight of what she'd been told pressed like a wall of bricks on her spirit. Kelly needed time to absorb it all, time to figure out how to balance her world again. And she needed to do that alone.

"You're not feeling well again, are you, Kelly? Don't lie, I can tell from the pea-green color of your face. We need to go." Ross gathered the dishes, slid them into the dishwasher, wiped the table and rinsed out the coffeepot in a few practiced moves. "I'll leave the rolls in this container, in case you get hungry."

"Thank you." She knew Sandra was waiting…for something. "I'm sorry to cut this short, but thank you for dragging up the past enough to tell me. I'd still like to know exactly who my father is."

"Maybe I'll be able to tell you someday. Are you sure you don't want to go to the hospital? Your hands are shaking."

"I'll be fine." She rose, walked behind them to the front door. "You don't have to worry about me. Good night."

"Good night, Kelly." Sandra gave her one last look then pulled her collar up and stepped out the door.

"Thanks for the soup," she called out belatedly. "It was delicious."

"Anytime." Sandra wanted to say more but Kelly saw the look she exchanged with Ross and was grateful for the almost imperceptible shake of his head. She hurried toward her car.

"Call me if you need anything. Promise?" Ross kept glancing over his shoulder until Sandra was safely inside her car, then he closed the door, his gaze intent as he stared down at her. "I do mean anything."

"I'll be fine. I just need to think things through."

"I know. It's unexpected and you've got to adjust. But you're not alone, Kelly. Sandra will be here in a flash if you ask her. So will I."

"Thank you. I may take you up on that. But for now I need to pray about this."

"Why?" His eyes hardened. "What do you think God is going to do, change the past?"

"He's going to help me find a way to get through this, to put my life back together," she told him simply. "I don't understand why any of this happened."

"I do. A creep abused the trust a young woman put in him and God let her child be taken away."

"You're very angry at God, aren't you?" She leaned against the wall, weary but willing to listen if it would help him. "Why is that?"

"It's too long a story and you're too tired. Maybe another time." Ross brushed a tendril of hair off her face. His hand stayed cupped around her jaw, feathering against her skin. "You're a strong woman, Kelly. I admire you for listening tonight. It can't have been easy." He leaned forward, brushed his lips against hers. "Sleep well," he whispered, then left.

Kelly touched her lips with her fingers, but her roiling stomach drew her attention from his kiss and she didn't linger. She locked the door quickly behind him, then began turning out the lights. She'd reached the bottom step before the question blew through her mind. She'd made sure all the doors were locked, so how had Ross been able to get inside?

She picked up the phone and called him.

"The side door of the garage was open," he explained. "But I locked it behind me."

"Oh. Thanks. Good night."

Kelly walked back to the door that opened onto the garage. She stood looking at it while her mind played back her actions of earlier today. It had been locked. She knew it had.

So if Ross found it unlocked, that meant someone else had been inside—someone who was able to move freely through her house whenever they wanted. That thought sent chills up her spine.

She locked the door once more, then dragged the heavy mahogany hall table in front of it. Fatigued beyond description, she started up the stairs once more. The phone rang but she ignored it until the answering machine kicked in to record the caller's voice.

"Better forget about the past and think about your future. If you want to have one."

Chapter Eight

"**I**'d like all the locks changed, please."

Ross's hand, raised to rap on Kelly's office door, froze midair. He'd thought she was alone.

"As soon as you can. Yes, that will be fine. Thank you."

Locks changed? The little tic at the side of his neck that always signaled trouble began racing a mile a minute. Something had happened. He tapped on her door while trying to tamp down his frustration.

Why hadn't she called him?

"Come in."

"Hi."

"Hi, yourself." Kelly stared at him. "You look angry. What's wrong?"

"You tell me. You're the one who's having your locks changed. I didn't listen in deliberately, I just happened to be there at the right moment." He flopped down in a chair and glared at her until she told him about the phone call and the door. "You're sure you locked it?"

She nodded. "Positive. Zach said they're trying to trace the call but all they've been able to find so far are pay phone numbers. They have no clues about who was in here the night I got stuck in that closet, either."

"Huh." He didn't assimilate much of what she said, he was too busy admiring her formfitting red suit. Sick or healthy, Kelly Young was a lovely woman. "You look beautiful," he murmured.

"Thank you."

"And tired," he added, noticing the droop to her eyes. "Did you get any sleep?"

"Some." She shrugged at his disbelieving look. "Okay, I dreamed a lot. Staying awake seemed preferable."

"You said that before," he reminded her. "That you dreamed. What was it about last night?"

She sank into the big chair behind her desk, folded her hands on top. Her face seemed to pale even more as she spoke.

"It was about a fire and someone burning to death. Then the fire came toward me, only it wasn't a fire, it was a person, and they had my parents tied up." She shook her head. "It's just a dream. It doesn't make sense."

In a way it did. She'd tied together Sandra's story of her mother dying in the diner fire to her own parents. The very basic psychology courses Ross had taken at the police academy taught him how to defuse hostage and drug situations. Applied to this situation he realized Kelly was afraid that accepting Sandra would cost her the happy memories of her parents.

"Did you work out how you feel about Sandra?"

She smiled. "That isn't going to take me one night, Ross. It's a process and I have to get there in my own way."

"I know. You're doing fine."

"I'll talk to her in a day or so."

"Okay. In the meantime, I came to ask you out for dinner."

"Oh." Something flared in her eyes, then was dampened. "I'd better not. I was planning to clean out that closet tonight. Or at least make another start."

"You have to eat." He squinted at her. "You haven't stopped eating as well as sleeping, have you?"

"It's easier not to eat than to be sick all the time." She unscrewed the lid of a container and tapped out three tablets which she took with a glass of water.

"What's that?"

"Penicillin. I had an ear infection a few weeks ago. I'm just finishing the medication."

"Maybe that's what is making you sick."

"The drug?" She frowned. "I've never had a problem with it before."

"Things change, Kelly. This has gone on too long. I think you should see a doctor."

"I second that opinion." Pilar stood in the doorway, frowning. "I've been trying to tell her that all day. I even made an appointment for her at the office down the street."

"When is it?" Ross asked.

"In ten minutes. Guess I'd better go cancel." Pilar turned away.

"Wait." Ross rose, reached out to touch Kelly's hand. "Come on, I'll go with you." She frowned. "What's it going to hurt, Kelly? Worst-case scenario, he says you've got the flu and Mrs. Know-it-all Morrow is proven right. Come on."

"I agree with Ross. You should get this bug checked out, Kelly. We don't want to pass on anything contagious to the baby that's coming in next week."

Kelly's eyes widened and she stood. "I'd never want that," she whispered.

"So we go." Ross turned, winked at Pilar, who gave a

thumbs-up, then grabbed Kelly's coat and held it out. "Time's a wastin'."

"You two are so pushy," she complained, sliding her arms into the sleeves. "Give you an inch and you take a mile."

"Exactly." Pilar stood back as they passed. "See you tomorrow, Kel. If the doctor says it's okay."

"I'll be back tonight no matter what he says. I want that storage closet empty."

"Why? What's so important about it?"

She blinked, shook her head. "Put it down to my need to tie up loose ends. Besides, there are some things that we could store there for use when the children come in."

"Or we could just say you're an obsessive compulsive who has to have everything in its place," he teased.

"We could. But we're not going to say that, are we?" She gave him the same look his seventh grade teacher had when he'd smart-mouthed her.

"No, Miss Young," he agreed placidly as they walked down the stairs. Ross held out his arm when they reached the icy street, relishing the touch of her fingers on his sleeve. She was gorgeous in the long black coat, the perfect foil for her golden hair. He felt about ten feet tall when several passing males turned for a second glance at her.

"This must be the place," he said, reading the nameplate in the window. He pulled open the door, waited for her to pass through.

"You know what I hate the most lately?" she whispered as they walked toward the desk.

"No, what? And why tell me now?"

"Because I just realized that I've lost control of my life. You and Pilar talked me into this. I'll have to think of payback." She gave him an arch look, then began to explain her presence to the receptionist, who directed her to a room down the hall.

Ross would have preferred to go with her to find out exactly what the doctor had to say, but he made do with sitting in the waiting room, watching the people who came and went. One of those who was going was Dr. Eli Cavanaugh, whom Ross knew was a pediatrician at the Children's Hospital in Richmond.

"Hey, Ross. Good to see you again. You sick?"

"No, I brought Kelly in. She hasn't been feeling well." He studied the other man more closely. "I didn't know you worked here."

"Don't usually. I didn't have a clinic today so a buddy of mine asked me to stand in for him here. He doesn't get a lot of time off. I thought I was finished for the day, but I'll check with the desk." He held a hurried discussion with the receptionist, then returned to Ross. "Dr. Klein is backed up. Rachel's not expecting me home for another hour or so. I can see Kelly if she wants to see me."

"I'm sure she'd be happy to talk to you." He wasn't sure of any such thing but Ross had a hunch that Eli might be able to wiggle more out of Kelly than someone she barely knew.

"Sit tight. It shouldn't take us long."

But it did take a long time and Ross, alone in the waiting room, had just checked his watch for the tenth time when the two finally emerged.

"Everything okay?" he asked Kelly as he helped her with her coat.

"You should ask Eli that."

The doctor's face bore a serious expression. "I don't think it's flu, Kelly. I think it's more in the nature of an infection of some kind. The blood work will tell me and I'll call you about it as soon as I have the results. In the meantime, I'm giving you this prescription. I want you to take it until it's all gone."

"More pills. I don't think I've swallowed this many drugs in years."

"Well, you're getting older," Eli teased. "We all are. We break down quicker."

"That's encouraging." She made a face at him, pulled on her gloves. "You'll let me know the results?"

"As soon as I have them. Don't overdo it, get plenty of rest." He glanced at the chart in his hands. "You might think about going back to your water aerobics classes as a way to get rid of the stress. Anyway, I know how much you love the water so an hour of splashing around in it shouldn't be a hardship."

"I do not 'splash around,'" she told him with a grimace. "But I stopped because of the time factor. There's so much to do."

"I thought January was your slow season."

"Slow for clients, but busy for us because we try to get all the odds and ends cleaned up in the office. Have to keep Tiny Blessings running like a well-oiled machine, you know," she said cheekily.

"I'm more concerned about keeping you up to par. You're too stressed, Kelly. You have to relax a little."

"I'll help with that," Ross volunteered. "Dinner with me. No cooking, no cleaning. Just relaxing."

"Exactly what I'd prescribe." Eli grinned. "Take it easy, you two."

"Thanks, Eli."

On the street outside the clinic, night had fallen, bringing with it a fine dusting of powdery snow.

"Isn't it pretty?" Kelly raised her face and stuck out her tongue.

"I'm taking that as a sign that you're hungry," Ross told her. "Come on. I know just the place."

He chose the Starlight Diner for two reasons. One, the special tonight was Sandra's meat loaf and he'd never tasted anything better. But more importantly, he had a hunch that because of their meeting last night, Kelly would avoid the diner, or perhaps feel she should. He wanted to go with her to help her realize that in spite of what she'd learned about herself and Sandra, nothing had really changed, that she was still Kelly Young and Chestnut Grove was still the place she called home.

"It's hard to believe there was ever a fire here, isn't it?" Kelly's big brown eyes were focused on the long chrome counter. "Even the jukebox with its Elvis songs seems authentic."

"That's because it is." He didn't bother with the menu, he already knew what he wanted. "Thirty-three years ago there was still a lot of '50s memorabilia available. Sandra said her father was able to replace the soda fountain from a bankrupt business and they collected the posters on a trip to Hollywood. Sandra has had the booths reupholstered since then, of course, and the walls repainted to keep things fresh. But overall she wanted to keep the diner much the same as her parents had it."

"It looks great. And I love this bright blue vinyl." She ran her hand over the back of the booth. "But how can she keep it up? That stuff must be getting hard to find now."

"I guess. But don't forget the retro look is back in vogue so things like that milk shake mixer have probably been replaced." He watched her scan the menu. "See anything you'd like?"

"I think I'll have some soup and toast."

"That's it?"

"For now." She grinned. "I don't want to tempt fate, or rather my stomach, by giving it too much. Besides, I love vegetable beef soup. My mom—" She paused, swallowed. "My mother used to make the beef so tender your mouth would water. She always put in pot barley. I love pot barley." She looked away from him, focused on the wall.

"Don't do that, Kelly. She was still your mom. She'll always be your mom. Nothing can change that. And you don't really want it to."

"No," she admitted. "I don't. But clearly you've done all the research, checked and rechecked your facts?" She lifted one eyebrow, silently asking for confirmation.

"Yes, I have. The DNA says you are Sandra Lange's daughter."

"Then you know who my father is, too, don't you?" Her brown eyes dared him to deny it.

"You know I can't say any more than that, Kelly. I promised to keep Sandra's confidence and I won't go back on my word." Why had he ever made that stupid promise? It wasn't right or fair that he should know and she shouldn't.

"Fine. You know what? For tonight, just for a few hours, let's forget about me and my problems. Let's talk about you." She paused, gave her order to the waitress, waited for him to do the same. "Milk shakes? As in plural?"

"We're in a diner. We have to have a milk shake." He grinned, pleased that she'd lost that sad look. "Besides, you love milk. Every time I see you you're drinking it. You have it in tea, dip gingersnaps in it, make hot chocolate with it. You—what did I say wrong?"

"I didn't make the hot chocolate with it," she explained. "I used some packets of gourmet stuff I bought before Christmas. So call me lazy." She frowned when he didn't smile. "There's something wrong with my gourmet chocolate? You seemed to like it before."

"No, nothing wrong. I was just thinking about something." He pulled out his notebook, scribbling a memo to himself. "Anyway, one milk shake won't hurt you."

"That's where Eve got in trouble, if I remember my Bible correctly," she teased. "Just one little bite—isn't that how it went? And look what happened to her."

He did laugh then. "Your sense of humor sneaks out at the oddest times. Under all that sober responsibility I expect you're rather a brat."

"How did you know? But we're not talking about me. So don't try to change the subject." She accepted her vanilla shake from the waitress and sipped it. "It's good. Thank you."

"You're welcome," the waitress said, moving back to the counter where several diners were waiting.

"Ross, last night you admitted you were angry with God. You said it was a long story."

"So?" He couldn't look at her.

"I'd like to hear it. It would do me good to get my mind off my problems and onto someone else's."

He opened his mouth to decline and realized he didn't have a leg to stand on. He'd poked his nose into her life big-time, was even keeping the name of her father from her. Clearly it was payback time.

"It's boring stuff. Somebody who grew up the way you did probably has no idea how rough life can be for kids." Her brows drew together and Ross knew he'd said the wrong thing. "That didn't come out right. I'm sure you hear of it all the time, in your line of work. What I meant was, it's a different thing to experience it."

"Life can be tough in mansions, too, Ross. We get parents wanting to adopt and mothers wanting us to find good homes for their children from all over the country, from all economic stratas. If I've learned anything at Tiny Blessings, it's not to judge a person by outward appearances. Scars don't always show." She reached out, touched his restless fingers. "Just tell me."

He stared at their hands, aware that this was the first time she'd actually initiated contact. And he liked it. A lot.

"It's not really something I've ever talked about." He couldn't figure out how to explain his doubts about God without hurting her feelings. Kelly was a woman of faith, it influenced her life. He, on the other hand, found it difficult to believe God cared one whit about him or his life.

"Start with something simple then. Did you grow up going to church?"

He laughed. "Sure. Christmas Eve, sometimes Easter, weddings. When my parents were sober enough and they weren't verbally beating each other's brains in. I even took Trista to a girls' club at a church when she was in grade school. They had a boys' club, too. I went once or twice."

"And you didn't like it?" Kelly leaned forward, intent on what he was saying.

Ross liked that about her. It wasn't idle curiosity that brought on her questions. She really was interested.

"I didn't hate being there, if that's what you mean. But I hated it when Trista started believing what they were saying, that God was interested in every detail of her life. That He'd be there for her." He raked a hand through his hair, shifted his feet under the table as the old anger boiled just beneath the surface. "I'd see her kneeling by her bed, praying and praying that there'd be enough food in the fridge to take a lunch to school, enough milk to go on the three-day-old porridge I'd been meting out in bites."

"So you were angry at God for not removing you from that situation?"

"Or maybe for putting us in it!" He pushed the milk shake container away. "How many times have you seen couples desperate to have kids? How many people have spent millions of dollars on any procedure they think will help them have a child? And yet here we were, two healthy kids stuck with two of the lousiest parents God ever created. Why?"

"I don't know. Why don't you ask Him?"

"What?" He paused middiatribe to glare at her. "What do you mean?"

"Well, in any court of law, the defendant gets to question his accuser. You've condemned God without asking for His side of the story." She leaned back against the seat, her face calm, her eyes intent.

"Are you joking?"

Kelly shook her head. "I wouldn't joke about something that touches you so deeply, Ross."

"Then I don't get it." He leaned back to allow the waitress to serve them. The meat loaf he'd anticipated with such pleasure suddenly seemed less important than finding out what Kelly was talking about. "I know other kids had it tougher. My little sob story doesn't compare with what I saw on the street when I was a cop. Our dump seemed like a mansion compared to some of the squalid tenements I've been inside. But none of that answers my question. Where was God? Kids, little kids shooting up on anything they could get their hands on just to be free of that hellhole for a little while—where was God then?"

She'd lifted a spoonful of the rich tomato-based soup to her lips, but Kelly put it back in the bowl, met his anger with a soft smile. "He was there, Ross. He's here, too."

"I've heard that before. But why didn't He do something?"

"How do you know He didn't?"

Her faith was just like everyone else's—based on gullibility. She was kidding herself about God.

"Don't get mad at me for saying this, okay? But we're going round and round in circles here. You're not answering my questions, just asking more." He took a bite of the meat loaf, chewed it long enough to cool down a little. "You claim to believe in this God of yours but you can't explain Him to me. Is that about the gist of it?"

"Ross, God isn't like a package of instant pudding that I can open and say 'add two cups of milk, stir and you'll get pudding.' He's God. Big, all-knowing, loving, righteous—a whole host of things. But if you really want to, God *is* knowable. The reason He created us was to love us. Don't you think a God who made you wants you to understand what He's like?"

"I...don't know."

"Then take my word for it. God loves you, He wants to build a relationship with you. But in order to do that, you have to get to know Him. Personally. You can't build a personal relationship with me by talking to Sandra. Why would you think you could do it with God?"

She tasted her soup, added a bit of salt, then slowly began to eat, closing her eyes as she savored each bite. "This is excellent."

Ross decided to give her some space, let her enjoy her meal before he plied her with yet more questions. He had a thousand of them. Such as, would getting to know God bring the answers to his questions, would he finally understand why a pit of despair like the slums of Brooklyn was allowed to exist?

He glanced up, stared at the figure lounging against the

counter. He was almost certain it was the same person he'd seen in Lindsay Morrow's garden the night of the party.

"Ross?"

"Yes?" He kept his attention on the counter, begging the person in the black coat, hat and boots to turn around so he could get a better look.

"What are you staring at?" She twisted in her seat, trying to follow his stare. "Why are you so interested in Andrew Noble?"

"Is that who it is? I can't see his face clearly."

She took a second look, nodded. "I think so. It looks like him. I asked Rachel what he does. She said a lot of things, but she never did tell me what Andrew was doing in town, or what he does for a living. He's a curious fellow, our Andrew. The prince of Chestnut Grove."

"Why do you call him that?" He glanced at the man, his curiosity whetted. But Andrew never looked his way, simply whipped up the take-out package, dropped a ten-dollar bill on the counter and left.

"You know the Nobles are wealthy? Well it's not just Rachel's parents that have the money. The whole family is well-heeled. Hey!" She dropped the spoon she was holding, jerked back as it hit the dish with a clang. "I just thought of something."

"What?"

"That night you picked me up—I don't remember which night. Since I've been sick, the days kind of run together. Anyway, there was a person who ran out from the side of the house. Remember I told you I'd seen someone. Well that person was dressed head-to-toe in black."

"Him?" Her jerked a thumb the counter.

"Maybe." She bit her bottom lip, her forehead creased. "I couldn't swear to it in court, but it is an odd coincidence that we've seen him several times in the last few weeks. Before Rachel's wedding I don't think he was in town for ages, a year or more, and even then only for a night."

It would look too obvious to take out his notebook now, but Ross made a mental note to check up on Mr. Andrew Noble. Something about the guy was off.

He finished his mashed potatoes then leaned back against the booth seat and watched her carefully remove the crusty edges from her toast. She caught him and blushed a rich rose that lent her cheek a healthy glow and brought more color to her face than he'd seen in days.

"My mother would lecture me if she was watching." She slid the last piece away, popped a bite of the golden bread into her mouth. "She always insisted I eat my crusts. But she's not here to see me so…" She frowned at him. "You probably think that's an awful thing to say."

"Why would I?" He was curious about her sudden guilt. "If you don't like crusts, why eat them? You're an adult, after all. No reason you can't make those choices for yourself. Isn't that what parents are supposed to raise kids to do—make their own decisions?"

"I guess." She chose another of the delicately cut bits and chewed on it. "Is that what your parents did?"

"You could say that." He almost snorted with laughter at the question until he realized she was serious. "It wasn't quite like that. When they got on the bottle, we pretty much had to fend for ourselves. I don't recommend it as a child-rearing method."

He was trying to be flip but he was pretty sure Kelly wouldn't let him get away with it.

"I'm sorry you had to go through that," she murmured. "It must have been very hard. Didn't you have any grandparents you could turn to?"

"No." He didn't want to talk about his past anymore. "Did you?"

"My parents were both only children. They were older when they adopted me. Their parents died when I was a baby. I never met them. I used to wish I had." Kelly's voice dropped, grew a little husky. "All the children's stories that talk about going to Grandma's house, having Christmas dinner with cousins and aunts and uncles—I used to imagine that kind of idyllic life for myself."

"Sounds fun."

"That's what I thought." Her smile was self-deprecating. "Not that I had anything but lovely Christmases. I have no right to complain at all. But they were very quiet."

"This year must have been hard."

"It was a bit." Her eyes grew too bright, glossy with tears. "But I don't wish them back. Mother developed COPD. Chronic obstructive pulmonary disease. She'd always been so active and the disease stole all that from her. In the end she was really struggling. It's actually a relief to know she's not suffering anymore, that she's in Heaven with Dad and that they're with God."

There she went with that faith thing again.

"You sound pretty sure about this Heaven thing."

"I am. The Bible says that if we are a follower of Christ, we can be assured that when we die our spirits will go to live with Him. It says there will be no more pain there." She met his gaze. "My parents were strong Christians. They taught me so much and I miss them every day. But they weren't healthy in their last years here and I can't wish them back to a life of suffering. I know they're at home in Heaven. Now I'm all alone."

"But you're not alone, Kelly. You have Sandra now."

She glanced at him, her gaze pensive. "It's not quite the same," she said quietly.

"You don't have years of history together, that's true. But you could." He saw the hesitation, knew she wasn't quite ready to let Sandra into her heart. "It won't be the same. Sandra can't replace your mother, and she doesn't even want to try. But she could be a friend."

"I know." She pushed away her dirty dishes, planted her elbows on the table and set her chin in her hands. "It's just—I never thought of myself as the child a father wouldn't want anything to do with. That I'm the product of that kind of tawdry, sordid relationship is hard to accept."

"Do you blame Sandra?" A protectiveness burst up inside, which surprised him. He'd known he felt it for Sandra—but for Kelly, too? Ross couldn't decipher it. He only knew he wanted these two women to find some common ground.

"Of course I don't blame her. I've heard her story too many times—young women used by unscrupulous men. If anything, I blame him. He was committed in another relationship. What right did he have to tell her lies and cheat her out of knowing her child—me?" She gulped, stared at him. "Why won't you tell me who he is? I'd like to face him down, ask him if he knows what he missed out on by not being my father."

"I'm sorry." He reached out and brushed a tear from her cheek but Kelly jerked away.

"Yeah. Sorry. Aren't we all, Ross?" She wiped away the tears, smoothed a hand over her hair, then met his stare. "I have to get back to the office. I want to get that closet cleaned out tonight."

"Okay." He walked toward the cash counter, aware that he wasn't her most favorite person at the moment. As he

drove back to Tiny Blessings, Ross shuffled through a
dozen subjects, none of which seemed appropriate conversation topics for this moment. He pulled in beside the curb.

"Thank you for dinner. It was good." She reached for
the door handle.

"Kelly?"

"Yes?" She refused to look at him, kept her gaze
straight ahead.

"If I push you and Sandra together a little too hard,
maybe it's because I don't want you to lose the chance I
never had."

She frowned. "I don't know what you mean."

"I told you my parents never had their act together."

She nodded. "Yes?"

"Actually my father was gone a lot of the time. Mostly
I'm talking about my mother. I tried to forgive her for ne-
glecting us, and that is what it was. I tried to reconcile the
past, to move on, to understand that she had her own problems, that she didn't feel valued or worthy or loved. I tried
all that."

"But you still can't understand why she didn't act as if
she loved you?"

"Before I came here, I made a trip especially to see her,
to ask her the things I've struggled with for years. Why she
didn't try harder, why the booze always came first, why
Trista and I never mattered enough for her to get sober, you
know?" He turned slightly so she couldn't see his face,
couldn't see the anger and frustration that ate at him.

"What did she say?"

"Nothing." He heard himself bark out a laugh and wondered if she heard the pain behind it. "She didn't even know
who I was. My own mother and I was a stranger to her."

"It wasn't her fault, Ross. It's the disease. Alzheimer's

affects the memory part of the brain. I'm sure the doctors told you that."

"They told me." She didn't understand and he couldn't explain it properly, not without letting her see how much it hurt. "I prayed. Did you know that?" The words grated out of him and he was glad to release some of the anger. "I begged your loving God to let me talk to my mother, just one last time. I went to church, I confessed my sins, I did all the things you're supposed to do. Do you know what happened?"

"She still didn't know you."

"Right! Some answer to prayer, huh?" He did face her then. "That's why I'm not buying into your loving God religion. If it works for you, I'm glad. But it's not part of my life anymore. I can't go through that again, weeks of hoping, praying, trying to have faith and then getting smacked down. It's a fool's game. You're kidding yourself if you think God is going to change one single thing in your life. If there even is a God, He must be sitting up there snoozing or playing cards or something, because He sure doesn't seem one whit interested in what's happening here."

"Oh, Ross." Her voice brimmed with sympathy that he didn't want to hear.

"What I started out to say was that you've got this second chance with Sandra. She's survived her cancer. She really cares about you. Don't throw that away. It doesn't happen very often."

Kelly remained silent for what seemed like eternity. He wondered if she was regretting going with him tonight, of being subjected to his personal problems. But maybe, just maybe, it would be worth it if she would let go of her fears and really get to know the woman who was her mother.

"I promise I'll think about what you said, Ross." Then

she opened the door, stepped into the snow and shut the door behind her.

He sat waiting until she'd unlocked the door and was safely inside. When the light came on in her office, he shifted into gear and did a U-turn on the deserted street, thinking that Kelly had no idea how much better off she was not knowing who her father really was. But Ross knew that kind of creep, knew a hundred others like him.

He should. Tonight he'd trail yet another loser who had abandoned his wife's love and was on his way to creating a world of pain and heartache for those who loved him.

As far as he was concerned, it was time God got out of His Heaven and did something about the trouble on earth.

Chapter Nine

"Hey, Pilar. You're working late."

"I had a few things to clean up. I'm almost done." She closed one file, picked up another. "I love getting this stuff from last year cleared away so I can plunge into the new year. What's your excuse?"

"That's why I'm here, too. I intend to clean that closet out tonight no matter what." Kelly raised her head at the noise from down the hall. "Is someone else here?"

"A friend was here fixing that broken drawer in Anne's desk. He wanted to do it before she got back. I think Florence is still here, too. Don't talk to her," Pilar warned. "She's in a foul humor."

"Like that's new?" Kelly sighed. "I'm not up to reprimanding her again. I guess I'll just keep to myself in my little closet."

"You're feeling better?"

"Much. Eli was there, did some tests. I'll get the results in a few days but he seems to think it's some kind of infection. I had some soup and toast for supper. My stomach seems to have settled down at last."

"That's good. We need you here, Kelly. As the new director of Tiny Blessings Adoption Agency, you've made us a more cohesive group and I love the atmosphere. Take care of yourself, *chica.*"

"I'm trying. Thanks, Pilar." She waved, then continued down the hall to her own office. Divested of her coat, Kelly changed into the spare pair of jeans and T-shirt she kept for just these occasions. Then she dived into her work.

It took four trips to the basement to get rid of the mops, brooms, pail and other cleaning supplies that were left. Then she relocated the old paint cans there, too. She'd have to ask Florence to dispose of them properly.

Finally there was nothing left in the small space but the filing cabinet. Though she tried using every possible muscle group she could think of, the cabinet would not budge from its location inside the closet. Maybe Pilar would help.

"Pilar?" Kelly walked down the hallway hoping someone was still in the building, but the farther she got, the stronger the realization grew that she was alone.

"Okay, shades of last time," she muttered heading for the front door. It was locked. One by one she checked each of the fire doors, the emergency exit, every single entrance that led to outside. They were all as they should be.

Heaving a sigh of relief, she returned to the closet, stood in the doorway staring at the cabinet.

"Fine. If you won't move, I'll open you where you are. Whatever you've got inside you must weigh a ton. If it's garbage, I warn you, I'm chucking it out."

She returned to her office, found a pair of scissors and tried prying open the lock. Hopeless. She tried jimmying it with the same lack of success. Just in case brute force might work, she used a heavy metal paperweight from her desk against the bulky cabinet. Nothing.

"You're beginning to bug me," she muttered as she carried the scissors and paperweight back to her office. The ringing phone broke her survey of the office shelves for something to use. "Tiny Blessings Adoption Agency," she answered.

"Hey, it's me." Ross's voice held none of the anger she'd heard when he dropped her off. "I was just over at Sandra's and she has a cold. I thought I'd tell you in case you were thinking of visiting. She's going to be laid up for a day or two, but if you wanted to see her after that, I'm sure she'd be happy to have you visit."

"She's not…seriously ill, is she? She didn't catch whatever I had?" A flutter of panic assailed Kelly. Maybe she shouldn't have been so stubborn about getting to know Sandra.

"She says it's just a cold. Nothing serious."

"Oh, good." Kelly glanced into the hall. An idea emerged. "Where are you, Ross?"

"About three blocks away. Why?"

"Would it be too much to ask you to help me out? I've got the closet cleaned out but I can't get the filing cabinet to move—or open, for that matter," she added. "I don't know if it's rusted or something but the lock will not budge."

"I'll be there in a couple of minutes. Can you let me in the front door?"

"Sure. Thanks, Ross."

"No prob."

She walked downstairs and stood in the lobby, watching the street. It took a few moments for her eyes to adjust, but from her position at the side of the big door, Kelly could see a figure standing across the street.

"Who is that?" she murmured. She knew she was hidden

by the shadows since most of the lobby lights were still off, so she shifted just a little to the left to get a better look. "Andrew?" she whispered, as car lights flashed across his face.

Ross pulled up by the curb and climbed out of his car carrying a small box under one arm. When she glanced back across the street, Andrew was nowhere to be seen.

"Kelly?" Ross rapped on the door and she hurried to open it.

"Sorry." She waited for him to step inside, then relocked the door. "I saw someone across the street."

He whirled around, peered into the night. "Who?"

"Andrew Noble."

"That's three times. This is obviously more than mere coincidence. What is the guy up to?" He took a second look, shook his head. "Looks like he's gone now."

"Maybe he's working for one of the people whose records were falsified by Barnaby Harcourt. I don't know if you remember but when I first found out my own adoption papers were falsified, I also found a history of deception in our files. Maybe there's someone like Sandra who wants to know the truth and he's helping them." She led the way upstairs.

"Could be, I suppose. Though I would think he could ask first. Wasn't there an article in the *Gazette* about that?"

"Yes. Jared printed it after I'd gone to the police. He interviewed me so I could explain how I discovered the problems. We hoped that would do some damage control for the agency. Our reputation has been growing and I didn't want to see it ruined by something that happened before I was there."

"I remember. I read the piece. I think it cleared Tiny Blessings pretty well."

"Thank you. But maybe somebody else doesn't think so.

Maybe they think I'm hiding something. That could be the reason they want me to leave."

Ross shook his head. "If they're looking for the truth, they'd want you to stay, to dig deeper. But those phone calls told you to leave. It's more likely someone doesn't want something known. There was a break-in a few months ago, too, wasn't there?"

"Don't remind me." Kelly saw him clamp his lips together and realized he hadn't meant to speculate aloud. He probably thought he was scaring her, but in fact it made her feel better to think there could be a reason behind the calls, that they weren't just because someone wanted to drive her out of town for no reason.

"There it is, the stubborn beast." She pointed to the cabinet. She stared as Ross opened the small box he carried and displayed the curious tools inside. "What are those?"

"Things I need to pry open this cabinet." He set to work and in a matter of moments the lock popped open. He pulled the top drawer out. "What have we here?"

Kelly reached in and lifted out two of the many cassette tapes that were stacked inside. She was very familiar with the writing on them.

"These were Barnaby Harcourt's," she said. "I wonder what's on them? And look at these notes!" She lifted out a yellow legal pad and tried to decipher the scrawl. A sudden burst of sound made her freeze. "What's that?" she whispered.

"I don't know, but I intend to find out. Put those back and we'll lock the drawer again." He waited till she'd returned the notes and tapes, then closed the drawer and relocked it. "Do you have the key to lock the closet door?"

She pulled it out of her pocket, shoved it into the knob. "I always wondered why someone had a lock on a closet. Now I guess we know."

"Okay, let's go. Stay behind me, okay?"

She nodded, realized he couldn't see. "Yes," she whispered.

"I think it came from the floor below. Let's check there first." They crept down the stairs and into the lobby. Suddenly Ross stopped. Kelly bumped into him, wondered why he didn't go ahead. She moved to the side, but his arm held her back.

"What is it?" Kelly murmured, tilting forward so her lips were less than an inch from his ear. His arm dragged her against his side, his fingers pressed against her mouth to stop further speech. He pointed.

A figure in black was standing on the sidewalk, surveying the smashed window.

Ross stepped forward. "Hold it!"

The words hadn't even left his lips before Andrew disappeared. At least that's who Kelly thought it was.

"He's gone. I'll call the police. Don't touch anything." Ross pulled out his cell phone, began to dial, then froze.

Kelly moved so she could see what he was looking at and gaped. Red fluorescent letters were spray painted on the wall underneath the gold letters of the agency.

Forget the past, KY. Leave this town.

Her fear was full-blown now. "What did I do?" she whispered, unable to control her shaking limbs. "What did I do wrong?"

"Kelly?"

She heard his voice but couldn't take her eyes off the horrible words that marred the marble surface. The old bank building was a pleasure to work in even with its cranky heating system. Granite floors, marble surfaces, oak woodwork—it would have been too costly to build, but Tiny Blessings had acquired it for a song when First City

Trust moved to its new premises. Now it was ruined, because of her.

"Kelly, listen to me."

She heard what he said but it didn't sink in. Why would anyone do this? What if she'd been alone? Would they have come upstairs? Was Andrew Noble watching her every move?

"Kelly?"

Ross's big hands rested on her arms for a minute, then he drew her against him, held her. The warmth of his body chased away the chill of shock and after a moment she was able to draw a deep breath. His solid presence and strength empowered her. For the first time in a very long time she no longer felt utterly alone.

"It's okay, honey. You're all right. Nobody's here but you and I."

"And the police," she told him as a flashing red light pulled up in front of the building.

"Yes. We're going to have to talk to them. Can you manage that?"

"I think so." She jerked her head to stare at him as panic rose like a tidal wave. "Where are you going?"

"I'll be right here, Kelly. I'm not going anywhere." He set her gently away, then grasped her hand. "We'll do this together."

And they did. First Kelly—then Ross—explained that they'd been working upstairs when they'd heard a noise and come to investigate. But it was Ross who mentioned Andrew to Zach when he arrived a few minutes later.

"I don't know what he was doing here, I can't imagine why he would break a window and then write that on the wall." He jerked a thumb at the ugly painted words. "But we both saw him standing on the sidewalk. And he knew we saw him. Kelly thought she saw him earlier, across the street. Maybe he was watching the building for an opportunity."

"Andrew Noble. You're sure?" Zach gave them a funny look. "Why would he bother with graffiti?"

"Why would he want me to leave town? I don't even know the man." Kelly shuddered, the shock of having someone after her finally settling in.

"We'll pick him up, ask some questions. Want me to call Ben Cavanaugh, see if he can come and board up that window? It will probably take a few days to get someone from Richmond to do the repairs."

"That would be great. Thanks, Zach." Kelly stared at the gaping hole in what was left of the glass. "You know I've lived in this town most of my life, but this is the first time I've felt afraid."

"It's good to be wary, to check things out before dashing ahead," Zach said. "Just don't let your fear take control. We're only a phone call away. Ross here seems like he's doing a pretty good job of being Johnny-on-the-spot. You might want to keep him nearby, too." He gave them a teasing grin then excused himself to speak to one of the other officers.

They didn't have very long to wait before Ben showed up with several sheets of plywood on the back of his truck. He and Ross worked together to cover the open space. By the time they'd finished, the clock on the wall said eleven.

"Thanks so much, Ben. You send Tiny Blessings a bill right away. And make sure you charge for your labor. I appreciate you coming out this late, especially since I'm sure you'd rather spend your evenings with your bride."

"Not a problem, Kelly. I just hope they find whoever did this. I don't like to see this kind of thing happen in Chestnut Grove. I want my kids to grow up safe and sound, like I did."

"Me, too." She watched him leave, noticed that most of the police had left. Ross was talking to Zach by the front door. The conversation seemed fairly heated. "Something wrong?" she asked, walking up to them

"I had someone check. Andrew Noble claims he was across the street but that he was just out for a walk. He denies being anywhere near here when the window was broken. And he has an alibi."

"He's lying. We saw him."

"You said you saw someone in black clothing. That doesn't make it Andrew. Besides, at stressful times like these, perceptions can get distorted."

"I was a cop, Zach," Ross countered, his face grim. "I'm used to 'times like these.'"

"Whatever. The alibi seems pretty solid. Anyway, I'll do some more checking but I have to tell you, I was a little skeptical it was him in the first place." Zach turned to Kelly. "You know as well as I do that the Nobles have all the money anyone could want. As far as I know we've never had any of their kids involved in any criminal activities. Andrew is hardly a kid anymore so it seems unlikely he would bother with something like this."

"True." Kelly saw Ross's face and knew he wanted to argue but she forestalled him. "Can I lock up soon? I'd like to get home and get some rest."

"Sure. We're finished here." Zach glanced around. "A team will show up in the morning to do some wrap-up but we won't have to bother you."

"Great. I'll just go upstairs and get my coat." She left the two men to climb the stairs to her office. It was a simple thing to gather up her work clothes and stuff them into a bag she'd shoved into the credenza underneath the window.

Kelly paused there for a moment, staring down into the

street below. Everything looked calm, peaceful. But somewhere someone was up to evil. She caught a movement out of the corner of her eye and turned her head to catch a glimpse of a figure in black turning the corner on a street two blocks away. She grabbed Ross's jacket and her stuff and raced down the stairs.

"Someone's out there," she called as she hurried into the street. "I saw them turn the corner onto Main Street."

"Go home." Zach jumped into his car and raced down the road, lights flashing.

Ross accepted his jacket, his eyes on the disappearing police cruiser.

"Was it Andrew?" he asked, his mouth tight.

"I don't know. I think the person wore black but he was far away and it's not exactly bright out tonight." She slid her arms into her own coat, raised her keys toward the door. "Should we go?"

"Might as well."

Once she'd set the alarm and locked the door, Ross drove her home without saying a word. Kelly wasn't sure what she'd expected, but it sure wasn't this stony silence with only the hum of the car heater fan to break the chasm that seemed to yawn between them. Then suddenly he said the one thing she didn't want to hear.

"I'm heading back to Richmond next week."

"Already?" Could he hear how much she didn't want him to go?

"I'm pretty much finished that infidelity case I took on when I wasn't making much progress with Sandra's. Tomorrow I'll see the wife, tell her what I've learned, show her the pictures. After that it's just a matter of closing up shop."

"Oh." Kelly gulped. "I'll be sorry to see you leave," she

murmured. "I've enjoyed getting to know you." The height of understatement.

The realization that Ross wouldn't be there to call on the next time she needed someone to talk to, to help open a stuck filing cabinet or get her out of a closet, to bring her soup when she felt like death—it hit her fully in that moment with the horrible sinking lurch of loss.

"I thought you'd be celebrating that I'm not going to be pestering you about Sandra anymore." His dark gaze rested on her.

Kelly forced herself to sound normal, hide the shock that she'd felt at his words.

"I know you were concerned for her. I think that's rather nice." She tried to keep her voice normal, her face impassive. "I'm sure she's appreciated all you've done for her."

"I don't know about that but I'm really going to miss her when I go. She's been like a mother to me. Or at least what I imagined a mother would be like."

"Well that's good," she said, infusing her voice with a cheerfulness she didn't feel. "Before you go I want to have you over for dinner. It's the least I can do to repay you for feeding me so often."

"You don't have to do that."

"I want to. Tomorrow night?"

"Sure."

"Would you like me to invite Sandra?" Kelly hoped he'd say no. Maybe it was silly, but if she was going to be alone in this, she'd better learn to handle this new life on her own. She wanted to meet with and talk to the other woman on her own, without Ross watching. Maybe Sandra would give away something about her father, though why she felt this need to know was something Kelly didn't fully understand. She certainly hadn't wanted Sandra's disruption to her calm, careful life. But wasn't it better to know the whole truth up front instead of living afraid, as if something might fall on her head when she least expected it?

"I don't think she's in any shape to go out just yet." Ross turned onto her street. "Tonight she looked pretty weak. I think the chemo left her more vulnerable than she lets on."

"I hope she didn't catch anything from me."

"I doubt it. You don't have a cold." He pulled into her driveway, turned to study her. "Are you going to be all right?"

"In my own home?" She nodded, only half-certain herself. "I'll be fine. I've felt much better today. Maybe it's my cooking that's making me sick."

"Oh? In that case I might have to reconsider your dinner invitation," he said with a teasing smile.

Ross Van Zandt could be fun when he wanted. She would miss that dry wit and the funny glint in his eyes.

"Come on, I'll walk you to the door."

He was around the car before she'd undone her seat belt and he insisted on carrying her bag of clothes. Kelly fumbled with her keys, nervous for some reason as he stood watching her. She shoved open the door and hit the light switch. Everything looked normal.

Ross leaned in to drop her bag on the floor. As he straightened, his face passed within inches of hers. Kelly froze, mesmerized by the look on his face.

"Actually, I'd like to join you for dinner. There's nothing better than sharing a meal and you are a very beautiful woman, Kelly Young. Inside and out." He tilted forward, pressed a butterfly-light kiss against her lips. "I'll see you tomorrow."

"Yes," she breathed, watching as he walked out of the

house and down the walk. "Good night." Suddenly she realized she was standing there like a moonstruck teen. She
moved inside, closed and locked the door.

But she wasn't ready for bed yet. There were too many
things to think about—most of all why the disorganiza-
tion that filled her neat little world suddenly didn't seem
so important.

Free of her coat, she moved into the kitchen, poured herself a glass of milk, then curled up in front of the fire as if
it held the answers to her questions.

Knowing Ross was leaving meant a return to loneliness.
There'd be no one forcing her to see a doctor the next time
she was sick, no one to tell her she was smart and beautiful. No one to gather her up and hold her when life got
scary. The future suddenly seemed bleak.

Kelly turned off the gas fire, emptied her glass and
climbed up the stairs to bed. Her dreams were filled with
figures in black peering around corners, holding her pris-
oner and dumping her in a land where she knew no one.
She tossed and turned until five, then finally got up to
make coffee.

She'd intended to water her plants but the sight that met
her stopped Kelly cold on the threshold. The entire room
had been ransacked, every plant stripped of its foliage and
tossed to the floor. Nothing usable remained. Even the
sculpture she and Ross had won at the Morrows' lay over-
turned on the floor, the head dented and smashed.

But worst of all were the orange spray-painted words
on her windows.

No past. No future. Leave.

Chapter Ten

"**I**'m sorry you've had such a horrible experience, but I'm delighted you suggested this impromptu lunch." Sandra took another bite of the sandwich Kelly had bought from a deli near her office.

"I hope you didn't feel you had to let me come over." She'd deliberately kept the details of the break-in at Tiny Blessings from her. No point in worrying her when she already had so much to think about.

"I wanted to see you," Sandra insisted.

Kelly watched her face closely, looking for signs that Sandra might regret having her here. "I could come another time if you're not feeling well."

"I have a cold, that's all." Sandra leaned back in her chair, her eyes pensive. "There's the one thing about this disease that medicines can't deal with—the fear. People look at you differently after you've had cancer. As if they're afraid they can catch it."

"I didn't mean—"

"No, no. I didn't mean you. I was speaking generally." She nibbled on her pickle. "Do you feel vulnerable now, knowing someone was inside your house? You could always move into my spare room until they catch whoever did it."

"Thank you, that's very kind. But I'm sure I'll be fine once the locks are changed."

Sandra stared at her. "You think they had a key?"

Kelly castigated herself for letting that slip. "Truthfully, I don't know. But the police suggested it and I decided it was a good idea. The locks are the same ones that were there when I bought the place. Someone the previous owners knew could have a key, or maybe there's one floating around. I think it's just safer if I get them changed. I should have done it long ago, but—"

"It never seemed necessary before. I understand." Sandra leaned forward, placed her hand on Kelly's knee. "You look tired, dear. Is something else bothering you?"

Kelly was tempted to brush off her concern but right at the moment she was weary beyond measure and having someone to listen was very tempting.

"A lot of things are bothering me. It's not just the burglary," she admitted after a long pause. "I don't know what's wrong but I feel lousy most of the time. I can't seem to rest because I have terrible dreams at night. And on top of all that there's a case at the agency that's got me concerned." She made a face. "I'm sure you don't need to hear all this."

"But I'd like to listen, if you want to tell me."

"It's just—a host of things seem to be going wrong. Nothing in my life is the way I want it to be and I can't seem to get it back on track. Every time I turn around there's something new to think about."

"And then I came along and pushed my way in." Sandra shook her head. "I'm sorry, Kelly. I was only thinking of myself when I asked to see you, not of the way any of this would affect you. I guess I'm not really mother material after all."

"Don't say that." She debated whether to bring it up and decided she'd rather not skirt the issues between them. "It's not your fault that I was taken from you."

"Maybe not. But the whole idea of me as your mother is upsetting to you. I can see that. And I think I know why." Sandra's smile appeared. "In some ways you're exactly like me, Kelly. You want to control your world, anticipate what could happen so you'll be prepared. You like organization, routine. I was the same."

"You're not now?" Kelly stared at her, wondering what had changed.

"To some extent." Sandra leaned her head back, stared at the ceiling. "The only way I could make sense of my world after the fire at the diner killed my mother was to regain control of it. I had to nail down every detail from the scheduling to the grocery orders. I guess I had this notion that if I could assess the situation and keep everything in check, nothing bad would happen to me again." She straightened, looked at Kelly. "I think you've been doing the same thing."

Had she? Kelly frowned. "What's wrong with being organized, prepared?"

"Nothing. To a point. It's when it spills over into a need to control, into a fear of what could or might happen— that's when it becomes a negative." Sandra laid a hand on the Bible that sat on a table at her elbow. "You see, honey, the hard truth I didn't want to face is that I'm not in control. Neither are you."

"But—"

"May I ask you something very personal, Kelly?"

"I guess." Nervousness about what that question might be had her shifting on the love seat.

"When you became engaged to Simon, did you ever think about what might happen if it broke up, if the two of you decided to split before you got married?" Sandra's stare seemed to burn through the barriers she wanted to erect. It was as if she could see her soul.

Kelly felt her cheeks burn, but she nodded anyway. "I did think about it, yes."

"And you made some plans for that eventuality, didn't you?"

"I didn't plan to break up with him, if that's what you're saying. I thought we would get married."

"I know. But did you ever consider a worst-case scenario? I mean, you bought the house so you obviously knew you wanted to live there with or without him. You were prepared for that."

"Are you saying that was wrong?"

"No. You're a sensible person and I'm guessing that you've always weighed your options, put some effort into looking ahead." Sandra leaned forward. "What I'm getting at is a feeling I have that deep inside, maybe in the very back of your mind, you probably had some plan about how you'd handle things if your birth mother—me—ever showed up."

Kelly opened her mouth to protest but Sandra continued.

"Maybe it was unconscious, maybe not. But I think a fear was there that your perfect world might be upset someday. When you couldn't come up with a way to deal with it you tucked it away and kept everything else under control to compensate."

"Maybe." This was a time for truth. Kelly took a deep breath. "When I was seven or eight," she whispered, "I used to have dreams that someone would come and take me away from my mother and father. I asked my mother about it and she said that it didn't matter if anyone came, that no one could pull out the love we had for each other, no one could unmake our family."

"But that secret fear didn't leave you, did it?"

"I guess not." She'd never told a soul that she'd harbored that worry. Until now. Until Sandra, who seemed to see into her heart as easily as she looked outside the window.

"And then Ross came along and told you I was your mother and your worst nightmare came true. No wonder it's been so difficult for you to accept." Sandra tossed her a grin. "I felt exactly the same when the doctor told me I had breast cancer. I'd done everything right—diet, exercise, vitamins, all of it. And it didn't matter one bit. I had no control over the cancer. It was here," she tapped her chest, "in *my* body and I couldn't do a thing about it."

Kelly felt a rush of empathy as tears filled Sandra's green eyes. "I'm sorry."

"Don't be." The words burst out of Sandra with a fierceness that surprised Kelly. "I needed to learn that lesson, I needed to understand that my security doesn't come from eating the right things, walking on my treadmill, taking vitamins. My security comes from God. He and He alone decides how many days I'll spend on this earth. The problems that come to me happen only because He allows them. And if I rest in His strength, I can do whatever He asks me to do."

"But my father—what he did to you." Kelly stared at her, frowned. "Aren't you angry at him? Bitter?"

"Not as much as I was," Sandra told her. "I blamed him terribly for what happened, but one day I looked at the truth and accepted that the fault was just as much mine. I was trying to control the future by demanding he leave his wife and marry me. I thought ruining someone else's life would make my world more secure. I wanted to show my parents that I wasn't the silly child they thought, that I had a plan. Your father was my means to an end."

Sandra leaned back in her chair, closed her eyes.

"That isn't love, Kelly," she said sadly. "That's using someone to get what you want. I wanted a home for my baby, legitimacy, a host of things. I wanted my own way. I didn't love him the way a woman should love a man she intends to marry."

"I'm sorry."

"No, it's good to face the truth, to let it cleanse you." She met Kelly's glance, nodded. "The hard truth is, I couldn't have been the mother to you that Carol Young was. She understood the demands of a child, was prepared to sacrifice her own needs so that you would have the security and stability you needed."

"She was a wonderful mother," Kelly whispered.

"And you loved her dearly." She smiled at Kelly's surprise. "I don't envy her that, my dear. She helped shape you into who you are today. If she were alive I could never thank her enough for loving you. She gave you a precious gift of motherhood that you'll pass on to your children and they'll pass on to theirs. God knew I couldn't have managed that and so He worked it out so that you would benefit from my willfulness."

"I never thought of it that way." God had a *reason* for doing this? She mulled that over until Sandra began speaking again.

"Do you remember the Wednesday afternoons when Carol would bring you into the diner for a milk shake before your ballet class?"

Kelly nodded. "Very well."

"I used to watch the two of you, chattering a mile a minute, and I'd think, there's a woman who's completely in tune with her child. She's not thinking about what to make for dinner or how she'll pay for the new carpeting. She's let all of that go and she's just basking in your presence."

The memory was too poignant, Kelly couldn't speak for the tears clogging her throat.

"That's how our relationship with God is supposed to be, honey. We're not supposed to fret about what could happen, what might take place next Thursday. We're supposed to do the best we can with what we've got and give the rest to God. Then we can bask in His presence, really get to know Him and not just recite lists of what we need to keep our life exactly the same."

"But I hate change, I hate not knowing what to expect."

"But change is the only way we grow. Ross was telling me about a poinsettia you have. He thought it was so odd that you were disappointed it didn't bloom at Christmastime when he couldn't believe that it had actually bloomed at all. Do you see what I mean?"

"A matter of perspective." Kelly nodded, her thoughts racing. "You mean I'm getting too caught up in the what-ifs and missing the what-ares."

Sandra laughed. "Exactly."

"I don't know if I can let go of my need to control that easily," she admitted. "It's disconcerting to be tossed out of my comfort zone."

"But my dear, what you're really saying is that you can't trust God to handle things, to be there when you need Him."

"Am I?" She'd never thought of it that way before.

"I think so. And I think you do that because you fear change. Somewhere in your experience change became something to be afraid of. But look at the changes that have brought you where you are today." She ticked them off on her fingers. "You had to leave home, go to college, take courses, pass exams, meet new friends, interview for jobs, learn how to run Tiny Blessings, get engaged, break it off. Those are all big changes, Kelly. But they're also part of growing into adulthood, of leaving your mark on the world."

"I never thought of it that way." Kelly frowned as the ideas swirled in her mind. "You're saying that moving away from home to go to college didn't mean I was losing a home, it meant I gained a degree. Am I getting it?"

"Smart girl."

Kelly studied her, decided to admit the truth. "I had this idea that acknowledging you as my birth mother, letting you into my life—I felt that would somehow negate the past I had with my parents. But if I look at it from your viewpoint, maybe that past was a preparation for today."

"I like to think so. But, Kelly, please don't ever think I want to take away what Carol and Marcus gave you. They were your parents, they were there when you needed them and they loved you with all their hearts. Treasure that."

It took a lot of courage but Kelly looked her straight in the eye and voiced the question that had raced around inside of her for the past week.

"Where do we go from here?"

"Wherever you want. I'd like to think we could become friends, that maybe we could share lunch sometimes, talk like we have today. But that's totally up to you. I'm not going to press you to pretend anything you don't feel. I'm just delighted God allowed me to know you better."

Tears welled at the words. How could she be grateful for so little? Kelly didn't know. She did know that she'd learned a lot about herself today, that she'd allowed a few of her fears to see the light and found out nothing was as bad as she'd anticipated. Sandra had helped her realize that.

"I have to go," she mumbled, glancing at her watch. "I've got a client coming in a few minutes. But I really enjoyed this."

"So did I, my dear. I hope we do it again soon." Sandra rose, walked her to the door. "I hear you're cooking Ross dinner tonight."

Kelly nodded, slightly embarrassed that she knew.

"He's a wonderful man, Kelly. I don't think I've ever known anyone more honest or loyal. He doesn't play games, he doesn't pretend to be someone he isn't. I'd trust him with my life."

Kelly frowned. "But?"

"He's got some issues with God that need sorting out."

Kelly chuckled. "Believe me, I know. We've talked about them several times. He has this idea of God as some kind of fairy godmother."

"Not so different from our own view sometimes, is it?" Sandra murmured, then chuckled at Kelly's downcast face. "But we're learning. That's a good sign."

"More change." Kelly pressed a hand against her stomach as a spasm clenched it painfully. "I sure hope the doctor figures out what's wrong with me. I'm getting sick of feeling nauseated all the time."

"I'll be praying."

Kelly couldn't help herself. She leaned over and hugged the short, frail-looking woman. "Take care of yourself, Sandra," she whispered.

Sandra hugged her back, her arms tight before she finally let go. "You, too, my dear."

"Bye." Kelly drove back to the office thoughtfully. She

didn't really notice the broken glass in the lobby, wasn't aware of the voices in the offices beyond. All she could think about was that she'd finally faced one of her fears and the experience had left her empowered.

Ross leaned against the porch column of Kelly's house and tried to get his nerves under control. Since when did eating dinner with Kelly make him as nervous as a schoolboy?

Since he'd realized he didn't want to leave Chestnut Grove, didn't want to return to the emptiness of his former life in Richmond, didn't want Kelly to face whoever was targeting her alone.

The people here were friendly, the town charming, life more simple. But it was more than that, and he knew it.

The thing that made his day worthwhile, that made his spirit perk up, was imagining Kelly. She had this way about her that made him feel strong—protective and yet cared about. He had no college degree, no special training in anything but police work and yet she'd never looked down on him or made him feel the way some people did about his job as a private investigator.

Kelly accepted him for who he was, that was the thing that Ross liked the most about her. And of course there was her spirit. Green at the gills or dressed to kill, Kelly Young faced up to life instead of looking for the easy way out. Unlike him.

"What are you doing standing out here, Ross? Afraid of my cooking?" She stood in the doorway, her smile wide, a flicker of fun dancing in her eyes. "Wanna come in, or do you need some more time to think about it?"

"Ha-ha! You're calling me a coward?" He stepped inside, shrugged out of his jacket. The aroma tantalized his nose. "Something smells delicious."

"Roast chicken," she told him. "It's not quite done so we can sit by the fire for a while if you want."

"Sure." He accepted the glass of punch she handed him and followed her into the den. The fire flickered, casting its golden glow on the comfortable room. In the background soft orchestral sounds hinted at hidden speakers.

"It's funny, I kind of thought your house would be more…feminine, when I first knew you lived here. But this room is a guy's room."

"Is it?" She looked startled, glanced around. "Why?"

"Maybe that was the wrong way to describe it," he backtracked, embarrassed by his outburst. "I just meant that some places are more feminine. Like at Sandra's, I always worry I'll bump one of those fancy vases over or sit down too hard and her furniture will collapse." He waved a hand. "This room is all about comfort. Something funny about that?"

"I think so. When we first looked at the house, Simon mentioned he'd love to turn this room into a media room. He said it should be a place where he could bring his friends over and they could watch football games together."

Ross glanced around. Not a television in sight. "I'm not much into sports, but I guess a television would be okay."

"I'm not into them, either, at least not watching them on television. But I did put a TV in here, I just hid it." She touched a panel beside the fireplace, which opened to reveal a black screen. "Simon's idea ranged more in the neighborhood of five feet by six." She made a face.

"Ah. A big-screen man."

"I guess. I'm not fond of dedicating a room to a TV. If I want to watch the news or something, it's there, but I'd much rather sit and talk to the teen group when they come over to plan what they're going to do at Tiny Blessings."

"What could they do?" An adoption agency didn't seem

the kind of place where teens would want to go in their spare time.

"You might not have noticed but we have a little playground and sort of picnic area at the back. Sometimes they come after school or during the summer to watch the children while our staff holds meetings with the mothers and parents-to-be." She smiled. "From time to time they get industrious and decide we should hold an open house where people can come in and learn about what we do. We usually ask the teens to do the tours and host the coffee room. They have a baking session and bring in the treats to serve to the visitors. Things like that."

Ross had no idea she'd involved so many members of the community in the agency. A new thought came to his mind.

"Could it have been one of the kids who trashed your sunroom last night?"

She lifted her brows.

"Oh, yeah, I heard all about it from Zach. I'm just sorry I wasn't around. I had to make a quick trip to Richmond this morning or I'd have been over here."

"I was fine, Ross. Shocked a little, I guess. But I've had the locks changed. Ruth Fraser, our pastor's youngest daughter, came over and cleaned up for me after school so it isn't such a disaster zone anymore. Just a little empty." She swallowed the hurt. "I had to throw the plants out. They were ruined. Even The Thing got its head bashed in."

"Now there's a loss." He lost the smile. "I'm sorry, Kelly."

"So am I. But I can get some more plants. And I'll choose my own statuary, next time. There was nothing precious lost." Except her privacy, her peace of mind, her security.

She rose. "I'll go check on that chicken."

Ross stood, followed her. "I can help. I know a little bit about a kitchen."

At least he knew how to carve a chicken. Two years of after-school work in a butcher shop had taught him the fine art of deboning. Ross laid the pieces on the platter she provided, content to sneak glances as Kelly drained and mashed the potatoes, placed tiny green peas in a serving bowl and pulled a salad from the fridge.

She wore a long black skirt that flowed whenever she moved. She'd paired it with a printed green blouse tucked into a wide leather belt that emphasized the narrowness of her waist. Her sleeves had been folded back to reveal her forearms, and on one of those she wore a small silver bracelet with a jade-colored stone in the middle. Her golden hair was pulled to the top of her head and held in a matching silver clip, though here and there a tendril had escaped and now caressed her cheek or her slim neck.

"This is quite a spread," he murmured, when at last she bade him take his place at the beautifully set table in her dining room. The soft light of candles, the glistening china and sparkling silver all added to the beauty of the meal.

"I almost never eat in here so when someone comes over, I like to use this room. I hope that's okay."

"It's fine," he said. "But I was actually talking about the food. It looks like a Thanksgiving banquet."

"Confession time. I love chicken salads, chicken sandwiches, roast chicken. I always buy the biggest bird I can find so I'll have lots of leftovers." She grinned at his surprise. "It isn't much fun to cook for only one person."

"True." He waited while she said grace in a soft natural tone that told him it was part of her normal routine, then helped himself to everything. "This is excellent," he told her appreciatively.

"Thanks." She served him a little more punch from the crystal decanter.

Ross found himself relaxing, totally content to enjoy the meal seated next to her at one end of the table, the clink of silver on china a companionable punctuation to his thoughts.

"Did you get another look at the stuff in that cabinet?" he asked.

She set down her fork, her face startled. "Actually I forgot all about it," Kelly admitted.

"Oh." Vague disappointment washed over him. He'd hoped she'd find something in there that would make him feel less guilty about keeping her father's name from her.

"Which is really silly when you consider what could be in there." Kelly shook her head. "I guess I've been a bit busy. But I'll take a look tomorrow, I promise." She frowned at the sound of the phone.

Ross saw the faint flicker of worry fill her face and knew she thought her phantom caller might be on the other end. "Shall I answer it?"

"Thanks," she murmured, relief washing over her face, though she remained perched on her chair as she watched him move toward the phone.

Ross picked up the receiver. "Young residence. Oh, hello, doctor. Yes, she's here. Just a minute please." He walked back into the room, handed the phone to Kelly. "Dr. Cavanaugh."

"Thank you." Her long narrow fingers brushed his as she accepted the telephone. "Eli? Hi. You're working late. Oh, that was Ross. I invited him over for dinner."

Ross heard the doctor's voice but couldn't tell exactly what he was saying.

"I bought everything this afternoon. I've sort of let my

groceries run down after the holidays. I wasn't feeling well so—why are you asking me this?" As she listened her eyes lost their glow, her face grew paler than he'd ever seen. "Are you serious? But—how?" She listened for a few minutes then held out the receiver. "He wants to talk to you."

Ross took the phone. "Van Zandt."

"Listen to me carefully, Ross. The results from Kelly's tests are in. There are fairly high levels of arsenic in her system. Too high to be acceptable. Ben told me that someone had broken into Tiny Blessings and then into her house. Is that right?"

"Yes." He kept watch on Kelly, who had slumped in her chair and was staring at the food. "There have also been some threatening phone calls and other incidents."

"For the levels to build this high, she's probably consumed it in her food. If someone's been in her house, they may have contaminated it."

"What?" He couldn't believe what he was hearing. "You mean that's why she's been sick?"

"Yes. Don't get crazy on me now. You should both be all right if you only ate what she bought today."

"Yeah. Okay. Just a minute." He held the phone so Eli could hear. "Kelly, is everything on this table fresh from the store or did you use something you already had here?"

"I bought the chicken, peas, potatoes, salad stuff—it's all fresh. Except for the milk. I bought too much before New Year's and I've been trying to use it up, but it's probably spoiled by now. I didn't use it in the potatoes because I got fresh cream for that."

"You heard that?" Ross checked with the doctor on the other end of the line.

"Yes. Okay. Go ahead and finish your meal. I'm quite certain it's not the source. But I have a hunch that something there has been contaminated and I'm going to find out what. I've contacted Zach since Ben said he was handling her case. Zach requested a medical team from Richmond. They'll be there some time within the next hour. They'll take samples and find the source. Until then no one is to consume anything else in that house. Do you hear me?"

"Loud and clear." Ross thought a moment. "What about the water?"

"I checked with the municipal office. They flushed their lines right after New Year's as per standard procedure. It isn't coming from them. Is she using some kind of filtration system or bottled water?"

Ross asked Kelly, who shook her head. He relayed her response.

"Then water is probably not the source. Those antibiotics she was taking for her ear infection might have saved her life. God was protecting her there." Eli's voice hardened. "We've got to find out where this is coming from. Right away."

"No kidding." Ross wasn't ready to give God any credit. He could have stopped the whole thing.

"Let me talk to her."

Ross touched Kelly's shoulder to draw her attention, then handed her the phone.

"Yes?"

Eli's voice was clearly audible. "Kelly, I've asked the pharmacy to deliver a new prescription for you. I want you to take two of these pills three times a day—breakfast, lunch and dinner until they're all gone. Some people are coming to do tests. Until then, don't eat any more meals at home. Nothing, do you understand?"

"Yes." She looked like a little girl who'd just lost her best friend. Ross felt the old anger seethe inside at the pain someone was causing her.

"I want you to go back to the clinic every day after work for the next week so we can monitor the levels in your blood. It's important that we clear this up fast."

"Yes."

"You'll be okay, Kelly. It was high but I think we got it in time. There's no evidence of liver breakdown."

"Yes. Thank you."

"No problem. You just take care of yourself." He paused, then lowered his voice. "Rachel said to tell you she's got a prayer line going."

"Thanks. I guess I need it." She glanced sideways at Ross, half turned away from him and whispered, "Who would do this, Eli? What did I do wrong?"

"It's not your fault. Somebody's sick is my guess. You just stick close to Ross. He'll watch out for you."

"Yes. Okay. Thank you."

"Take care."

Kelly pushed the off button, then laid the phone on the table. She glanced at the beautiful meal she'd prepared, then pushed away her half-eaten plate. Ross didn't blame her. Who wouldn't be afraid to eat after news like this?

The doorbell rang. He rose, answered it, paid the delivery boy from the drugstore. Then he went to the kitchen tap and ran it for several moments before filling a glass. He handed the white bag and the glass to Kelly.

"Here are your pills. You're supposed to take two now, right?"

"Yes." She took two from the bottle, put them in her mouth, then swallowed them with a huge drink of water. The doorbell rang again.

Ross opened the door to Zach and a team of individuals who asked how to get to the kitchen, then set to work.

"Where is she?" Zach asked sotto voce.

Ross motioned to the dining room next door.

"Let's get her away from this. Where do you suggest? I need to ask her some questions."

"She's pretty fragile at the moment. She just talked to the doctor." He swallowed his questions. There was no way he would hinder the process that would expose whoever had done this. "Go to the den," he suggested. "I'll bring her in a minute."

Zach nodded, talked to the technician in charge. Ross went back into the dining room. He hunkered down beside her, kept his voice soft as he touched her arm to draw her attention from whatever she was staring at.

"Kelly, Zach is here. He needs to talk to you. He's in the den. There are a bunch of people in the kitchen, too. They're testing for the arsenic."

"Oh. Yes. Okay." She rose, tossed her napkin on the table. "I'm sorry to cause you so much trouble. It seems like something bad happens every time we're together."

He tried for humor. "Are you kidding? You're the most exciting date I've ever had."

She smiled but her eyes were sad, hopeless.

Date? Who was he trying to kid? He wasn't the kind of man Kelly Young would date. Besides, by next week he'd be long gone.

Who'd watch out for her then?

Chapter Eleven

Kelly stood at the front door as the last of the technicians left. Zach was at the end of the line, his face grim.

"I don't have to tell you not to eat anything from here, do I?"

"Not hardly," she snapped, then smiled apologetically. "I get it, Zach. Really I do. Someone is trying to poison me, though I have no idea why. I'll start throwing stuff out right away."

"No!" He touched her arm, his eyes hard. "When they find the source, I want the evidence. Just put everything back where it belongs and go to bed. I'm sending Glynis Barnes to stay with you tonight. You remember her?"

"Of course." The presence of the quiet police officer who'd stayed when this ugliness first began brought a wave of relief. Kelly felt the tears well up and had to swallow hard. "Thank you, Zach. I'm sorry I'm weepy. It's all been a little bit much, I guess."

He slung an arm around her shoulder, hugged her. "That's an understatement if I ever heard of it. I'm amazed you've been so strong." Zach glanced at Ross.

"This woman is one of the most courageous I've ever seen."

Kelly saw Ross nod. "I know it," he whispered, his gaze resting on her.

"You need me for anything, anything at all, you call. Anytime. No excuses. The three of us are going to figure out what's going on and we're going to put a stop to it."

"Yes." She was beginning to feel better. "A man is coming to change the locks tomorrow morning. He was supposed to come earlier, but—"

"Have you thought about having a security system installed?" Zach frowned when she shook her head. "They're not impervious to break-ins but they sure slow the perps down."

"Okay, I'll look into that tomorrow. Thanks."

"You take care of yourself." Zach left shortly after, promising that Glynis would be over within the hour. Until then he ordered Ross to stay.

"You don't have to stay," Kelly said when he'd left. "I'll be fine."

"You think I'm disobeying him?" Ross shook his head, eyes dancing. "I'm not that dumb."

"Well then, let's go sit down by the fire while we wait for Glynis." Once they were seated across from each other, Kelly began to feel the impact of the night. She had trouble swallowing her tears. "I just can't believe someone would put arsenic in my food."

"There are all kinds of kooks in the world, believe me. I've seen it."

"You always get that look in your eyes when you talk about your past," she said quietly, watching him. "Is it so hard for you to let go of it?"

He blinked as if he were surprised she'd figured that out. "I guess it is."

"Why?"

He shrugged, looked away. "Regrets, I suppose. Things I should have done and didn't."

"Like what?" There was something hidden under that facade of capability and Kelly had a feeling she was getting closer to understanding how it affected Ross even today. "You were a cop, you did your job, what more could you do?"

"Stayed there, kept trying."

The despair in his words made her sit up straight.

"Ross, you said—or at least hinted—that you were burned out. How could you do anyone any good in that condition? You had to get away to preserve your own peace of mind."

"What about the kids that are still there, still getting sucked into the misery of that place? Who's going to help them?" He shook his head, his jaw hardened. "I hated the waste and stench of evil that clung to those streets, but I knew them better than most of the guys. Maybe I could have done something more, helped one more kid."

"At the risk of losing yourself?" Kelly moved to sit beside him, took his hand. "Second-guessing yourself is a sure way to go crazy and believe me, I do know whereof I speak. In that moment, at that time, you were maxed out. You had to get away for the sake of self-preservation. No one blames you for that. Besides, no matter how hard you tried, you could never save them all."

"No." His fingers threaded through hers. "But what I do now—sometimes it seems pointless. Telling some poor woman her husband is cheating on her—what kind of a job is that?"

"Then why do you do it?" she asked, loving the feel of his strong fingers around hers.

"Because I don't have to get involved. I can follow the guy, take pictures, record who he sees and when, but it doesn't involve me." He turned his head, stared at her. "I'm running away." His eyes went wide with surprise.

"Sometimes you have to," Kelly agreed. "I tried to do it when you told me Sandra was my mother. I pushed the knowledge away as hard as I could."

"Why? She's a nice person."

"It wasn't about her, it was about me. I hate disorder, I hate not having all the ends neatly tied up. Not knowing what to expect drives me nuts." She slid her feet out of her slippers, lifted them to the sofa and snuggled her toes between the chenille cushions.

"Comfortable?" Ross teased, then he lifted his arm and wrapped it around her shoulders, drawing her against his side.

"Now I am. Thanks." Kelly glanced at him, smiled. "You're a good friend."

She saw the surprise flare in his eyes and changed topics quickly.

"I was talking to Sandra about it and she said that my need for control really means I don't trust God. I've been thinking about that. Maybe she's right."

"Well that doesn't apply to me," he murmured, his breath feathering over her hair. "God had nothing to do with my decision."

"How do you know? Maybe He wanted you to get away, to take a second look at your life, to do something different. Maybe it was God that sent you to help Sandra find me."

"God?" He sounded skeptical.

"He's not just judgment and condemnation, Ross. He lovingly created us, we're His children. He wants us to include Him in our daily lives."

"Why would God care about me?" he asked in disbelief.

"Because He loves you. He wants to see you succeed, to press ahead to the things He's planned. He wants to teach you. That's what I didn't understand." She cleared her throat, tried to clarify her thoughts. "I was so afraid that I almost missed my opportunity."

"You're saying that you're ready to accept Sandra as your mother?"

"I'm ready to get to know her. Thinking of her as my mother is difficult because it feels like I'm trying to replace the mother I had. Sandra told me she doesn't want that. She helped me realize that ours is a completely new relationship, it has nothing to do with my past."

"That's good."

"Yes, it is. But the same thing applies to you. You saw the misery, the problems, the death and drugs. Maybe what you have to do now is figure out how you can use that to help other kids."

"I don't think I can go back there, Kelly."

"Maybe not today, maybe not next week. But I think you will someday, and I think you'll say, 'This is where I tried to do some good. Sometimes I helped, sometimes I didn't. But I didn't give up, I moved on.'"

Ross was silent for several moments, then his fingers tightened against her shoulder. "Do you have faith in everybody you meet?" he asked brusquely, staring down at her.

Kelly returned his scrutiny, kept her voice soft. "I have faith in *you*, Ross. I believe that you have what it takes to make a difference. Don't stop asking God questions. He has the answers, He wants you to hear them. It just might take a while to learn how to trust Him."

He reached up to touch her cheek with his other hand. "Thanks for believing in me."

"My pleasure." An electric current sent tiny darts of delight from his palm to her cheek. They lit up a path of joy all through her body. "I'd like to be your friend, Ross."

"Sweet Kelly." He bent his head. "I think I'm interested in more than friendship," he whispered a second before his lips touched hers.

Kelly leaned into his kiss, delighting in the way he made her heart race. Her hands lifted to touch his face, to draw him closer, trying to shut out the ringing.

"It's the doorbell," Ross murmured as he drew away. "Glynis must be here."

"Her timing stinks," Kelly muttered as she lifted her legs off the sofa and felt with her toes for her slippers. She glanced at Ross, saw his shoulders shaking with laughter.

"Oh, Miss Young," he chided, eyes dancing. "The language you use."

"Hush." She bumped him with her shoulder, smiling as she walked beside him to the door. Sometimes life was funny.

"Hi, Glynis. Come on in." They chatted for a few minutes, then Glynis asked if she could put her things in a bedroom. Kelly pointed to the stairs, told her which room and Glynis disappeared.

"It's late. I'd better go." Ross grabbed his jacket, shrugged into it. "You'll be all right with her here?"

"Yes. Thank you." She stood in place, peering up at him. "Ross, please think about what I've said. I know it's hard to understand why things happen the way they do, but the only person who can truly answer your questions is God. If you keep asking Him for answers, I know you'll find them."

"It's that important to you?"

"No." She shook her head, stood on tiptoe and brushed her lips against his cheek. "It's that important to *you*," she whispered, then took a step back before things could go any further. "Good night."

He stared at her for several moments, then nodded and pulled open the door. "Lock this," he ordered.

"I will." She watched him walk toward his car, waited till he'd climbed inside and driven away before she closed the door, locked it, then slid the dead bolt home just to be sure.

"Everything okay?" Glynis stood at the top of the stairs.

"Everything's locked up," Kelly told her quietly.

She didn't know if everything would ever be okay again.

The banging woke her.

Kelly forced her eyelids up, stared at the clock. 8:10. She'd slept in and then some. A rap on her bedroom door scared her until she remembered Glynis had stayed overnight.

"Coming," she called, dragging a housecoat over her gown. She opened the door. "Who is banging?"

"It's the front door. That P.I. that was here last night won't let up. I didn't want to allow him in without asking you."

"Ross?" Kelly raced down the stairs. "For Ross to make a noise like that something has to be wrong." She unbolted the door, yanked it open. "What's wrong?"

"Sandra. Someone attacked her last night."

"Oh, no!" She stepped back as he moved inside, shocked by his haggard face and the words he'd just said. "Is she all right?"

"Don't know yet. I found her about an hour ago. She was still unconscious when I left the hospital. I thought you'd like to know."

"I want to see her." The words burst out of her without conscious thought. Kelly looked at him. "Can you take me? My car's not back yet."

"That's why I'm here. I brought this." He held out two cardboard cups, megasize, which sent the fragrant aroma of coffee straight to her nose. "One's for Glynis."

"Thanks for the thought but I don't drink coffee." Glynis stood on the bottom step, her blue uniform shirt untucked, her hair mussed. It was the worst dressed that Kelly had ever seen the officer. "You go ahead and have it, Mr. Van Zandt."

"Okay, I will. Thanks." He glanced at Kelly. "You going like that?"

"No." She lifted the lid, took a sip, then set the cup down on the hall table. "I'll change. Give me five minutes."

Kelly dragged on a pair of jeans and a sweater, brushed her hair as smooth as she could get it after washing her face. She spared a minute to phone Tiny Blessings and tell them she wouldn't be in till later, then hurried down the stairs. Glynis was waiting.

"I've contacted Zach. He asked me to stay here until further notice. Is that all right with you?"

"Of course. Make yourself at home." Kelly blinked as the memory of last night returned. "But the food—what will you have for breakfast?"

"My partner is bringing something over. Don't worry about me."

"Thanks for doing this." Kelly dragged her boots out of the closet and pulled them on, snatched her jacket from a hanger and looked at Ross. "I'm ready."

He said nothing, merely held the door open, then followed her out.

Kelly's heart ached for the silent, taciturn man seated beside her. In the short time he'd been in Chestnut Grove, Sandra had become his closest friend. He'd said she was the mother he never had.

"How bad is she?"

"Coma. It looked like someone had broken into her place, hit her with something."

"Wouldn't she have heard them?" Kelly couldn't imagine tiny little Sandra trying to defend herself against an attacker.

"She takes pills sometimes, to help her sleep. If she had one of those in her system…" He let the sentence trail away. "What I don't understand is why? There's been some crime in the area, sure, but petty stuff. No assaults." He glanced at her sideways. "Suddenly the two women I know are victims."

"It's not your fault. Sometimes things happen. We just have to believe it will work out." It sounded too pat. Kelly was having trouble believing that herself.

"Yeah." Anger simmered under the surface of that one word.

They pulled into the hospital parking lot. The ground was slippery with the mix of sleet and rain that was falling. Kelly stumbled as they walked, then gladly accepted Ross's outstretched hand as they hurried toward the entrance.

Zach was leaving when they arrived.

"She's stable but still out," he said before Ross could ask. "I'm going over to her place now, but from what I've been told she was hit from behind with a brass lamp. Lucky they didn't kill her."

"Luck didn't have anything to do with it, Zach," Kelly corrected.

"No, you're right. It didn't. And I know it." Zach peered into her face. "Are you okay?"

"I'm fine. I just want to see Sandra. Will they let me?"

"I think so." He stopped a passing nurse, spoke to her. "Wanda will take you up, Kelly. Ross, can I talk to you for a minute?"

"Sure." Ross looked down at her, a question in his eyes. "Will you be okay?"

"I'm fine." She squeezed his hand, then let go. "See you later."

"I'll bring you some more coffee and something to eat."

"Thanks."

Kelly followed Wanda until she stood in the doorway of Sandra's room, then her attention focused on the woman lying unconscious in the bed. Her heart lodged in her throat—this woman had given her life, and someone had tried to take hers.

"Why did it happen to her, God?" she whispered as she slid her hand underneath the lifeless fingers. The question reminded her of Ross's need for answers about his own life experiences.

"Wouldn't it be easy if we knew all the reasons behind things?" Reverend Fraser stepped out of the shadows and patted Kelly's shoulder. "But then we wouldn't have to learn how to trust."

"Hi, pastor." She received his hug, sat down on the chair he offered. "I don't understand what you're saying. Surely it would be easier to trust if we understood why things happen the way they do."

"Would it?" He smiled, his eyes twinkling. "What kind of faith would that be, Kelly? Adam and Eve were in the garden, they had everything their hearts could desire and yet still they wanted more. I think humans are like that. A little knowledge isn't enough. Soon we'd want to be like God, we'd be telling Him how to work it out."

"You're teasing me."

"Maybe just a little," he chuckled. "But I am serious about the faith issue. We can choose to believe God is still in control even though we don't understand why things happen. That takes some pretty strong faith, a lot of grit and determination not to be swayed."

"Yes."

"Or we can fuss and worry about how He's going to handle it and what it will do to our plans and schemes and whether or not we'll be called upon to get out of our comfort zone. But that's not faith, that's worry."

"All well and good," a voice said, "but surely if God loves His children as much as Kelly tells me, He wouldn't want one of them hurt." Ross stood in the doorway, his face masklike. "Sandra is supposed to be one of His."

"He would never want to see Sandra hurt," Reverend Fraser stated clearly. "But God didn't do this to her. People did. People who have a choice, who can decide for themselves whether they're going to use their lives to make a difference or to bring grief and pain. If God stepped in and stopped them, what good would free will be, Ross?"

"You know who I am?"

"Oh, yes. Sandra had spoken of you often. She loves you like a son, my boy."

Ross stared at the pale face surrounded by swaths of gauze. "She's like the mother I never had," he whispered.

"Then you must know how much she trusts her Lord." Pastor Fraser waited for Ross to nod. "Can't you trust Him to do what is best for her?"

"But—" Ross's voice dropped so low it could barely be heard. "What if she dies?"

"Then she goes to live with God. What could be better than that?" John Fraser waited a few moments before he moved beside the bed, bowed his head and closed his eyes. "Father, I come to You in Jesus' name to ask You to be with Sandra. Bless her and keep her safe in the palm of Your mighty hand, we pray. Amen." He smiled at them. "I've got to go. I want to make sure everything's running smoothly at the diner. Sandra would want that."

"Thank you for thinking of it, pastor." Kelly took his hand squeezed it. "Will you get the prayer line going?"

"It's already working, my dear." He turned from her to Ross. "Think about what I said, young man. And remember, trusting God doesn't mean that He'll give you everything you ask for. Trusting Him—real faith in God—means He's God, not you. You don't get to tell Him what to do. You have to turn everything over to His control."

The pastor left quickly, his long stride quickly eating up the distance in a rhythmic tapping that gradually faded down the hall.

Ross watched him leave, his face pensive. Finally he seemed to become aware of Kelly's scrutiny.

"I almost forgot." He held out a brown bag and a cup. "Zach asked me to go to Sandra's right away, see if I'd notice if anything was missing. Can I leave you here for a bit?"

"I'm not leaving," she told him firmly. "Not until we know something more."

"I'm glad." He wrapped his arm around her shoulder and hugged her. "It could be a while though, Kelly. The doctors said that with this kind of injury, a person can stay in the coma for a long time or wake up the next minute."

"Then I'll pray for the next minute. And the one after that." She buried her nose in his coat, felt his lips brush her forehead. "I—I can't lose her, Ross. Not now. Not before—"

"I know." He held her for several long moments until finally she drew away.

"Go," she insisted. "I'll be fine."

But he stood there, looking down at her, his eyes dark and searching. "Don't beat yourself up," he whispered. "There was nothing you could have done to prevent this."

"I know. But it still hurts." She stood on tiptoe, kissed him, then backed away. "You'd better get going."

"Go where?" he asked in pretended confusion, a smile tipping up the corners of his mouth as he brushed a finger across her nose. "Oh, yeah. I remember. I'll see you later."

"Yes." Kelly watched him leave with a lump in her throat. Then she gathered herself together, angled her chair so that she could sit beside Sandra and lean against the bed. She tucked Sandra's hand into her own. "You're a fighter, Sandra. You didn't let *him* beat you down, don't let this get you, either. Come on, wake up."

The sounds of the busy hospital faded into oblivion as Kelly stared into Sandra's pale face. In the space of a few short hours everything in her life had shifted, changed again. Nothing was as it should be. Why? Why was it all happening?

Kelly recalled her own words to Ross about the things he'd gone through. It had seemed so easy to tell him that God was working things out. The words had tripped off her tongue as if she knew exactly what she was talking about in his case, yet she'd fought every step of the way to accept Sandra as her mother.

Such a silly thing to cling to! Who said a woman could only ever have one mother? Women got married all the time, adopted their husband's mother as their own. It didn't diminish their own mothers, make them any less loved. So what was it that she'd feared so much about letting this woman into her life?

Alone in the hospital room, the truth would not be silenced. Kelly had never admitted to anyone the feeling of alienation she'd carried hidden inside for so long. Her parents had loved her dearly and she'd loved them back, but she'd always believed that she was somehow different. Then along came Sandra with an explanation that should have explained everything. And yet from the first moment since she'd found out Sandra was her biological mother, Kelly had fought against the truth.

Why?

Because you don't trust. Because you've never really believed that God would care for you no matter what.

The truth startled her, but with it came a rush of relief. Yes, that was it. She'd pushed Sandra away for several reasons, but one of the biggest was because she allowed a thread of doubt to corrode her faith. She'd let herself believe that God would take this mother as He'd taken Carol and Marcus Young away from her. But what if, instead of being a threat to her carefully controlled life, Sandra had been a gift from God, a path to security she'd never even imagined?

Kelly closed her eyes, let her brain create a collage of hours spent together discussing Sandra's parents, her history, her hopes and dreams—the stories every family passed down. She didn't even know if Sandra had a sister or brother. Perhaps there were relatives of which she'd never heard. She'd deliberately closed that door because she was afraid.

Sandra had been ready and willing to open her heart and her life to the child she'd lost so many years ago. Wasn't it time she, Kelly, stopped clinging so tightly to what she thought she had, and let go so she could experience what *might* be?

"I messed up, God," she whispered. "I have no right to be talking to Ross or anyone else about faith when my trust in You is so meager. Forgive me, Lord. All this time I've been so afraid I would lose everything. Now I understand that You are the Giver of life. You have a better plan for my life than I could even dream of. Teach me to trust."

She stared into Sandra's face and felt a soft sweetness

unfurl inside her heart. This was her mother—a second mother who had promised to be there whenever Kelly needed her.

"Please God, let me have a second chance. Let us have a future together."

A noise at the door startled her. She glanced up, saw the fury on Ross's face.

"How can you pray, Kelly? How can you trust in a God that would allow this?"

"Because He's also the God that brought us together. What else can I trust in, if not in Him? King David said something like this—who else knows me, the very inside heart of me? God saw me before I was born, while my bones were knitting together, He knew what I would be like, what I'd need." She smiled up at him. "I made a big mistake in pushing Sandra away, Ross. I'm not going to do that again. Whatever happens, God will take care of me just like He did when my parents died, when Simon and I broke up. Just as He took care of me when someone tried to poison me. He cares, Ross. He really cares. For me and for you."

She sensed he needed time to think it over, so she didn't say anything more, simply sat by Sandra's side and waited for God to work. After a while she felt his hand curl into hers and she gave a sigh of thanks. God was at work and she could depend on Him.

"Mr. Van Zandt?" A nurse stood in the doorway. "The police are on the phone. They'd like to speak to you."

Ross rose, squeezed her hand, then left the room. The door whooshed closed behind him. Kelly eased her body to a different position in her chair, marveled at the time. She'd been here most of the day. From the hallway, the hustle and bustle of a shift change could be heard. The door opened. Ross must be back.

"What did Zach want?" she asked, leaning over to adjust Sandra's blankets.

"He wants you gone. Just like I do."

There was a burst of excruciating pain, a shower of crystal stars, then Kelly felt nothing.

Chapter Twelve

Ross paced up and down the hallway but his attention was focused on the room in which a cluster of people worked on Kelly. When the doctor emerged, he moved to block his path.

"Is she all right?"

"Stable condition, conscious, a bit wobbly but I think she'll be fine." The doctor massaged one shoulder. "They hit her fairly hard. She's lucky. The damage to her head and neck could have been much more serious."

"She'd tell you luck had nothing to do with it," Ross muttered.

"Probably right. I contacted Dr. Cavanaugh about the arsenic levels. We're treating that as well. I can tell you that she'll probably be in here a couple of days, until I'm satisfied that her system is back up to par."

"Thank you." Ross moved out of his way as a page over the speaker announced the doctor was needed, stat. As the man in the white coat scurried away, Ross resumed his course back and forth down the hall until a nurse motioned him to come inside.

"We're going to keep her in the same room as Sandra. We can watch both of them." She smiled at him. "She'll be all right, but you can stay for a while if you want."

Ross did want. Kelly was right. Bad things didn't happen only in New York City. Two women had been attacked right here in Chestnut Grove, Virginia. He'd done everything he could think of to keep both of them safe and he'd failed. A question rose in the back of his mind. Had Kelly's attacker been after her or Sandra?

Ross waited patiently while the staff prepared the room the way they wanted, only venturing to grasp Kelly's hand when the last of them had left and they were alone.

"How are you feeling?" he asked quietly, staring into her big brown eyes.

"Like someone hit me over the head." She touched the bandage, then her hand dropped back down to her side. "It hurts. Is Sandra all right?"

"She's fine. The same." He couldn't let go of her fingers until he knew for certain that she was all right. "Did you see who it was?"

She began to shake her head, stopped, winced, and said "No. I thought it was you coming back from your meeting with Zach. I never even turned to look. I asked you what Zach wanted. A voice said, 'He wants you gone. Just like I do.' Then everything went black."

So they *had* been after her. Part of him wanted to be glad Sandra was safe, part of him raged that someone would dare to accost Kelly in a public hospital.

"I'm fine, Ross. Just a headache."

"That's good to hear." Zach stood in the doorway, his face drawn tight so that the fan of lines around his eyes was emphasized. "You couldn't place the voice, maybe remember something else that would identify this person?"

"I was just telling Ross that I didn't see anything."

"Are you sure?"

"Well there was one thing." She rubbed her temple, eyes closed as she tried to catch the elusive thought. "It was the same voice as on the telephone, I think," she managed at last. "I'm pretty sure it was the very same person."

Zach nodded. "Okay, we'll work with that. From now on you've got a full-time guard. Glynis is officially taking over now."

The officer walked into the room, her uniform as clean and spotless as if she'd just pressed it.

"This is getting to be a habit, Glynis," Kelly grumbled. "I feel like a kid."

"I hope you don't expect me to read to you."

Everyone stared at Glynis, but Ross saw the twitch at the corner of her lips.

"No, thanks. I'm assuming you brought that cross-stitch piece with you?"

"Right here." Glynis lifted out a hoop with some kind of stitching on it. "If you don't mind, I'll work on it for a bit."

"Good. I'm going to sleep. Maybe that will help this headache." She squeezed Ross's fingers. "You don't have to babysit me. Go and get something to eat, get some rest. You don't look well and there's no more room in here for another patient."

Her spunk caused a rush of tenderness to flood his insides. That gritty determination filled her face. She was plucky and sweet, but she probably did need to rest. He bent down, brushed his lips over hers.

"Get some sleep, slugger. I'll be back later," he whispered, staring into her eyes.

She nodded, but her hand did not release and he stayed where he was just in case she had something to add. Sure enough, a few moments later he saw the shine wash over her eyes and knew she was trying not to cry.

"Somebody is really upset at me, Ross. I just can't think why."

"Don't worry about it, Kelly. We'll figure it out later. Just get some sleep." He waited till she nodded, patted her hand, let it go, then walked out of the room before he burst into tears himself.

Zach followed. Ross let him trail behind until they were at the elevators and well out of range of Kelly's room.

"This is not going to happen again," he seethed, turning on the detective.

"I'd like to promise it won't, Ross. I'm not any happier about it than you are, but just how do you propose we stop whoever this is?"

"I'm going over to Kelly's. There has to be some evidence, somewhere. I intend to find it."

"I'll go with you."

Ross turned, ready to rant and rave at the detective until he saw the other man's face and knew that he, too, was affected. "Good. The two of us should be able to see something."

He caught a ride with Zach, who wheeled out of the parking lot like a man on a mission.

"I had Glynis stay this morning until the locksmith came. I have a key to Kelly's house."

Ross glanced at the cop, surprised. Zach grinned. "Even us small town hicks have our moments. I'm thankful we had that bit of snowfall during the night. If anyone was snooping around outside after we left last night, we should be able to see."

"As long as the light holds up." Ross didn't feel much hope.

"You don't know Kelly's place very well," Zach told him. "The couple she bought it from had a thing about burglary. They put in floodlights all the way around. We should be able to get a pretty good look."

And they did. Enough to find footprints to a small basement window almost hidden by a pile of snow.

"They got in here. Somebody tried to hide the evidence, but I'm pretty sure we'll find enough inside to prove it. Careful where you step," Zach warned. "There are more tracks here. Small male, I'm guessing. Maybe a teen, or a woman." He pulled out a flashlight, followed the prints toward the back of the yard. "The padlock is broken."

"Kelly saw someone," Ross remembered aloud, cursing himself for not believing her when she'd told him. "It was a while ago, but she said she saw a figure come out from the side yard and go down the street."

Zach said nothing, merely scanned the area some more using his flashlight to highlight the dark spaces. "Nothing else here, that I can see. Let's check it out inside."

He unlocked the front door. They slid off their shoes, moved through to the den, the kitchen—which was now clean and spotless—through to the dining room and the living room.

"Clear," Zach said with a sigh.

"Who was in here?" Ross asked. "Everything's been tidied."

"Rachel, Pilar, Meg—the whole bunch of them told me they were not letting Kelly deal with the mess on her own when she came home from the hospital." Zach made a face. "You'd think I was trying to preserve everything the way they talked. Anyway, once my men were finished, they swooped in this afternoon and scrubbed the place down."

The telephone rang as soon as he finished speaking.

Ross frowned. If the women knew Kelly was in the hospital, they'd know she wasn't going to answer.

"Could be our mystery caller," Zach said. He picked up the phone and held it so Ross could listen.

"You see what can happen? Next time someone dies."

"Who is this?" Zach demanded. The caller hung up immediately. Zach punched *69 but the number could not be given. He hit his radio. "I want to know the number and location of the last call to this number immediately." He recited Kelly's telephone number. "Call me back."

They waited for several minutes before the answer came. A pay phone four blocks away. He ordered a patrol car in the vicinity to check it out but they saw no one.

"So whoever that was on the phone couldn't have seen we were the ones who were here," Zach told him, brow furrowed. "You can't see this block from there."

"Maybe they drove past the house first, saw the lights, decided to call."

"Maybe." Zach motioned to the basement door, flicked on the lights. "Let's check that window. I'm getting really tired of this game. This isn't some random nutcase, Ross, and you know it. This person is clearly intent on keeping his word."

"Did you notice something about the voice?" Ross couldn't quite place the niggling in his mind.

"No. What are you thinking?"

"That whispery tone—I thought—" He shook his head. "I don't know."

"There's the window. It's unlatched." After checking the floor for evidence and finding nothing, Zach secured the window. "She's got a toolbox over there. See if you can find a hammer and a couple of nails. I'm going to make things a little more difficult for this phantom visitor."

Ross handed over the items, watched Zach nail the window shut.

"It's not a very big space," he mused. "Our perp can't be too big around or he wouldn't fit through it."

They worked together to drag an old tallboy to stand in front of the window and thereby prevent anyone from opening it.

"Even it someone smashes the glass, they can't get in," Ross said with grim satisfaction.

"We'll leave the outside lights on tonight, just so my men can clearly see if anyone is hanging around." Zach led the way up the stairs and to the front door. "I'm going home to get some sleep. You should do the same."

"I will, but—" he paused, studied Zach. "Would you mind checking with your officer at the hospital first? I want to make sure Kelly is okay."

Zach gave him a funny look, but made the call. "She's asleep. Everything's fine," he reported.

"Thanks."

"You really care about her, don't you?"

"Yes." He couldn't stop the words even if he'd wanted to. "I care about Kelly Young a lot," he admitted. "But I'm not the kind of guy someone like her needs."

"You mean you're not a Christian," Zach interpreted.

"There's that." Ross nodded. "I just can't wrap my head around her religion."

"It's not a religion, Ross. It's faith. Believing in Someone bigger, smarter, more capable than yourself. And it's not really that hard. You make the decision to trust, you ask for His forgiveness and you are His child. Then you learn how to do what He wants."

"It's funny, you know." Ross pressed his clenched fists against his thighs to control his emotions. "Last time I went to see my mother she rambled on and on about God, how He loved her, how she was going to Heaven."

"Uh-huh." Zach leaned against the foyer wall, waited.

"This is my mother I'm talking about. Drunkard, abandoner, out of her mind most of the time now thanks to Alzheimer's. She doesn't even remember me." He shook his head, anger threading through him. "Dooon't remember me, but she knows all about Heaven. My mother thinks that just by believing in God she can wipe out the past, get a clean slate."

"That's what the Bible says, Ross. 'Though your sins be many they shall be white as snow.'"

"It's too easy."

Zach's rueful smile softened his harsh features. "You want her to suffer some more, is that it?"

"We did." Ross bit his lip at the childishness of that response.

"Would her suffering more fix any of the past? Would it undo what happened to you?" Zach shook his head. "That's the thing about God, Ross. He doesn't give a fig for the past. It's over with. It's today and tomorrow that matter to Him. *Your* tomorrow."

"I guess."

"You don't have to guess. You can know. Just ask Him to help you understand." He pulled the door open. "I've got to get going."

"Yeah, me, too. Thanks for checking things out with me. At least we know the place is safe for now."

Zach locked the door, drove him back to the parking lot at the hospital and parked alongside Ross's car, engine running.

"They're getting closer," he mused. "Whoever is doing this is also getting bolder. A hospital is a pretty public place. But they can't hide forever. Sooner or later they're going to make a mistake."

"I just hope it's not too late for Sandra or Kelly."

"A few prayers couldn't hurt." Zach gave him a pointed look, waited till he'd stepped out of the car then raised a hand and drove away.

Ross resisted the urge to go to Kelly's room. This yearning inside was bigger than her, bigger than anything he'd experienced before. Sandra, Zach, Kelly—they all seemed confident, certain that their God would accept him.

That was something he needed to find out for himself.

Kelly glared at Glynis.

"It's not that I'm ungrateful, it's not that I want to be anyone's target, but I've missed way too much work," she whispered, glancing at Sandra to be sure she wasn't disturbing the other woman. But Sandra hadn't moved. She lay still and white, lost in the coma that bound her in some place Kelly couldn't reach.

"I'm no help here, but there are things I have to do. So I'm going to Tiny Blessings. If you want to come along, you're more than welcome. But I *am* going!"

"Fine." Glynis stuffed her handiwork into the bag by her feet and rose. "My orders are to stay with you, so that's what I intend to do."

Once the paperwork was done, Kelly and Glynis left the hospital.

"I forgot, I didn't bring a car. Wait here, I'll get a cab."

"No need. I have wheels." Glynis led her to a small coupe. "You want to go home first and change?"

"Yes, please."

They actually made it to the office just in time for morning coffee break. Kelly accepted the warm wishes of her staff, returned a few hugs and finally entered her office. There were several pressing matters but once they were clear, she headed for the hall closet.

The memory of those cassettes and papers had threaded through her dreams all night. She intended to satisfy her curiosity before anything else happened to deflect her attention from them. She grabbed her keys and opened the closet door.

Grateful for Glynis's presence, Kelly lifted out the stacks of papers, which she handed over. She gathered up the cassettes herself and carried them into her office. One last check ensured that the bottom drawer of the small cabinet held only empty case files and two very large stones.

"Somebody didn't want that cabinet going anywhere," Glynis mused.

Kelly nodded, sank into her seat and began scanning the pages of notes.

"I'm thinking this is private. I'll wait outside. I have to call in anyway."

"Okay. There's a room right next door you can use. I promise I won't go anywhere without telling you. And thanks. Really." Kelly moved around the desk to hug her. "I do appreciate everything you've done."

"That's my job."

"You've gone above and beyond."

Once Glynis had gone, Kelly returned to reading the material. After ten minutes she asked reception to hold all her calls, spent a few minutes praying for strength, then returned to the papers. What she read was more shocking than anything she could have imagined.

Sometime later a knock disrupted her thoughts. Glynis must have arranged for lunch because she brought in a sandwich and a glass of orange juice. Kelly ate absently, her thoughts busy as she began to put the pieces together.

She scribbled notes as she read, checked them against the tapes, until everything made sense. Finally she leaned back in her chair, pressed her fingers against the throbbing spot at the back of her head and sighed.

"Oh, Lord, this is more than I can bear."

She spent a long time alternately praying and weeping. When a hand pressed on her shoulder, she stifled a scream. It was Ross.

"Oh, Ross, it's so awful." She threw herself into his arms and sobbed on his shoulder as she told him the whole awful mess. "Barnaby Harcourt didn't run Tiny Blessings for any good or generous or kind reasons. He used other people's problems to fulfill his own greed."

She pulled away, waved a hand over the stacks of papers, tapes, notes.

"Look at this, a horrible history of extorting people who came to him for help. Look at these names—a who's who of prominent people who brought him unwanted babies. He changed their records, altered everything he could to make it as difficult as possible to trace these children back to their prominent parents. Including me."

"What do you mean?"

"I know who I am, Ross." She glanced up into his face, her voice hard. "You wouldn't tell me, but I know. I'm the daughter of our illustrious mayor. Gerald Morrow is my father."

"Yes." Ross nodded, his eyes sad. "I'm sorry I couldn't tell you, but I'm glad you know the truth. No one can live with a lie forever."

"It's about time Barnaby's lies came out," she vowed, dashing away the tears. "I knew him, you know. He seemed like an innocent grandpa who loved kids, but he was a user. Greedy, dishonest—words don't begin to cover what he did."

Ross frowned. "What all did you find?"

"He blackmailed these people for years after he so generously got rid of their unwanted children." She couldn't stop the anger that rose up inside for the innocent babies who'd been used by this unscrupulous man. "Some of his 'clients,' like Gerald, he kept on the hook for years afterward. Barnaby Harcourt profited from misery and in doing so, if these notes are accurate, took in a fortune!"

"It sure looks like it." Ross whistled as he scanned the pages she'd highlighted, read her notes. "There's no mention of Ben Cavanaugh's parents here."

"No. Actually, I found very little in here about him. Just when he was brought in, his age, weight, that kind of thing. It doesn't mention his parents. There's only this curious notation beside his name—see ANM. I haven't been able to find out what that means." She took a deep breath, planted her hands on her desk to steady herself.

"Are you okay?"

"I'm not sure. I want to talk to Gerald Morrow. I want to ask him why he forced Sandra to do what he did." Kelly fought to keep the tears from her voice. "I want to know if he ever gave a thought to the child he gave away all those years ago. If he ever wondered what I'd become, who I was."

"Is that really what you want to ask, Kelly?" he asked her softly.

"No," she admitted. "I guess what I really want to know is if he ever loved me."

"You may not get an acceptable answer to that question." He led her to a sofa, sat down beside her. "I need to tell you something, Kelly. Maybe it will help you with this."

"Okay." She stared into his eyes. Something was different.

"I never told you why I really left New York." His hands

held hers, his thumb brushed over her skin as if he needed the contact. His voice was tight, controlled. "The place was everything rotten that I told you about—and more. But that doesn't excuse what I did. I shot a kid, Kelly. A boy. He wasn't even a teenager yet and I gunned him down because I lost my focus, thought I saw a gun when I didn't. My bullet robbed that kid of life as he knew it."

"Oh, Ross." She squeezed his hands as tears formed at the corners of her eyes. "You didn't do it on purpose."

"It felt as if I did. I was so fed up, so sick of seeing the same thing over and over. I wanted it to stop and when I saw him reach for something, I was sure I saw the barrel of a gun. 'I'll stop the little creep,' I decided. So I took aim and I fired. Only he was turning away and the bullet lodged in his spine. He will never walk again, Kelly. Because of me, because of what I did. I'm no better than the punks I was chasing."

"The difference is here." She tapped his chest. "You didn't knowingly shoot him in the back. You were trying to stop a crime, you were doing your job."

"I was trying to be judge, jury and executioner. And I almost killed him." He shook his head, his lips tight. "But last night I realized something."

"Oh?"

"I'm forgiven, Kelly." He shook his head, eyes wide with disbelief. "It seems impossible to me and yet, when I talked to Reverend Fraser this morning, it all came together. He and Zach helped me see that I can't change the past. What I did, my childhood—all of it happened. It was what it was and there's no way I can rewrite history."

"I see."

"That would be sad, *if* that's all there was to it. But it's not." He grasped her hands tighter, leaned in, excitement filling his face. "You and I—we have trouble accepting what was, what is. But don't you see, it's what we make of what is now that matters."

"But I wanted—"

"I know." A sad smile lifted his mouth. "You want what we all want—to be loved and cared for by the people who should be doing just that. But despite the ugliness, despite our mistakes and dreams and wishes, God has a different plan. And it's what we do with that which can make or break our future."

"Are you saying you believe in God?" She could hardly believe it.

He nodded. "I believe in Him, I trust Him, I have faith that no matter how bad my past is, He's going to make it right, He's going to get me through."

A wash of shame spread over her. Ross was new to the faith, just learning and yet, he'd grasped what she hadn't.

"I'm very glad for you."

"Thanks." He leaned nearer, his gaze intent. "Kelly, if God can do that for somebody as messed up as me, don't you think He can work things out for you, too?"

"Yes. But I can't deny this need to talk to Gerald Morrow. I need answers." She rose. "I'm going to call him now, try and set up a meeting." She looked up the mayor's number, asked to speak to him.

"I'm sorry, he's not in at the moment. Who's calling?"

"I'm sorry, Mrs. Morrow, I should have said. It's Kelly Young. Do you know where I might reach him?"

"I'm sorry, I don't, my dear. But I do know that with the new year upon us, he's very busy trying to get municipal affairs in order. Is it something I could help you with?"

"No, thank you. I need to speak to Mr. Morrow. I'll try his office."

"My husband is a very busy man, Kelly, and extremely stressed at the moment. I'd prefer if you didn't trouble him today." The hostess voice dropped several degrees. "I really think you should try to handle whatever this is about on your own. That is why they made you director of that place, isn't it? So you could make the decisions and not bother others."

There was a soft click.

"She hung up." Kelly stared at the phone. "She told me he's too busy to see me and told me to handle it on my own. I've never heard her speak like that before. She was almost rude."

"She probably has her own troubles to deal with. I overheard them arguing the other day. I don't think their marriage is very smooth." Ross rose, reached out a hand. "Come on, I'm taking you out for dinner. You've had a long day, because you wouldn't stay put in the hospital," he added with arched brows.

"I couldn't. I had to get at this stuff."

"Maybe so. But you're in no shape to go grocery shopping and then start cooking. Come on, we'll celebrate my new decision."

"I really am very happy for you," she told him once they were riding down in the elevator. Glynis's replacement had taken over for a few hours and was behind them. "It's a decision that will change your life, Ross. When you go back to Richmond, you'll want to find a church where you feel comfortable. They'll help you learn more."

"Is that what you want?" he asked as he walked with her down the street toward a small café. "Would you be happier if I wasn't around?"

"That isn't what I meant." The appearance of the mayor's signature black luxury car distracted her. "Look.

Maybe Mr. Morrow will be having dinner here, too. I could ask him for a meeting."

"Maybe." Ross's face grew grim. Inside the restaurant they were seated at a table in a darkened corner where they could see the other patrons but weren't particularly noticeable. The policewoman who'd replaced Glynis declined to join them but seated herself at a table behind them.

"I hadn't realized it was so late," Kelly said as her stomach issued a loud rumble. "We're lucky to get a table. This place gets packed for dinner every night."

Ross was silent and she knew from glancing at his face that luck had nothing to do with it.

"You made a reservation?"

He nodded. "I wanted to talk to you."

"About leaving?" She told him what she wanted, which he relayed to the server. When they were alone once more, she folded her hands in her lap and tried to prepare herself for more bad news. "When are you going?"

"I'm not sure." He changed the subject, asked her a hundred questions about the information she'd uncovered that afternoon. When their food came, they ate heartily, enjoying the rich flavors of a chef who knew how to tantalize.

"I wish there was a way to get that extortion money to the children Barnaby Harcourt adopted out," she mused, laying down her fork. "Many of the families were wealthy ones and they don't need the money, but the children might welcome funding for college or to start a business."

"Is that what you want from Gerald?"

"Ross! How can you even ask that?" She stared at him, surprised by his hard tone. "No. I don't want his money. I just want a chance to talk to him. All this time he and Barnaby were working together and he never even tried to help Sandra. I want to know why."

"It was a long time ago. I doubt he knew that you were the child he had Barnaby arrange an adoption for. He probably paid heavily not to know."

"I never thought of that." She glanced around, saw the Morrows being seated near the windows in a prominent position. "Look who dropped in. You'd think with servants and a cook on staff they wouldn't have to eat out, wouldn't you?"

He turned slightly, watched the older couple. "The missus doesn't seem very happy tonight. In fact, it looks as though Chestnut Grove's society maven is furious."

Kelly agreed. Tonight Lindsay Morrow seemed unconcerned with her image. She ranted at the staff, refused to accept the salad she was brought and ordered her server to return her food to the fool who'd salted it too heavily. Mayor Morrow argued less loudly, but several times he placed his hand on his wife's wrist and forced it down to the table. Neither looked as though they even knew what they were eating.

"I'm having dessert. Want to share some?" She felt Ross's shock and grinned. "Well, you said celebrate. I'm having the Hawaiian cheesecake. I've only had it once before but I can tell you there's enough of it for two." She raised an eyebrow in question.

Ross nodded, beckoned one of the staff.

"Celebrating huh?" the young man asked.

"Yes. A new life," he answered.

But there was something wistful in his voice and Kelly found herself wishing that he wouldn't leave, that Sandra would wake up and beg him to stay in Chestnut Grove.

She was in love with him.

The awareness hit her without warning just as the cheesecake was set before them. She stared at him, realized she'd memorized every line of his face, knew exactly how his dark eyes glowed when he was excited, narrowed when he was trying to figure something out.

He'd been there for her every time she needed him. Who would she turn to when he left?

Chapter Thirteen

"Are you ready to leave?" Ross watched Kelly glance at the Morrows again and knew immediately what was coming.

"Can we stop by their table? I'm going to set a time to see him if I can."

"Sure." He walked behind her, stood silently while she greeted the unhappy couple.

"I was wondering if I might meet you privately, Mayor Morrow," she murmured, softly enough that no one else in the restaurant would overhear. "I have some things I need to discuss with you. I understand from your wife that you're busy but I'm afraid it can't wait. Would sometime this evening be convenient?"

"I'm afraid Gerald and I have plans for this evening, Kelly." Lindsay Morrow smiled but there was a bite to the brilliant gleam of those perfect teeth. "Can't your business wait until tomorrow?"

"I wasn't planning on going in to the office tomorrow," Gerald told Kelly. "But if it's important, I guess I could meet you there at ten-thirty."

"Why should you disrupt your day off, Gerald? You

need a break from that dreary office." Lindsay's glare was polished steel. "Come to the house, Kelly. I'm sure you can talk all you want there. I won't be home but Gerald can make you comfortable."

"Thank you very much, Mrs. Morrow. I do appreciate your help. And I apologize again for interrupting your dinner."

Ross felt anger simmering below the surface and told himself to get a grip. Why was he always so irritated that Kelly found this woman admirable?

"My dear, please don't apologize. It was a meal that needed interrupting. I can't think why Gerald suggested this place instead of the country club. It's so…common."

Implying they were, too, because they'd eaten here? Ross clenched his teeth.

"We'll be leaving then. Good night, Mayor. Mrs. Morrow."

Before anyone could say anything else he slid his arm around Kelly's waist and led her toward the exit.

"What's the rush?" Kelly mumbled, but she thrust her arms into the coat he held and walked outside with him. She walked back to the agency with him, never even protesting when he ushered her into his car. She was probably tired.

Ross turned to the cop who'd replaced Glynis.

"Officer, I appreciate your concern, but Miss Young and I are going for a drive and we'd like some privacy. Is that a possibility?"

The young woman stared at him for a full minute before her eyes flickered in understanding. "I think I can stay a reasonable distance away and still keep you in my sights, sir."

"Thanks." Ross drove out to the country club that Lindsay was so fond of, but went around the back way he'd used when tailing a cheating husband. He'd happened upon the most gorgeous view of Chestnut Grove and he wanted to share it. "Just look at this."

"It's a beautiful spot, isn't it?" Kelly leaned forward to peer out the window. "My friends and I used to hike out here when we were kids and the country club was having one of its summer galas. We'd sit and watch the beautiful people in their gorgeous clothes and dream of how one day we'd be part of them."

"Is that what you want? To be like Lindsay Morrow?" he asked.

"No. I saw something in her tonight that made me think of what you said after we'd been to that party. She was rude to her server, a nasty kind of rude that sent the girl sobbing into the back." Kelly's face was troubled. "I don't like to see other people's feelings trampled on."

Thank You, God. Russ heaved a sigh of relief that he hadn't misread her. He turned in his seat.

"At dinner you asked me when I was going back to Richmond."

"And you never answered." She stared at him. "Why?"

"Because I'm thinking of staying here, in Chestnut Grove."

"Really? Why?"

"I want to be near Sandra, to be around when she finally comes out of that coma. And she will."

"I see."

"I like the community, Zach and I have developed a friendship. I haven't let anyone get close for a long time and yet the people here—" He shrugged, trying to explain without using the words. "They're friendly, generous, they accept me."

"Good."

She wasn't offering him the opening he needed so Ross decided to be blunt.

"But most of all I want to stay so I can be near a certain woman who runs the adoption agency." He reached out, tucked a tendril of her hair behind her ear, brushed her cheek with his knuckles. "She's quite a lady, you know. She faces danger head-on, she goes out of her way to be kind and she's always ready to hand out another cup of hot chocolate."

"Ross—"

He shook his head, put his fingers over her lips. "Let me say what I need to, Kelly." He swallowed. "I fell in love with you ages ago. I don't know exactly when, but I think it was the day your car took out the curb and you climbed into mine and buried your toes in the carpet. You were so beautiful but so worried about being late for that wedding. I've never known anyone like you, Kelly Young."

He picked up her hands, wrapped his own around them.

"The hardest thing I ever had to do was break up your world, tell you that you weren't who you thought you were. I knew you'd love Sandra if you gave her a chance because that's the kind of person you are. It was like hurting myself to watch you struggle to figure everything out while some maniac broke into your house, sent those messages, poisoned you. But every time you regrouped, grew stronger and pressed on."

"Not quite true," she whispered.

"Your faith stymied me, Kelly. I couldn't understand it, couldn't see how you could let yourself believe in what I thought was mumbo jumbo. But then I found myself wanting what you had, desperate to have that inner certainty that it didn't matter if I fouled up." He cupped her cheeks in his hands.

"When I found you in Sandra's room, slumped over the bed with blood dripping on the sheet, I knew I couldn't leave this place. Not unless you left with me." He leaned forward, pressed a light kiss against her lips. "You're part of my world, Kelly Young. The most important part. I can't walk away from you. Not unless you tell me that's what you want."

"Are you crazy?" She looped both arms around his neck and drew him close, planted her lips on his in a kiss that told him he wasn't going anywhere. "You're like my knight in shining armor. Whenever I need help—boom! There you are. When I need a shoulder to cry on, someone to soothe my troubles or bolster up my confidence, I look for you, Ross. Your allegiance to Sandra, your insistence that I not hurt her—I loved knowing you were there for her when no one else was."

"Are you saying—" He leaned back, frowned, unable to believe what he thought she was telling him.

"I thought private investigators were supposed to be intuitive." She dragged a hand through his hair, loving the mussed up look that gave him a tough but tender appearance. "I love you, Ross Van Zandt. I didn't feel I had the right to care about you so much when our faiths differed. Knowing you share what I believe, that God is as big a part of your life as He is of mine—that means the world."

She pulled him forward, kissed him gently, tenderly, with her heart.

"You're not going anywhere now, Mr. P.I."

"Don't worry, I don't want to," he assured her, drawing her across the seat to sit beside him so he could wrap his arm around her shoulders and hold her close. "I want to stay here, Kelly. But I don't know if there'll be enough work for me here."

"Then we'll have to pray about it." She kissed his cheek then pointed to the gorgeous black velvet sky with its crystal display. "Let's walk for a bit."

"Will you be warm enough?"

She gave him a look that he couldn't argue with. He felt the same—as if a fire inside his heart kept him warm.

"Isn't it beautiful out here?" She twirled around. "I needed to come here, to be reminded that God created beauty and joy."

She almost toppled over and Ross caught her, set her on her feet. Then he knelt in front of her, in the snow, feeling utterly foolish, yet somehow gallant.

"Kelly Young, will you please marry me and help me figure out what to do with the future?"

"I want to marry you, Ross. I really do." She stood there, looking down at him, her face troubled.

Ross held her hands and shared her silence for a moment. "But? You're thinking about Sandra, aren't you?"

"She would be so happy about us." A tear trickled down her cheek. "How could I not have told her I loved her? How could I have let the opportunity slip away? She was so wonderful and I never even gave her a chance. What if it's too late? Maybe she'll never—"

"She will, Kelly. She's going to wake up with the giggles, she's going to be at our wedding and she's going to be there for our grandchildren."

"How do you know, Ross?"

He rose, tilted her chin toward the sky, then stepped behind her, wrapped his arms around her waist.

"Watch," he whispered in her ear. Several moments later a shooting star raced across the sky. "Would the God who created all this, who brought us together, who protected you—wouldn't He expect us to trust Him to do the best for Sandra?"

"I hope so," she murmured.

But Ross could tell she wasn't totally convinced that

something else wouldn't ruin their dream. And somewhere, deep inside, he was worried about that meeting with Gerald.

What if…?

Kelly tightened her fingers around Ross's hand.

"You're sure you want to do this?" he asked as the door-bell of the Morrow mansion chimed their arrival the next morning.

"I have to." She ignored the niggling voice inside her head that said this was not a display of trust and pasted on a smile as the door opened. To her surprise Gerald Morrow motioned them in. Lindsay was not in sight.

"Come on in. I've given everyone the day off so we're alone here." He took their coats, laid them over a nearby chair. "We'll go to my den."

Ross perched on the arm of Kelly's chair as if he needed to be near to protect her. "I suppose you know what this is about?" he asked.

"I can guess. But why don't you tell me anyway." Gerald sat behind his desk, his gaze fixed on Kelly.

"Yesterday I found some tapes and papers in an old filing cabinet at Tiny Blessings. They're Barnaby Harcourt's." She couldn't read the expression in his eyes so she pressed on. "According to him, you are my father. Apparently he was blackmailing you with that right until his death."

"Maybe you even had something to do with his death," Ross suggested. "Bad brakes, wasn't that the official cause of the accident? Strangely enough, Kelly had her steering tampered with, too."

"I had nothing to do with either of those!" Gerald rose, walked around the desk toward Kelly. "I know this is prob-ably the worst way you could have found out and I apologize for that. I am your father. When I heard that the tests confirmed you were Sandra's child, I knew I should have stepped forward before, told you myself."

"Then why didn't you?" Ross wasn't cutting the older man any slack, but Kelly could see a sadness in Gerald's eyes and knew there was much he wasn't saying.

Gerald pulled up a chair so that he was facing Kelly. "I didn't tell her for the same reason I didn't marry Sandra thirty-five years ago. I wanted to keep Lindsay out of it."

"Or you wanted to hang on to her and the money she brought with her into your marriage."

"Maybe you're right." Gerald's shoulders sagged. "I'm not sure I know what was in my own mind, except that I was desperate for her not to know about Sandra or you. So I paid Barnaby's extortion and he handled everything. He told you you had been adopted by a couple in California. I never knew who they were, never dreamed you had moved back here. All I was told was that you were part of a happy, loving family."

"I was," Kelly agreed, ready at last to ask the questions that had bothered her for so long. "But that doesn't explain how you could do such a thing to Sandra. You knew she'd changed her mind, you knew she desperately wanted her baby back. Yet all these years passed and you didn't do a thing to help her."

"I tried. When she came back here from Richmond, I could see how unhappy she was. She wouldn't have anything to do with me but I knew I'd ruined her life." He hung his head. "I was ashamed of myself. I went to Barnaby, begged him to get you back. He wouldn't do it. Instead he hit me up for even more money, threatened to tell Lindsay the truth if I didn't make regular payments."

"And after he died, things had quieted down, and you

surely didn't want me opening them up again," Ross said. "So you broke into Tiny Blessings and tried to get a look at the files." His scathing tone made Kelly squirm.

"No."

Ross ignored him. "And when that didn't work, you started a fire in the place."

"No! I didn't do that. I heard about it, of course." Gerald's eyes begged them to understand. "I knew someone was up to something, but I swear to you that it wasn't me."

"Then who? Who else had the motive or cared?"

"I don't know." Gerald turned to Kelly. "You have to believe me. From the day he announced he was trying to find Sandra's biological child and that it was between you and Ben Cavanaugh, I knew you were my daughter. I knew Sandra's child was a girl."

"Then why didn't you contact me? Why didn't you say something?" she asked, half-afraid to hear the answer.

"I wanted so badly to go up to you and tell you who I was, that I was proud of everything you'd become, that I knew I didn't deserve it, but I wanted to get to know you better." He shook his head. "But I'd seen you with your parents. They were so important to you. I remember their funerals, how broken up you were. How could I expect you to accept me after having a father like Marcus?"

"Did you know that Kelly's been the target of someone's maliciousness? That her house has been burglarized, her food poisoned? That she's been personally attacked?" Ross wasn't letting Gerald off the hook so easily.

As she watched him interrogate the older man, Kelly gained new perspective on his abilities as a policeman. This same demeanor must have come in handy with rebellious teens in New York.

"I didn't know," Gerald gasped. "I didn't know any of

that! I heard about the agency being broken into, of course. Anyone can see the window's gone. But attacked—?" He stared at Kelly. "Who would do such a thing? And why?"

"That's what we'd like to know."

But Kelly realized she didn't care if she ever knew who. Now she only wanted the answer to one question.

"How could you do it?" she whispered. "How could you give away your own child? How could you do that to Sandra?"

"Fear," Gerald told her simply.

"I don't understand." She frowned at him, tried to make the pieces fit. "What would you have to be afraid of?"

"Exposure, condemnation, reprisals. I knew my affair with Sandra was wrong, I knew I wasn't going to marry her, that I only set her up in Richmond to keep her out of the scandal. I knew the people in Chestnut Grove wouldn't want someone like that representing their town." He leaned forward, his face intent. "I was centered on my career, Kelly, on how I could make it as a prosecutor. And I had political aspirations even then. I had to ensure that nothing interfered with my goals—not you, not Sandra, not even Lindsay. I know it was wrong but at the time I was blind to everything except my own goals." He half smiled. "You're my daughter, Kelly. Surely you must understand the need to control your life, to make things happen the way you want them to."

His words were like a knife to her heart because in that moment Kelly understood exactly what he meant. Controlling, manipulative—they weren't only Gerald's faults. She'd done it, too. Maybe she hadn't coerced someone into giving up her baby, but she'd refused to handle that case last week, wouldn't allow herself to become embroiled in a tough situation that might reflect badly on her, a case where the daughter wanted to give up her child for adoption and the mother wanted her to raise him. Why had she turned them away with some platitude instead of digging in and doing her best to help, if not to protect her reputation?

Because she couldn't foresee the outcome, because she would have had to become too personally involved.

In a flash Kelly saw what she'd missed for so long. She'd never really allowed herself to participate fully in life, she'd always held back a little, never fully committed to anything, Ross included, because the same fear that governed Gerald's actions also controlled her. Subconsciously or not, she knew that part of her was keeping a door open just in case it didn't work out between her and Ross, just as she'd done with Simon. She wasn't expecting God to give her the best, she was preparing for the worst!

"Kelly?"

"I'm fine," she reassured Ross, squeezing his hand. "I'm really fine. Just working it through."

"I guess I'm a slow learner, Kelly. Because it took me a few years to realize that all that I'd achieved didn't matter in the slightest when I looked into Sandra's eyes and saw the hurt and pain I'd caused. I was a big man, all right, but only in my own eyes."

The room was silent for several moments, though deep inside the house somewhere, a floor creaked.

"I apologize to you, Kelly. I had no right to do what I did. I'll say that to Sandra, too. It's time to stop trying to cover up the truth. The mayor," he spat out angrily. "Who cares about that when you've lost years of getting to know your own child?" He reached out, covered her hand with his. "What does any of it matter anymore?"

"It matters to me." Lindsay Morrow stood in the doorway, a small gun in her right hand. "Isn't this touching father-daughter reunion special! But I worked hard to achieve the status we enjoy in this town and I'm not prepared to let you ruin it with some maudlin fatherly sentiment. You were always weak, Gerald."

"Lindsay, what are you doing?" Gerald drew away from Kelly, turned toward his wife. "Put that gun away before someone gets hurt."

"*Before* someone gets hurt?" She chuckled loudly but it was a hollow motion. The intensity came from her blazing eyes. "I think it's a little too late for that, don't you, Kelly?"

"What do you mean?" She'd never seen Lindsay Morrow like this, fury radiating from somewhere inside her. "What are you saying?" she whispered as a thousand scenarios filled her mind.

"Tell me, my dear, are you completely off milk now?"

That voice, she knew that voice!

"How do you—" Kelly stopped, stared. "It was you. You put the arsenic in my food."

The woman she'd admired for so long nodded, her face shining with glee.

"That and so much more. You truly have no idea of the lengths I've had to go to in order to rectify my husband's little *mistake* with the diner floozy."

"You knew?" Gerald frowned. "But—"

"Not everyone is as stupid as you, Gerald. Of course I knew. From the very beginning. Did you really think you could hide it from me?"

"That's when you started to change," he remembered. "Before that you were so sweet, so loving and giving."

"And to repay me, you had an affair."

"It wasn't on purpose. It just…happened."

"So did she." Lindsay jerked her hand toward Kelly, aimed the gun directly at her. "You weren't even bright enough to tell Barnaby no when he kept sucking a fortune out of us. Well, when I found out I soon made sure he didn't collect any more of my money."

"Lindsay, what are you saying?" Gerald blanched.

"You had some shady pals before I got you that prosecutor's position, darling." She shrugged, tossed her hair back. "I simply hired one of them to end Barnaby's extortion. Well, that and the diner fire."

"The fire at the diner?" Ross asked, glancing at Kelly as he did. His hand tightened around hers. "You were responsible for that?"

"Of course. I couldn't have that floozy poking around, making accusations that would cover us in scandal." She preened. "And it worked. She stopped asking questions. Everything was fine until you came along and started working for sweet little Sandra." She thrust the gun in Ross's direction.

"But that fire killed Sandra's mother."

"Collateral damage, isn't that what they call it?" Lindsay looked unconcerned. "The old goody two-shoes was always talking about Heaven anyway. Now she's there. Everybody's happy."

"You were behind the break-in and the fire at Tiny Blessings a few months ago, weren't you?" Ross shook his head as it began to sink in. "The graffiti, the broken glass the other night—you did that, too. And I was trying to pin it on Andrew Noble."

"Andrew?" Lindsay twittered with laughter. "Oh, my, no. Dear Andrew has…other fish to fry, shall we say?"

"The phone calls to my house—the threats, that was you, wasn't it?" Kelly couldn't believe she'd ever thought the woman attractive. Now she looked vicious and mean, her eyes blazing with hate.

"Of course. What did you expect? I couldn't give up everything I'd worked so hard to achieve just because Gerald's brat was going to be exposed." Lindsay pointed the gun at her, her aim steady. "You should have listened, my dear, and left town as I told you. Everything would have been so much simpler. Sandra's out of the way, or she will be soon if she comes out of that coma. All that remains is to tie up a few loose ends."

"Lindsay, this is crazy!" Gerald stretched out his hand. "Give me that gun."

"Crazy? How dare you call me that?" She turned on him as if berserk. "I dragged you out of that dinky law office and made you into somebody. Because of *me,* you've been able to hold your head up, to meet with the elite, the powerful. It was my money that made you into what you are, my family's status that got you the position as mayor."

"Yes," he agreed. "You did all that. But it wasn't for me. You kept pushing me because you wanted to be the queen of everything. You could never be satisfied with what I provided. You always wanted more."

"I certainly wanted more than my husband engaging in some tawdry affair, fathering some illegitimate baby. Did you honestly think I was going to let you ruin me with your nasty scandal? You are not worthy of me."

She waved the gun in his direction, all the while her eyes grew wilder, more desperate.

"You mentioned a plan, Mrs. Morrow." Ross's voice emerged calm, soothing. Kelly glanced at him, realized he was trying to divert her attention. "I'm sure it's a clever one. Tell us about it."

She laughed hysterically. "Tell you? Oh, you're going to learn firsthand."

"But if you tell me, I can make sure there aren't any holes in it. Remember, I was a cop once. Zach is pretty thorough. I can make sure you haven't forgotten anything."

"I seldom forget the details," Lindsay told him. "I've spent years perfecting my life. But all right, if you must know, I'll tell you. What we'll have here is a vicious attack by a masked gunman. He's going to have robbed us, been surprised by Gerald and you two whom he kills. I'll be injured, of course, as I rush to my husband's side. The sole survivor and a grieving widow. Brilliant, don't you think?"

Her evil smile sent shudders down Kelly's spine.

"It's pretty good," Ross agreed. He tapped one finger against his chin as if he were thinking deeply. "And you do have a knack for this kind of thing. Nobody ever suspected that you'd tampered with Barnaby's car, or Kelly's for that matter."

"Sometimes Gerald's connections do come in handy."

"I'm sure. Were they the ones who got into Kelly's house through the window?"

Kelly stared at him, shocked by the knowledge.

"No. I did that. I couldn't get a key, at first. But then everyone takes off their coats at church. No one ever thinks about what's in their pockets."

"No, I don't suppose they do. Very clever."

"It is, isn't it?" Lindsay leaned forward, her voice a mere whisper. "She left her keys in her coat. So careless. I simply removed them, had a second set for her house and the office cut and returned them to her home. She never even knew."

"And the poison?"

"Carol Young once told me that Kelly loved milk, that she often drank a glass before bed. Simple, really."

"But where did you—" He stopped, stared. "I saw you at the hardware store one day. You were buying some pesticide."

"Yes." Lindsay shrugged. "But you couldn't put it together. Tsk, tsk. Why do you think you should advise me about my plan, Mr. Van Zandt?" She moved around until she was on Kelly's other side, unprotected by Ross. "Now then, if we do this well, the entire event will be past by the time the Valentine's gala arrives. I'll be the belle of the ball and achieve my goal."

"What goal is that, Mrs. Morrow?" Ross let go of Kelly's hands, stood and rubbed the back of her neck with an intensity that surprised her. She tried to pull away, but he wouldn't let go. "Please, will you tell us? I haven't quite got it all clear in my mind."

"That's because you're a man. Men are so stupid about these things." She tapped one foot on the hardwood floor, shook her head at him. "Especially men from the gutters of New York."

"Yes, it was pretty gross. But I'm trying to learn. You can't fault me for wanting to better myself," he said softly as he took a step backward so the sofa was in front. He pressed Kelly's hand one last time, then let go.

Kelly listened, terrified to turn her head and watch him lest she draw Lindsay's attention.

"No, I think it's admirable to enrich one's education in all things. It's unfortunate Gerald couldn't understand how important social pedigree is." She shot her husband a nasty look. "I guess mixing in with the riffraff does that to you."

"Yes. He lowered his standards." Ross took another step.

Kelly's heart was in her mouth. Lindsay had only to turn a little and she'd have point-blank range on him. What could she do?

Nothing, she realized. She had absolutely no control in this situation. All she could think of was that Ross would be hurt and she'd never get to tell him how much she truly loved him.

I am the way. Trust Me.

Yes, that was all she had left. But it was also the best way. God knew Lindsay's heart. He would lead Ross, help him find a way to talk this demented woman down.

Please, God, keep him safe.

"What about the gala, Mrs. Morrow? Why is that so important?" Another step, just a little closer.

"Because it's going to put me on the state list of who's who in Virginia."

"And that's important?"

"My dear fellow, you really don't have a clue, do you?" Her tone grew condescending. "But with your background, why would you? That list is my ticket out of this burg, away from the pettiness I find here. Once I'm settled in Richmond, I'll be able to move in better circles, among those who are like me." The gun aimed for his chest. "Don't bother with your tricks, Mr. Van Zandt. It's not that hard to shoot this gun."

"I'm not going to try anything." Ross stepped back, sat on the back of the sofa behind Kelly. "But there is a flaw in your plan."

"What flaw?" Lindsay frowned. "My plans are always most detailed."

"Of course they are." Surreptitiously, his hand slid down, grasped Kelly's and lifted it to rest on his jacket pocket. "But you've forgotten something this time," Ross explained. He gave Kelly a funny look then held out his hands toward Lindsay. "The police will do a GSR test."

Kelly felt a shape under her hand, slid her hand inside the pocket which was blocked from Lindsay's view. Ross's cell phone. He wanted her to call for help.

"GSR? What's that?"

"Gunshot residue. It's standard procedure. If you fire

that gun you'll have it on your hands and they'll know you were the shooter."

"Ah. The details of police work." She stared at her hands for a minute. "Fortunately, I brought my gloves along." She stepped back, reached toward a small marble-topped table that stood by the door. "I'll wear these, then dispose of them. Thank you, Mr. Van Zandt. You do have your uses after all."

When Lindsay turned away to pick up the gloves Kelly dialed 911. The older woman had one glove on, was pulling on the other when an operator answered.

"The Morrow mansion. Hurry!"

Lindsay looked up, strode closer, saw the phone. "Just the authenticity we need," she murmured, her smile pure evil. She turned, pointed her gun at Gerald. "You first, darling."

A shot rang through the room. Gerald gasped, turned gray. Kelly closed her eyes and prayed harder than she'd ever done. Surely she hadn't found Ross and her father just to lose them.

Trust me.

"Yes, Lord."

Chapter Fourteen

The dull thud of a bullet making contact scared the daylights out of him, but Ross couldn't turn to see who it had hit. He only knew he had to get that gun or no one would be left to tell the truth.

I trust in You, he prayed mentally as he burst forward with speed he hadn't used in a long time.

"You will not ruin this!" Lindsay screamed as she battled with him for the gun. A second shot pumped into the ceiling.

"God help us!" Ross felt himself stumble on the edge of the carpet. It was now or never. With a twist of his wrist he heard Lindsay cry out, then the gun dropped to the floor. He grabbed it, trained it on her. "Kelly?"

"I'm fine. Gerald's been hit, though."

"It's not serious. Just a shoulder nick. I'm fine." Gerald wobbled into view, leaning on Kelly. "Oh, Lindsay, I'm so sorry."

He tried to reach out and touch her, but Lindsay turned away, sank down into a chair and stared blankly across the room. All life seemed to drain away from her. Ross kept the gun on her, asked Kelly to call an ambulance. It wasn't long before the screech of sirens could be heard outside. A moment later Zach came charging into the room. Five minutes after that Lindsay was being escorted out to a waiting police car.

When it was finally safe, Ross wrapped his arms around Kelly, content just to hold her while he thanked God for His help and Kelly silently wept on his shoulder. Gerald stepped toward them.

"I'm so sorry," he whispered, his face haggard. "My behavior caused problems for everyone, ruined so many lives. I don't know how I'll ever make it up to you."

"It's over, Gerald."

"I have to go with her now. After that I'm going to resign as mayor. But I would like to see you again, Kelly. Is that possible?"

She studied him for several moments, then glanced at Ross.

"Zach said we have to go and make a statement at the station so we'll probably see you there later. But until then I want to tell you that Mrs. Morrow helped me learn something." She looked him straight in the eye, glimpsed the shame that filled him. "We can't make up for the past, or change it, but we can make the most of the future. Call me whenever you like. I promise to listen."

"Thank you." He shook Ross's hand. "And thank you. Without your quick action, Lindsay might have hurt us all."

"Just doing what I've been trained to do."

"Maybe you should talk to your friend. We could use another good man on the police force."

"We'll see." Ross tightened his grip on Kelly. "We don't have our future all ironed out, but God knows. He'll show us a way."

Gerald nodded, then left.

Ross stared at the beautiful woman in his arms, felt a rush of joy that she was his. "I love you, Kelly Young. Don't forget it."

She wiggled a little to get her arms free then lifted them around his neck. "I love you, too, Ross. More than life. I'm so glad God brought you into my life." She stood on her tiptoes to kiss him. "I'm never letting you go so don't try it."

"As if!" After an appreciable amount of time had passed, Ross loosened his grip on her, stood back to study her. "What now? The police are going to want details after the last thirty-five years of secrets. Should I drop you at work first?"

"You know what?" She looped her arm through his and walked with him to the foyer. "I think I work too much. I love my job but sometimes I let it control me. I think I'll take today off. After all, we have wedding plans to make. Sooner or later we'll get to Zach, answer whatever we can."

"I vote for later." Ross held her coat, helped her into it, then waited while she buttoned it up. All the while his mind was racing. Once they were in his car, Ross headed downtown, stopped in front of a store.

"What are you doing?"

"You said you wanted to get started on wedding plans."

"Yes." She glanced at the store. "This isn't a wedding store."

"Sure it is." He climbed out of the car, went around to the other side to help her out. "You make your very first plan for the future right here." He led her inside the jewelry store. "*My* plan is to get a ring on that finger that will make it really hard for you to back out. Then we're going to see Sandra, visit my mother and call up my sister. Wedding plans. Do you like them?"

"Oh, yes." Kelly patiently tried on every ring he chose and finally agreed that the emerald-cut solitaire set in platinum was the nicest ring she'd ever seen.

"It's awfully expensive," she whispered when the jeweler left them alone for a minute.

"I'm only doing this once," he told her with a grin. "I intend to do it right And that ring looks exactly right."

Once they were out in the car again, Kelly held out her hand, admiring the sparkle of the sun against the facets of the gorgeous diamond.

"It's beautiful. Thank you." She leaned over and kissed him. "What's next on your list?"

He patted his pocket. "Wedding rings chosen. Next we visit Sandra. Then my mother."

"I'm going to New York?" Kelly stared at him.

"No. She's in a place in Richmond. I wanted to be able to see her more often so I had her transferred there before I came here. The doctors thought that might help her."

"I'm glad." She slid over next to him. "You know I was just thinking," she murmured as he headed for the hospital.

"Uh-oh. That spells trouble."

"Be nice." She leaned her head back on the seat, closed her eyes. "It's a good thing I already gave the controls over to God because it seems like nothing is under my control any more."

"Does it have to be?"

"No." She grinned at him. "As long as God's working it out, I'm perfectly happy. After all, He brought you here. Now I've got a new mother and maybe a father, too. As director of Tiny Blessings, I couldn't have arranged anything better myself."

Chapter Fifteen

"Have you ever seen a better day for a wedding?" Leah Cavanaugh looked to her friend Anne for confirmation. "June is always so lovely. It's the perfect bridal month, with flowers blooming and everything so lush."

"I'm just glad the Harcourts got their public apology out of the way yesterday. It was noble of them to apologize for Barnaby's actions. Now the focus is fully on Kelly and Ross. As it should be," Meg Kierney interjected before greeting the group. "Hi, all."

"Yeah, that's all well and fine for the Harcourts," Ben muttered. "But I'm not so sure about their promise to investigate the other falsified records. Who knows what else lies buried in time?"

"Relax, Ben." Jared Kierney thumped him on the shoulder. "Whatever it is, I promise to be discreet about publishing it in the *Gazette*."

"You look tired, Jared. Fatherhood keeping you a little busy these days, Dad?" Ben teased. "Where is Hope anyway?"

"Grandma's. We'll pick her up after the reception. We'll

probably leave early because Meg doesn't like being away from our new baby too long." Jared glanced around the people preparing to enter the church. "I've been trying to locate Andrew Noble for ages. Anybody seen him?"

"Have to ask Rachel and you can't right now because she's inside fussing over the flower arrangements." Pilar lowered her voice. "Who is that?"

They all turned to survey the young woman who stood staring at the church.

"That's Trista, Ross's sister and Kelly's matron of honor." Zach walked over to talk to her, before leading her to the group. "Trista, here are some of our friends. There's too many of them for you to remember now, but don't worry. You'll get to know us all in time."

"Thank you. I intend to visit Ross often now that I'm living in Richmond." She seemed to teeter a little bit, her face paled.

Zach grabbed her arm. "You all right?"

"A little nervous?" One hand fluttered to her stomach.

"You're not by chance pregnant, are you?" Anne leaned in and whispered when the focus had shifted from Trista to another guest. "I only ask because I am and you looked exactly how I felt this morning."

"I don't know how you guessed, but yes, I am."

"Come on, then," Anne murmured. "Let's get you inside and out of the sun. You can sit down for a few minutes before the ceremony. I'm Anne Williams, by the way. My husband Caleb is the youth minister for Chestnut Grove Youth Center. Welcome to our church."

"Thank you." Trista waited while Anne called her husband over, then they mounted the stairs together.

Leah heard the sound of a car, turned, caught her breath as Sandra Lange stepped out of a cab.

"You look fantastic, Sandra," she said, grasping the other woman's hand to help her.

"Thank you, Leah. Though it's only been a week since I really woke up, I'm feeling much better. It was so kind of all of you to visit and send your encouragement," Sandra told them, including the group in her smile. "Is Sunday brunch still on?"

"Of course. We'll see you tomorrow. And we'd love it if you joined us," Pilar offered.

"I might just do that." Sandra turned and hesitated when she saw Gerald walking toward the group.

Leah saw him also and motioned to the others to leave the couple alone.

By the time Gerald reached Sandra, the sidewalk was clear. They were the only ones standing there.

"I'm glad to see you looking so well, Sandra."

"Thank you." She didn't know what to say to him.

"I've been meaning to write but I think what I need to say should be done in person. It's probably too late, but I apologize for everything I did, all of it. And for what Lindsay did, too. I won't blame you if you hate me." He looked at his feet. "Some days I hate myself for taking her away from you."

"I couldn't have given her the life Carol and Marcus did," she told him softly. "God knew what He was doing. Besides, I've gotten to know Kelly better now and I couldn't be happier."

"Can you ever forgive me?"

His eyes were so sad. Sandra felt a rush of warmth for the suffering he'd endured.

"Of course I forgive you. And Lindsay, too. Pain sometimes makes us want to strike out, let others feel what we feel. How could I blame you for trying to protect her?"

"I don't know if that's what I was doing," he said honestly. "Maybe I was just protecting myself. But you'll be safe now. Lindsay will never hurt you again."

"I just hope she can get some help. But the past doesn't seem as important now, does it? It's over. It's the future we're here to celebrate. Her future," she murmured as a car arrived with Kelly inside.

"I should go," Gerald whispered. "I thought she was already inside. I didn't know—" He stopped, stared at Kelly as she emerged from the car, clad in brilliant white. "She's so beautiful," he whispered.

"That's God's work. Turning ashes to beauty." Sandra smiled at her daughter. "You're a lovely bride, Kelly Young."

"Thank you." Kelly brushed her cheek with her lips, then turned to her father. "Hello."

"I should be going. I never meant to intrude." He turned, walked a few steps before Kelly reached out to touch his arm.

"Don't go." She drew Sandra to her other side. "You're my parents. I care for both of you. This is the happiest day of my life. I want you both to share in that. Will you walk me down the aisle, Mother? Father?"

Sandra's heart welled with joy and pride. She nodded at her daughter. "I'd be honored. Gerald?"

She could see the sheen of tears in his brown eyes. He gulped, then nodded. "Yes," he said huskily.

"Thank you. Both of you. This wedding is everything I ever dreamed of, and more."

Like a beam of light, Kelly led them up the stairs. They paused in the foyer while Rachel straightened her train, Trista helped her adjust her veil and handed her a bouquet of richly fragrant lilacs gleaned from the Nobles' yard.

Kelly glanced toward the front of the church, saw Ross

waiting for her and smiled. Everything in her world was under control, thanks to her Lord. She glanced at her parents.

"It's not the past and its secrets that matter," she whispered. "It's the present and the love we share."

She nodded at Trista, who stepped out to lead the way, followed by the Kierney twins, Chance and Luke, who proudly carried satin cushions with golden rings. Then Kelly slipped her arms into her parents' and together they walked down the aisle to meet the future. One full of possibilities only God could fathom.

* * * * *

Dear Reader,

Welcome back! I hope you've enjoyed visiting Chestnut Grove once more as Kelly deals with a lifelong insecurity that has kept her from relaxing in God's love. In each of us there is a kernel of disbelief that, if not checked, can grow until it saps our trust and faith in God and His divine plan for our lives.

My prayer for you is that you will lean on Him when life gets too much, that you will trust even though the struggles seem too hard. Know that He is there, waiting for you to call on Him. He will answer.

Blessings,

Lois
Richer

Brendan Montgomery switched his beeper to vibrate and slid it back inside his shirt pocket. Nothing was going to spoil Manuel DeSantis Vance's first birthday party—and this large Vance and Montgomery gathering—if he could help it.

Peter Vance's puffed-out chest needed little explanation. He was as formidable as any father, proudly displaying his beloved child. Peter's wife Emily waited on Manuel's other side, posing for the numerous photographs Yvette Duncan insisted posterity demanded. Apparently posterity was greedy.

Judging by the angle of her camera, Brendan had a hunch Yvette's lens sidetracked from the parents to the cake she'd made for Manuel. Who could blame her? That intricate train affair must have taken hours to create and assemble, and little Manuel obviously appreciated her efforts.

"Make sure you don't chop off their heads this time, Yvette." As the former mayor of Colorado Springs, Frank Montgomery had opinions on everything. And as Yvette's mentor, he'd never been shy about offering her his opinion, especially on all aspects of picture-taking. But since Yvette's camera happened to be the latest in digital technology and Frank had never owned one, Brendan figured most of his uncle's free advice was superfluous and probably useless. But he wouldn't be the one to tell him so.

"Don't tell me what to do, Frank," Yvette ordered, adjusting the camera. "Just put your arm around your wife. Liza, can you get him to smile?" Satisfied, Yvette motioned for Dr. Robert Fletcher and his wife Pamela, who were Manuel's godparents, and their two young sons, to line up behind the birthday boy.

Brendan eased his way into the living room and found a horde of Montgomery and Vance family members lounging around the room, listening to a news report on the big screen television.

"Alistair Barclay, the British hotel mogul now infamous for his ties to a Latin American drug cartel, died today under suspicious circumstances. Currently in jail, Barclay was accused of running a branch of the notorious crime syndicate right here in Colorado Springs. The drug cartel originated in Venezuela under the direction of kingpin Baltasar Escalante, whose private plane crashed some months ago while he was attempting to escape the CIA. Residents of Colorado Springs have worked long and hard to free their city from the grip of crime—"

"Hey, guys, this is a party. Let's lighten up." Brendan reached out and pressed the mute button, followed by a chorus of groans. "You can listen to the same newscast tonight, but we don't want to spoil Manuel's big day with talk of drug cartels and death, do we?"

His brother Quinn winked and took up his cause. "Yeah,

what's happened with that cake, anyway? Are we ever going to eat it? I'm starving."

"So is somebody else, apparently," Yvette said, appearing in the doorway, her flushed face wreathed in a grin. "Manuel already got his thumb onto the train track and now he's covered in black icing. His momma told him he had to wait 'till the mayor gets here, though, so I guess you'll just have to do the same, Quinn."

Good-natured groans filled the room.

"Maxwell Vance has been late since he got elected into office," Fiona Montgomery said, her eyes dancing with fun. "Maybe one of us should give him a call and remind him his grandson is waiting for his birthday cake. In fact, I'll do it myself."

"Leave the mayor alone, Mother. He already knows your opinion on pretty much everything," Brendan said, sharing a grin with Quinn.

"It may be that the mayor has been delayed by some important meeting." Alessandro Donato spoke up from his seat in the corner. "After Thanksgiving, that is the time when city councilors and mayors iron out their budgets, yes?"

"But just yesterday I talked to our mayor about that, in regard to a story I'm doing on city finances." Brendan's cousin Colleen sat cross-legged on the floor, her hair tied back in the eternal ponytail she favored. "He said they hadn't started yet."

Something about the way Alessandro moved when he heard Colleen's comment sent a nerve in Brendan's neck to twitching, enough to make him take a second look at the man. Moving up through the ranks of the FBI after his time as a police officer had only happened because Brendan usually paid attention to that nerve. Right now it was telling him to keep an eye on the tall, lean man named Alessandro, even if he was Lidia Vance's nephew.

There was something about Alessandro that didn't quite fit. What was the story on this guy anyway?

A phone rang. Brendan chuckled when everyone in the room checked their pockets. The grin faded when Alessandro spoke into his. His face paled, his body tensed. He murmured one word, then listened.

"Hey, something's happening! Turn up the TV, Brendan," Colleen said. Everyone was staring at the screen where a reporter stood in front of city hall.

Brendan raised the volume.

"Mayor Vance was apparently on his way to a family event when the shot was fired. Excuse me, I'm getting an update." The reporter lifted one hand to press the earpiece closer. "I'm told there may have been more than one shot fired. As I said, at this moment, Maxwell Vance is on his way to the hospital. Witnesses say he was bleeding profusely from his head and chest, though we have no confirmed details. We'll update you as the situation develops."

Love Inspired® SUSPENSE

RIVETING INSPIRATIONAL ROMANCE

A Time To Protect

by Lois Richer

Nurse Chloe Tanner stopped a would-be assassin from killing the mayor of Colorado Springs, and it is FBI agent Brendan Montgomery's job to protect the single mom. No one said anything about protecting his own heart....

Faith at the Crossroads: Can faith and love sustain two families against a diabolical enemy?

Don't miss this first book in the Faith at the Crossroads series.

On sale January 2006

Available at your favorite retail outlet.

On Sale December

LILAC SPRING
by Ruth Axtell Morren

As the daughter of a wealthy nineteenth-century shipbuilder,
Cherish Winslow loves everything about the sea, including her
father's apprentice, Silas. Silas also loves Cherish, but as a poor
apprentice, he feels that she is beyond reach. When a stolen
kiss between the two finds Silas on the street, he must fight
for his life, as well as for a life with Cherish.

Steeple
Hill®

Please visit your local bookseller.

Love Inspired®

TITLES AVAILABLE NEXT MONTH

Don't miss these four stories in January

A FAMILY TO SHARE by Arlene James
Connie Wheeler's relationship choices landed her in jail.
Yet the single mother's new job caring for Kendal Oakes's
troubled daughter helped her blossom, even as it brought
her closer to the little girl's father. But would he stand by
her when her past was revealed?

HOME TO YOU by Cheryl Wolverton
Faced with a devastating diagnosis, Meghan O'Halleran had
no one to turn to. Though she hadn't seen him in twenty years,
childhood friend Dakota "Cody" Ryder was her only hope.
The memory of that friendship shone like a beacon, guiding
her home once more. Would welcoming arms await her?

MATCHMAKER, MATCHMAKER... by Anna Schmidt
A fluff piece on Grace Harrison's Christian speed-dating program
was all well and good for reporter Jud Marlowe, but his instincts
told him a different story lay with her senator father. If only Grace
weren't so...*appealing*. With the article in question, it was up to
Jud to decide what was more important—a scoop or a sweetheart.

HIS BUNDLE OF LOVE by Patricia Davids
When the pregnant woman he'd taken to the hospital named
him as her child's father before slipping into a coma, EMT
Mick O'Callaghan was floored. He couldn't have children of
his own, and baby Beth melted his heart. And as the new mother
recovered, he couldn't help wanting to take care of her, too....

LICNM1205